ROADSIDE PICNIC

ROADSIDE PICNIC

ARKADY AND BORIS STRUGATSKY

TRANSLATED BY OLENA BORMASHENKO

Published by Chicago Review Press, Incorporated
814 North Franklin Street
Chicago, Illinois 60610
ISBN 978-1-61374-341-6

Library of Congress Cataloging-in-Publication Data
Strugatskii, Arkadii Natanovich, author.
[Piknik na obochine. English. 2012]
Roadside picnic / Arkady and Boris Strugatsky ; translated by Olena Bormashenko.
pages ; cm
Summary: "Red Schuhart is a stalker, one of those young rebels who are compelled, in spite of the extreme danger, to venture illegally into the Zone to collect the mysterious artifacts that the alien visitors left scattered around. His life is dominated by the place and the thriving black market in the alien products. But when he and his friend Kirill go into the Zone together to pick up a "full empty," something goes wrong. And the news he gets from his girlfriend upon his return makes it inevitable that he'll keep going back to the Zone, again and again, until he finds the answer to all his problems."— Provided by publisher.
ISBN 978-1-61374-341-6
1. Science fiction, Russian. I. Strugatskii, Boris Natanovich, author. II. Bormashenko, Olena, translator. III. Title.

PG3476.S78835P5513 2012
891.73'44—dc23

2012001294

Cover and interior design: Sarah Olson
Cover image: Still from the 1979 film *Stalker*, Mosfilm

Printed in the United States of America
16 15 14 13 12

FOREWORD

BY URSULA K. LE GUIN

Part of this foreword is taken from a review of *Roadside Picnic* I wrote in 1977, the year the book first came out in English.* I wanted to keep some record of a reader's response at a time when the worst days of Soviet censorship were fresh in memory, and intellectually and morally interesting novels from Russia still had the glamour of risk-taking courage about them. A time, also, when a positive review of a work of Soviet science fiction was a small but real political statement in the United States, since part of the American science fiction community had undertaken to fight the Cold War by assuming every writer who lived behind the Iron Curtain was an enemy ideologue. These reactionaries preserved their moral purity (as

---

* *Roadside Picnic* was first published in England and America in 1977, in a translation by A. W. Bouis. My review, "A New Book by the Strugatskys" is in *Science Fiction Studies* 12 (vol. 4, pt. 2, July 1977).

reactionaries so often do) by not reading, so they didn't have to see that Soviet writers had been using science fiction for years to write with at least relative freedom from Party ideology about politics, society, and the future of mankind.

Science fiction lends itself readily to imaginative subversion of any status quo. Bureaucrats and politicians, who can't afford to cultivate their imaginations, tend to assume it's all ray-guns and nonsense, good for children. A writer may have to be as blatantly critical of utopia as Zamyatin in *We* to bring the censor down upon him. The Strugatsky brothers were not blatant, and never (to my limited knowledge) directly critical of their government's policies. What they did, which I found most admirable then and still do now, was to write as if they were indifferent to ideology—something many of us writers in the Western democracies had a hard time doing. They wrote as free men write.

✦✦✦

Roadside Picnic is a "first contact" story with a difference. Aliens have visited the Earth and gone away again, leaving behind them several landing areas (now called the Zones) littered with their refuse. The picnickers have gone; the pack rats, wary but curious, approach the crumpled bits of cellophane, the glittering pull tabs from beer cans, and try to carry them home to their holes.

Most of the mystifying debris is extremely dangerous. Some proves useful—eternal batteries that power automobiles—but the scientists never know if they are using the devices for their proper purposes or employing (as it were) Geiger counters as hand axes and electronic components as nose rings. They cannot figure out the principles of the artifacts, the science behind them. An international Institute sponsors research. A black market flourishes; "stalkers" enter the forbidden Zones and, at risk of various kinds of ghastly disfigurement and death, steal bits of alien litter, bring the stuff out, and sell it, sometimes to the Institute itself.

In the traditional first contact story, communication is achieved by courageous and dedicated spacemen, and thereafter ensues an exchange of knowledge, a military triumph, or a big-business deal. Here, the visitors from space, if they noticed our existence at all, were evidently uninterested in communication; perhaps to them we were savages, or perhaps pack rats. There was no communication; there can be no understanding.

Yet understanding is needed. The Zones are affecting everyone who has to do with them. Corruption and crime attend their exploration; fugitives from them are literally pursued by disaster; the children of the stalkers are genetically altered until they seem scarcely human.

The story set on this dark foundation is lively, racy, unpredictable. The setting appears to be North America, perhaps Canada, but the characters have no particular national characteristics. They are, however, individually vivid and likeable; the slimiest old stalker-profiteer has a revolting and endearing vitality. Human relations ring true. There are no superbrilliant intellects; people are commonplace. Red, the central figure, is ordinary to the point of being ornery, a hard-bitten man. Most of the characters are tough people leading degrading, discouraging lives, presented without sentimentality and without cynicism. Humanity is not flattered, but it's not cheapened. The authors' touch is tender, aware of vulnerability.

This use of ordinary people as the principal characters was fairly rare in science fiction when the book came out, and even now the genre slips easily into elitism—superbrilliant minds, extraordinary talents, officers not crew, the corridors of power not the working-class kitchen. Those who want the genre to remain specialized—"hard"—tend to prefer the elitist style. Those who see science fiction simply as a way of writing novels welcome the more Tolstoyan approach, in which a war is described not only from the generals' point of view but also through the eyes of housewives, prisoners, and boys of sixteen, or an alien visitation is described not only by knowledgeable scientists but also by its effects on commonplace people.

The question of whether human beings are or will be able to understand any and all information we receive from the universe is one that most science fiction, riding on the heady tide of scientism, used to answer with an unquestioning Yes. The Polish novelist Stanislaw Lem called it "the myth of our cognitive universalism." *Solaris* is the best known of his books on this theme, in which the human characters are defeated, humbled by their failure to comprehend alien messages or artifacts. They have failed the test.

The idea that the human race might be of absolutely no interest to a "more advanced" species could easily lend itself to overt sarcasm, but the authors' tone remains ironic, humorous, compassionate. Their ethical and intellectual sophistication becomes clear in a brilliant discussion, late in the novel, between a scientist and a disillusioned employee of the Institute about the implications, the meaning, of the alien visit. Yet the heart of the story is an individual destiny. The protagonists of idea-stories are marionettes, but Red is a mensch. We care about him, and both his survival and his salvation are at stake. This is, after all, a Russian novel.

And the Strugatskys raise the ante on Lem's question concerning human understanding. If the way humanity handles what the aliens left behind them is a test, or if Red, in the final, terrible scenes, undergoes trial by fire, what, in fact, is being tested? And how do we know whether we have passed or failed? What is "understanding"?

The final promise of "HAPPINESS, FREE, FOR EVERYONE" rings with unmistakably bitter political meaning. Yet the novel can't possibly be reduced to a mere fable of Soviet failure, or even the failure of science's dream of universal cognition. The last thing Red says in the book, speaking to God, or to us, is "I've never sold my soul to anyone! It's mine, it's human! Figure out yourself what I want—because I know it can't be bad!"

ROADSIDE PICNIC

Goodness. . . . You got to make it out of badness. . . . Because there isn't anything else to make it out of.

—Robert Penn Warren

AN EXCERPT FROM AN INTERVIEW WITH DR. VALENTINE PILLMAN BY A CORRESPONDENT FROM HARMONT RADIO, AFTER THE FORMER RECEIVED THE 19— NOBEL PRIZE IN PHYSICS.

INTERVIEWER: . . . I suppose that your first important discovery, Dr. Pillman, was the celebrated Pillman radiant?

DR. PILLMAN: I wouldn't say so. The Pillman radiant wasn't my first discovery, it wasn't important, and, strictly speaking, it wasn't a discovery. It's not entirely mine either.

INTERVIEWER: Doctor, you must be joking. Everyone knows about the Pillman radiant—even schoolchildren.

DR. PILLMAN: That's no surprise. As a matter of fact, it was discovered by a schoolboy. I'd tell you his name, but unfortunately, it has slipped my mind. Take a look in Stetson's *History of the Visit*—he's an excellent source on the subject. Yes, the radiant was discovered by a schoolboy, the coordinates were published by a college student, and yet it was named after me.

INTERVIEWER: Ah, yes, you never can tell who'll get credit for a discovery. Dr. Pillman, could you please explain to our listeners . . .

DR. PILLMAN: Of course. The Pillman radiant is really very simple. Imagine taking a large globe, giving it a good spin, then firing a few rounds at it. The bullet holes on the globe would fall on a certain smooth curve. The crux of my so-called important discovery is the following simple observation: all six Visit Zones are positioned on the surface of the planet like bullet holes made by a gun located somewhere between Earth and Deneb. Deneb is the alpha star of Cygnus, while the Pillman radiant is just our name for the point in space from which, so to speak, the shots were fired.

INTERVIEWER: Thank you, Doctor. Dear listeners: finally, a clear explanation of the Pillman radiant! By the way, the day before yesterday was the thirteenth anniversary of the Visit. Would you like to say a couple of words on the subject?

DR. PILLMAN: What would your listeners like to know? Keep in mind, I wasn't in Harmont at the time.

INTERVIEWER: That makes us all the more interested in what you thought when you heard that your hometown was invaded by a highly advanced alien civilization . . .

DR. PILLMAN: To be honest, at first I assumed it was a hoax. I couldn't imagine anything like that happening in our little town. Western Siberia, Uganda, the South Atlantic—even those seemed possible, but Harmont!

INTERVIEWER: But eventually you had to believe.

DR. PILLMAN: Eventually, yes.

INTERVIEWER: And then?

DR. PILLMAN: I suddenly realized that Harmont and the other five Zones—actually, pardon me, we only knew about four at the time—I noticed that they lay on a very smooth curve. So I calculated the coordinates of the radiant and sent it to *Nature*.

INTERVIEWER: And you weren't at all worried about the fate of your hometown?

DR. PILLMAN: Well, by then I believed in the Visit, but I simply couldn't force myself to swallow the hysterical articles about burning neighborhoods, monsters that devoured exclusively women and children, and bloody struggles between the invincible aliens and the doomed yet heroic units of the Royal Armoured Corps.

INTERVIEWER: I have to admit, you were right. Our fellow journalists sure made a mess of things . . . But let us return to science. Have you made other discoveries related to the Visit? Was the Pillman radiant the first of many?

DR. PILLMAN: It was my first and last discovery.

INTERVIEWER: But you've probably been carefully following the progress of international research in the Visit Zones?

DR. PILLMAN: Yes, I periodically flip through the *Reports*.

INTERVIEWER: You mean the *Reports of the International Institute of Extraterrestrial Cultures*?

DR. PILLMAN: Yes.

INTERVIEWER: And what, in your opinion, is the most important discovery of the last thirteen years?

DR. PILLMAN: The fact of the Visit.

INTERVIEWER: Pardon me?

DR. PILLMAN: The fact of the Visit is not only the most important discovery of the last thirteen years, it's the most important discovery in human history. It doesn't matter who these aliens were. Doesn't matter where they came from, why they came, why they left so quickly, or where they've vanished to since. What matters is that we now know for sure: humanity is not alone in the universe. I'm afraid the Institute of Extraterrestrial Cultures could never make a more fundamental discovery.

INTERVIEWER: That's incredibly interesting, Dr. Pillman, but actually I was referring to technological discoveries. Discoveries that our Earth engineers can use. After all, many distinguished scientists believe that the items we've found could completely change the course of human history.

DR. PILLMAN: Ah, I'm afraid I don't belong to their number. And I'm not an expert on specific discoveries.

INTERVIEWER: But for the last two years, you've acted as a consultant to the UN Commission on the Problems of the Visit . . .

DR. PILLMAN: That's correct. But I'm not involved in the research on extraterrestrial culture. As a consultant, I, along with my colleagues, represent the international scientific community on decisions about the internationalization of the Visit Zones. Roughly speaking, we make sure that no one outside the International Institute gets access to the alien marvels discovered in the Zones.

INTERVIEWER: Why, are there others with designs on them?

DR. PILLMAN: Yes.

INTERVIEWER: You probably mean stalkers?

DR. PILLMAN: I'm not familiar with the term.

INTERVIEWER: That's what the residents of Harmont call the desperate young men who, despite the grave risks, sneak into the Zone and smuggle out whatever they find. It's quite the new career.

DR. PILLMAN: Oh, I see. No, that's outside our area of expertise.

INTERVIEWER: Of course! That's police work. Out of curiosity, what exactly is within your area of expertise, Dr. Pillman?

DR. PILLMAN: There's a constant leak of materials from the Visit Zones into the hands of irresponsible people and organizations. We deal with the consequences of such leaks.

INTERVIEWER: Doctor, could you be a little more specific?

DR. PILLMAN: Wouldn't you rather move on to the arts? Aren't your listeners interested in my opinion about the beautiful Godi Müller?

INTERVIEWER: Of course! But first let's finish up with science. Aren't you, as a scientist, tempted to study these alien treasures yourself?

DR. PILLMAN: Hard question . . . I suppose I am.

INTERVIEWER: So there's a chance that one day we'll see you back on the streets of your hometown?

DR. PILLMAN: Perhaps.

I.

REDRICK SCHUHART, 23 YEARS OLD, SINGLE, LABORATORY ASSISTANT IN THE HARMONT BRANCH OF THE INTERNATIONAL INSTITUTE OF EXTRATERRESTRIAL CULTURES.

The other day, we're standing in the repository; it's evening already, nothing left to do but dump the lab suits, then I can head down to the Borscht for my daily dose of booze. I'm relaxing, leaning on the wall, my work all done and a cigarette at the ready, dying for a smoke—I haven't smoked for two hours—while he keeps fiddling with his treasures. One safe is loaded, locked, and sealed shut, and he's loading yet another one—taking the empties from our transporter, inspecting each one from every angle (and they are heavy bastards, by the way, fourteen pounds each), and, grunting slightly, carefully depositing them on the shelf.

He's been struggling with these empties for ages, and all, in my opinion, with no benefit to humanity or himself. In his place, I would have bailed a long time ago and gotten another job with the same pay. Although on the other hand, if you think about it, an empty really is a puzzling and even a mysterious thing. I've handled them lots of times myself, but every time I see one—I can't help it, I'm still amazed. It's just these two copper disks the size of a saucer, a quarter inch thick, about eighteen inches apart, and not a thing between the two. I mean, nothing whatsoever, zip, nada, zilch. You can stick your hand between them—maybe even your head, if the thing has unhinged you enough—nothing but empty space, thin air. And despite this, there must be something there, a force field of some sort, because so far no one's managed to push these disks together, or pull them apart either.

No, friends, it's hard to describe this thing if you haven't seen one. It looks much too simple, especially when you finally convince yourself that your eyes aren't playing tricks on you. It's like describing a glass to someone or, God forbid, a wineglass: you just wiggle your fingers in the air and curse in utter frustration. All right, we'll assume that you got it, and if you didn't, pick up a copy of the Institute's *Reports*—they have articles about these empties in every issue, complete with pictures.

Anyway, Kirill's been struggling with these empties for almost a year now. I've worked for him from the very beginning, but I still don't get what he wants with them, and to be honest, I haven't tried too hard to find out. Let him first figure it out for himself, sort it all out, then maybe I'll have a listen. But so far, one thing is clear to me: he's absolutely determined to dismantle an empty, dissolve it in acid, crush it under a press, or melt it in an oven. And then he'll finally get it, he'll be covered in glory, and the entire scientific world will simply shudder in pleasure. But for now, as far as I know, he's nowhere near this goal. He hasn't yet accomplished anything at all, except that he's exhausted himself, turned gray and quiet, and his eyes have become like a sick dog's—they even water. If it were someone else, I'd get him totally wasted, take him to a great girl to loosen him up a bit, then the next morning I'd feed him more booze, take him to more girls, and by the end of the week he'd be A-OK—good as new and ready to go. Except this sort of therapy wouldn't work on Kirill. There's no point in even suggesting it; he's not the type.

So, as I said, we're standing in the repository, I'm looking at him, the way he's gotten, how his eyes have sunk in, and I feel sorrier for him than I can say. And then I decide. Except I don't really decide—it's like the words tumble out themselves.

"Listen," I say, "Kirill . . ."

He's standing there, holding up the last empty, and looking like he wants to crawl right inside it.

"Listen," I say, "Kirill. What if you had a full empty, huh?"

"A full empty?" he repeats, knitting his brows like I'm speaking Greek.

"Yeah," I say. "It's your hydromagnetic trap, what's it called? Object seventy-seven B. Only with some shit inside, blue stuff."

I can tell—I'm starting to get through. He looks up at me, squints, and there in his eyes, behind the dog tears, appears a glimmer of intelligence, as he himself loves to put it. "Wait, wait," he says. "A full one? The same thing, except full?"

"Yes, exactly."

"Where?"

My Kirill's cured. Good as new and ready to go. "Let's go have a smoke," I say.

He promptly stuffs the empty into the safe, slams the door, gives the lock three and a half turns, and comes back with me to the lab. For an empty empty, Ernest would give four hundred bucks in cash, and I could bleed the bastard dry for a full one; but believe it or not, that doesn't even cross my mind, because in my hands Kirill has come to life again—he's buzzing with energy, almost bursting into song, bounding down the stairs four at a time, not letting a guy light his cigarette. Anyway, I tell him everything: what it looks like and where it is and how to best get at it. He immediately takes out a map, finds this garage, puts his finger on it, gives me a long look, and, of course, immediately figures me out, but then that isn't so hard . . .

"You devil, Red!" he says, smiling at me. "Well, let's get this over with. We'll go first thing tomorrow morning. I'll request a hoverboot and a pass at nine, and by ten we'll be off. All right?"

"All right," I say. "And who else will we take?"

"What do we need another guy for?"

"No way," I say. "This is no picnic. What if something happens to you? It's the Zone. Gotta follow the rules."

He gives a short laugh and shrugs. "Up to you. You know better."

No shit! Of course, that was him being generous: *Who needs another guy, we'll go by ourselves, we'll keep the whole thing dark, and no one will suspect a thing.* Except I know that the guys from the Institute don't go into the Zone in pairs. They have an unwritten rule around here: two guys do all the work while the third one watches, and when they ask later, he vouches there was no funny business.

"If it were up to me, I'd take Austin," Kirill says. "But you probably don't want him. Or would he do?"

"No," I say. "Anyone but him. You'll take Austin another time." Austin isn't a bad guy, he's got the right mix of courage and cowardice, but I think he's already doomed. You can't explain this to Kirill, but I know these things: the man has decided he's got the Zone completely figured out, and so he'll soon screw up and kick the bucket. And he can go right ahead. But not with me around.

"All right, all right," says Kirill. "How about Tender?" Tender is his second lab assistant. He isn't a bad guy, a calm sort.

"He's a bit old," I say. "And he has kids . . ."

"That's OK. He's been in the Zone already."

"Fine," I say. "Let it be Tender."

Anyway, he stays there poring over the map while I race straight to the Borscht, because my stomach is growling and my throat is parched.

The next day I get to work at nine, as usual, and show my ID. The guard on duty is the beefy sergeant I pummeled last year when he made a drunken pass at Guta. "Hey," he says. "They're looking all over the Institute for you, Red—"

I interrupt him politely. "I'm not 'Red' to you," I say. "Don't you try to pal around with me, you Swedish ape."

"For God's sake, Red!" he says in astonishment. "But they all call you that!"

I'm anxious about going into the Zone and cold sober to boot. I grab him by the shoulder belt and tell him exactly what he is and just how his mother conceived him. He spits on the floor, returns my ID, and continues without any more pleasantries.

"Redrick Schuhart," he says, "you are ordered to immediately report to the chief of security, Captain Herzog."

"There you go," I say. "Much better. Keep plugging away, Sergeant—you'll make lieutenant yet."

Meantime, I'm shitting my pants. What could Captain Herzog want from me during work hours? Well, off I go to report. He has an office on the third floor, a very nice office, complete with bars on the windows like a police station. Willy himself is sitting behind his desk, puffing on his pipe and typing some gibberish on his typewriter. Over in the corner, some sergeant is rummaging through a metal cabinet—must be a new guy;

I've never met him. We have more of these sergeants at the Institute than they have at division headquarters, all of them hale, hearty, and rosy cheeked. They don't need to go into the Zone and don't give a damn about world affairs.

"Hello," I say. "You requested my presence?"

Willy looks at me like I'm not there, pushes away his typewriter, puts an enormous file in front of him, and starts flipping through it. "Redrick Schuhart?" he says.

"That's my name," I answer, feeling an urge to burst into nervous laughter.

"How long have you worked at the Institute?"

"Two years, going on the third."

"Your family?"

"I'm all alone," I say. "An orphan."

Then he turns to the sergeant and orders him sternly, "Sergeant Lummer, go to the archives and bring back case 150." The sergeant salutes him and beats it. Willy slams the file shut and asks me gloomily, "Starting up your old tricks again, are you?"

"What old tricks?"

"You know damn well what old tricks. We've received information on you again."

Aha, I think. "And who was the source?"

He scowls and bangs his pipe on the ashtray in annoyance. "That's none of your business," he says. "I'm warning you as an old friend: give up this nonsense, give it up for good. If they catch you a second time, you won't walk away with six months. And they'll kick you out of the Institute once and for all, understand?"

"I understand," I say. "That much I understand. What I don't understand is what son of a bitch squealed on me . . ."

But he's staring through me again, puffing on his empty pipe, and flipping merrily through his file. That, then, signals the return of Sergeant Lummer with case 150. "Thank you, Schuhart," says Captain Willy Herzog, nicknamed the Hog. "That's all that I needed to know. You are free to go."

Well, I go to the locker room, change into my lab suit, and light up, the entire time trying to figure out: where are they getting the dirt? If it's from the Institute, then it's all lies, no one here knows a damn thing about me and never could. And if it's from the police . . . again, what could they know about except my old sins? Maybe the Vulture got nabbed; that bastard, to save his sorry ass, would rat on his own mother. But even the Vulture doesn't have a thing on me nowadays. I think and think, can't think of a thing, and decide not to give a damn. The last time I went into the Zone at night was three months ago; the swag is mostly gone, and the money is mostly spent. They didn't catch me then, and like hell they'll catch me now. I'm slippery.

But then, as I'm heading upstairs, it hits me, and I'm so stunned that I go back down to the locker room, sit down, and light up again. It turns out I can't go into the Zone today. And tomorrow I can't, and the day after tomorrow. It turns out the cops again have me on their radar, they haven't forgotten about me, and even if they have, someone has very kindly reminded them. And it doesn't even matter now who it was. No stalker, unless he's completely nuts, will go anywhere near the Zone when he knows he's being watched. Right now, I ought to be burrowing into some deep dark corner. *Zone? What Zone? I haven't set foot there in months, I don't even go there using my pass! What are you harassing an honest lab assistant for?*

I think all this through and even feel a bit of relief that I don't need to go into the Zone today. Except how am I going to break it to Kirill?

I tell him straight out. "I'm not going into the Zone. Your orders?"

At first, of course, he just gawks at me. Eventually, something seems to click. He takes me by the elbow, leads me to his office, sits me down at his table, and perches on the windowsill nearby. We light up. Silence. Then he asks me cautiously, "Red, did something happen?"

Now what am I supposed to tell him? "No," I say, "nothing happened. Well, I blew twenty bucks last night playing poker—that Noonan sure knows how to play, the bastard."

"Hold on," he says. "What, you mean you just changed your mind?"

I almost groan from the tension. "I can't," I say through my teeth. "I can't, you get it? Herzog just called me to his office."

He goes limp. Again misery is stamped on his face, and again his eyes look like a sick poodle's. He takes a ragged breath, lights a new cigarette with the remains of the old one, and says quietly, "Believe me, Red, I didn't breathe a word to anyone."

"Stop it," I say. "Who's talking about you?"

"I haven't even told Tender yet. I got a pass for him, but I haven't even asked him whether he'd come or not . . ."

I keep smoking in silence. Ye gods, the man just doesn't understand.

"What did Herzog say to you, anyway?"

"Oh, not much," I say. "Someone squealed on me, that's all."

He gives me a funny look, hops off the windowsill, and starts walking back and forth. He's pacing around his office while I sit there, blowing smoke rings and keeping my trap shut. I feel sorry for him, of course, and really this is rotten luck: a great cure I found for the guy's depression. And who's to blame here? I am, that's who. I tempted a child with candy, except the candy's in a jar, out of reach on the top shelf . . . He stops pacing, comes up to me, and, looking somewhere off to the side, asks awkwardly, "Listen, Red, how much would it cost—a full empty?"

I don't get it at first, thinking he wants to buy one somewhere else, except good luck finding another one—it might be the only one in the world, and besides, he wouldn't have enough money. Where would a Russian scientist get that much cash? Then I feel like I've been slapped: does the bastard think I'm pulling this stunt for the dough? *For God's sake,* I think, *asshole, what do you take me for?* I even open my mouth, ready to shower him with curses. And I stop. Because, actually, what else could he take me for? A stalker's a stalker, the money is all that matters to him, he gambles his life for the money. So it follows that yesterday I threw out the line, and today I'm working the bait, jacking up the price.

These thoughts shock me speechless. Meanwhile, he keeps staring at me intently, and in his eyes I don't see contempt—only a kind of compassion. And so I explain it to him calmly. "No one has ever gone to the garage with a pass," I say. "They haven't even laid the route to it yet, you know that. So here we are coming back, and your Tender starts bragging how we made straight for the garage, took what we needed, and returned immediately. As if we went to the warehouse. And it will be perfectly obvious," I say, "that we knew what we were coming for. That means that someone was guiding us. And which one of us three it was—that's a real tough one. You understand how this looks for me?"

I finish my little speech, and we silently look each other in the eye. Then he suddenly claps his hands, rubs them together, and cheerfully announces, "Well, of course, no means no. I understand you, Red, so I can't judge you. I'll go myself. I'll manage, with luck. Not my first time."

He spreads the map on the windowsill, leans on his hands, hunches over it, and all his good cheer evaporates before my eyes. I hear him mumble, "Three hundred and ninety feet . . . or even four hundred . . . and a bit more in the garage. No, I won't take Tender. What do you think, Red, maybe I shouldn't take Tender? He has two kids, after all . . ."

"They won't let you out on your own," I say.

"Don't worry, they will," he says, still mumbling. "I know all the sergeants . . . and all the lieutenants. I don't like those trucks! Thirteen years they've stood in the open air, and they still look brand-new . . . Twenty steps away, the gasoline tanker is rusted through, but they look fresh from the assembly line. Oh, that Zone!"

He lifts his gaze from the map and stares out the window. And I stare out the window, too. There, beyond the thick leaded glass, is our Zone—right there, almost within reach, tiny and toylike from the thirteenth floor . . .

If you take a quick look at it, everything seems OK. The sun shines there just like it's supposed to, and it seems as if nothing's changed, as if everything's the same as thirteen years ago. My old man, rest his soul, could take a look and see nothing out of place, might only wonder why there isn't smoke coming from the factories—*Is there a strike on?* Yellow ore in conical mounds, blast furnaces gleaming in the sun, rails, rails, and more rails, on the rails a locomotive . . . In short, the typical industrial landscape. Except there's no one around: no one living, no one dead. Ah, and there's the garage: a long gray tube, the gates wide open, and trucks standing next to it on the lot. Thirteen years they've stood, and nothing's happened to them. Kirill got that right—he has a good head on his shoulders. God help you if you ever pass between those vehicles, you must always go around . . . There's a useful crack in the pavement there, if it hasn't filled with brambles. Four hundred feet—where's he measuring that from? Oh! Must be from the last marker. Right, can't be more than that from there. These eggheads are making progress after all . . . Look, they've laid a route all the way to the dump, and a clever route at that! There it is, the ditch where the Slug kicked the bucket, all of six feet away from their route. And Knuckles kept telling the Slug, "You idiot, stay away from those ditches or there will be nothing left to bury!" A real prophecy that was—nothing left to bury indeed. That's the Zone for you: come back with swag, a miracle; come back alive, success; come back with a patrol bullet in your ass, good luck; and everything else—that's fate.

I take a look at Kirill and see that he's watching me out of the corner of his eye. And the look on his face makes me do another one-eighty. Screw them, I think, let them all rot in hell, what can those toads do to me after all?

He doesn't need to say a thing, but he does. "Laboratory Assistant Schuhart," he says. "From official—I emphasize 'official'—sources I have received information suggesting that the inspection of the garage may be of great value to world science. I propose we inspect the garage. A bonus paycheck is guaranteed." And he's grinning from ear to ear.

"What official sources?" I ask, grinning like an idiot myself.

"These are confidential sources," he answers. "But I am authorized to tell you." Here he stops grinning and frowns. "Say, from Dr. Douglas."

"Ah," I say, "from Dr. Douglas. And which Dr. Douglas is that?"

"Sam Douglas," he says drily. "He perished last year."

My skin crawls. For God's sake! Who talks about these things before setting out? These eggheads never have a grain of sense . . . I jab my cigarette butt into the ashtray. "Fine. Where's your Tender? How long do we have to wait for him?"

Anyway, we drop the topic. Kirill calls PPS and orders us a hoverboot while I take a look at their map. It's not bad at all—made from a highly magnified aerial photograph. You can even make out the ridges on the tire lying next to the garage gates. If we stalkers had maps like this . . . then again, much good it'd do at night, when you're showing your ass to the stars and can't see your own two hands.

And here Tender shows up. Red in the face, puffing and panting. His daughter got sick, he had to go fetch the doctor. He apologizes for being late. Well, we hand him quite the gift—a trip to the Zone. At first he almost forgets to puff and pant, the poor guy.

"What do you mean, the Zone?" he says. "Why me?" However, when he hears about the double bonus and that Red Schuhart is coming too, he calms down and starts breathing again.

Anyway, we go down to the "boudoir," Kirill rushes off to get the passes, we show the passes to yet another sergeant, and this sergeant gives each of us a specsuit. Now these really are handy. Dye a specsuit any color other than the original red, and any stalker would put down five hundred for it without batting an eyelash. I've long since vowed to figure out a way to swipe one from the Institute. At first glance, it's nothing special, looks like a diving suit, with a helmet to match and a large visor at the front. Maybe it's not quite like a diving suit, actually, more like a space suit. It's light, comfortable, not too tight, and you don't sweat in it from the heat. You can go right through a fire in this thing, and no gas will penetrate it. It's even bulletproof, they say. Of course, fire, toxic gas, and bullets—these are only Earth perils. The Zone doesn't have those; in the Zone you have other worries. Anyhow, truth be told, even in their specsuits people drop like flies. On the other hand, without them it'd probably be even worse. These suits are completely safe from the burning fuzz, for example. And from Satan's blossom and its spit . . . All right.

We pull on our specsuits, I pour some nuts and bolts from a bag into my hip pocket, and we plod across the Institute yard toward the Zone entrance. That's how they always do it around here, so that everyone can see: *There they go, the heroes of science, to lay themselves down on the altar to mankind, knowledge, and the Holy Spirit, amen.* And sure enough, sympathetic mugs poke out of every window all the way up to the fifteenth floor; hankies waving good-bye and an orchestra are the only things missing.

"Keep your head high," I tell Tender. "Suck in your gut, soldier! A grateful humanity won't forget you!"

He gives me a look, and I see that he's in no mood for jokes. He's right—this is no joke. But when you're leaving for the Zone, it's one of two things: you start bawling, or you crack jokes—and I'm sure as hell not crying. I take a look at Kirill. He's holding up OK, only mouthing something silently, as if praying.

"Praying?" I ask. "Pray, pray! The farther into the Zone, the closer to heaven."

"What?" he says.

"Pray!" I yell. "Stalkers cut in line at the gates of heaven!"

And he suddenly smiles and pats me on the back, as if to say, *Nothing will happen as long as you are with me, and if it does, well, we only die once.* God, he's a funny guy.

We hand our passes over to the last sergeant—this time, for a change of pace, he happens to be a lieutenant; I know him, his pop sells cemetery fencing in Rexopolis—and there's the hoverboot waiting for us, the guys from PPS have flown it over and left it at the checkpoint. Everyone is gathered already: the ambulance and the firefighters and our valiant guards, the fearless rescuers—a bunch of overfed slackers with their helicopter. I wish to God I'd never set eyes on them!

We climb into the boot. Kirill takes the controls and looks at me. "Well, Red," he says, "your orders?"

I slowly lower the specsuit zipper on my chest, pull out a flask, take a long sip, screw the lid back on, and put the flask back. I can't do without this. God knows how many times I've been in the Zone, but without it—no way, can't do it. They're both looking at me and waiting.

"All right," I say. "I'm not offering you any, since this is our first time going in together, and I don't know how the stuff affects you. Here is how we'll do things. Everything I say will be carried out immediately and unconditionally. If someone hesitates or starts asking questions, I'll hit whatever is in reach, my apologies in advance. For example, say I order you, Mr. Tender, to walk on your hands. And at that very moment, you, Mr. Tender, must stick your fat ass up in the air and do as you are told. And if you don't do as you are told, you may never see your sick daughter again. Got it? But I'll take care that you do see her."

"Just don't forget to give the orders, Red," croaks Tender, who is completely red, sweating already and smacking his lips. "I'll walk on my teeth, never mind my hands. I'm no novice."

"You are both novices to me," I say, "and I won't forget the orders, don't you worry. Oh, just in case, do you know how to drive a boot?"

"He knows how," says Kirill. "He's good at it."

"Glad to hear," I say. "Then we're off. Lower your visors! Low speed along the marked route, altitude nine feet! At the twenty-seventh marker, stop."

Kirill lifts the boot to nine feet and puts it in low gear while I discreetly turn my head and blow over my left shoulder for luck. Looking back, I see our guards, the rescuers, are clambering into their helicopter, the firefighters are standing up in respect, the lieutenant at the door of the checkpoint is saluting us, the idiot, and above them all—an immense banner, already faded: WELCOME TO EARTH, DEAR ALIENS! Tender made a move to wave them all good-bye, but I gave him a sharp nudge in the ribs to knock the ceremonies out of him. *I'll show you how to bid farewell, you fat-assed fool!*

We're off.

To the right of us is the Institute, to the left the Plague Quarter, and we're gliding from marker to marker down the middle of the street. Lord, it's been a while since anyone's walked or driven here. The pavement's all cracked, grass has grown through the crevices, but here at least it's still our human grass. On the sidewalk to the left, the black brambles begin, and from this we see how well the Zone sets itself apart: the black thicket along the road looks almost mowed. No, these aliens must have been decent guys. They left a hell of a mess, of course, but at least they put clear bounds on their crap. Even the burning fuzz doesn't make it over to our side, though you'd think the wind would carry it around all four directions.

The houses in the Plague Quarter are peeling and lifeless, but the windows are mostly intact, only so dirty that they look opaque. Now at night when you crawl by, you can see the glow inside, as if alcohol were burning in bluish tongues. That's the hell slime radiating from the basement. But mostly it looks like an ordinary neighborhood, with ordinary houses, nothing special about it except that there are no people around. By the way, in this brick building over here lived our math teacher, the Comma. He was a pain in the ass and a loser, his second wife left him right before the Visit, and his daughter had a cataract in one eye—I remember we used to tease her to tears. During the initial panic, he ran in nothing but underwear all the way to the bridge, like his neighbors—ran for four miles nonstop. After that he got a bad case of the plague, which peeled his skin and nails right off. Almost everyone who lived here got the plague. A few died, but mostly old folks, and not all of them either. I, for one, think it wasn't the plague that did them in but sheer terror.

Now in those three neighborhoods over there, people went blind. That's what people call them nowadays: the First

Blind Quarter, the Second Blind Quarter . . . They didn't go completely blind but rather got something resembling night blindness. Strangely, they say they weren't blinded by a flash of light, though it's said there were some bright flashes, but by an awful noise. It thundered so loudly, they say, that they instantly went blind. Doctors tell them: That's impossible, you can't be remembering right! No, they insist, there was loud thunder, from which they went blind. And by the way, no one else heard any thunder at all . . .

Yeah, it looks like nothing happened here. That glass kiosk over there doesn't have a single scratch on it. And look at that stroller near the gates—even the linen in it looks clean. Only the TV antennas give the place away—they're overgrown with wispy hairs. Our eggheads have long been hankering after these antennas: they'd like to know, you see, what this hair is—we don't have it anywhere else, only in the Plague Quarter and only on the antennas. But most important, it's right here, beneath our very own windows. Last year, they got an idea, lowered an anchor from a helicopter, and hooked a clump of hair. They gave it a pull—suddenly, a *psssst*! We looked down and saw that the antenna was smoking, the anchor was smoking, even the cable itself was smoking, and not just smoking but hissing poisonously, like a rattlesnake. Well, the pilot, never mind that he was a lieutenant, quickly figured out what's what, dumped the cable, and hightailed it out of there. There it is, their cable, hanging down almost to the ground and covered with hair . . .

We glide slowly to the end of the street, at the bend. Kirill looks at me: *Should I turn?* I wave him on: *Go in lowest gear.* Our boot turns and drifts in lowest gear over the last few feet of human land. The sidewalk's getting closer and closer, there's the shadow of the boot inching over the brambles . . . Here's the Zone! And instantly a chill runs down my spine. I feel it every time, but I still don't know whether it's the Zone greeting me or a stalker's nerves acting up. Every time I figure I'll go back and ask others if they feel it too, and every time I forget.

All right, so we're drifting peacefully above the abandoned gardens, the motor under our feet is humming steadily and calmly—it doesn't care, nothing can hurt it. And here my Tender cracks. We don't even make it to the first marker before he starts babbling. You know, the way novices babble in the Zone: his teeth are chattering, his heart is galloping, he's out of it, and though embarrassed he can't get a grip. I think this is like diarrhea for them; they can't help it, the words just keep pouring out. And the things they'll talk about! They'll rave about the scenery, or they'll philosophize about the aliens, or they might even go on about something totally irrelevant. Like our Tender here: he's started in on his new suit and now just can't shut up about it. How much it cost and the fine wool it's made of and how the tailor changed the buttons for him . . .

"Be quiet," I say.

He gives me a sad look, smacks his lips, and goes on again, now about the silk he needed for the lining. Meanwhile, the gardens are ending, we're already above the clay wasteland that used to be the town dump, and I notice a breeze. There was no wind a moment ago, but suddenly there's a breeze, dust clouds are swirling, and I think I hear something.

"Quiet, asshole," I tell Tender.

No, he just can't shut up. Now he's going on about the horsehair. All right, no help for it, then.

"Stop," I tell Kirill.

He stops immediately. Quick reaction—good man. I take Tender by the shoulder, turn him toward me, and smack him hard on his visor. He slams nose first into the glass, poor guy, closes his eyes, and shuts up. And as soon as he quiets down, I hear: *crack-crack-crack* . . . *crack-crack-crack* . . . Kirill is looking at me, jaws clenched, teeth bared. I hold up my hand. *Don't move, for God's sake, please don't move.* But he also hears the crackling and, like any novice, feels the need to immediately do something.

"Go back?" he whispers.

I desperately shake my head and wave my fist right in his visor—*Cut that out.* For God's sake! You never know which way to look with these novices—at the Zone or at them . . . And here my mind goes blank. Over the pile of ancient trash, over the colorful rags and broken glass, drifts a tremor, a vibration, just like the hot air above a tin roof at noon; it floats over the mound and continues, cuts across our path right beside a marker, lingers over the road, waits for half a second—or am I just imagining that?—and slithers into the field, over the bushes, over the rotten fences, toward the old car graveyard.

Damn these eggheads, a great job they did: ran their road down here amid the junk! And I'm a smart one myself—what on Earth was I thinking while mooning over their stupid map?

"Go on at low speed," I tell Kirill.

"What was that?"

"God knows! It came and went, thank God. And shut up, please. Right now, you aren't a person, got it? Right now, you are a machine, my steering wheel, a lever . . ."

At this point I realize that I might be getting a case of verbal diarrhea myself.

"That's it," I say. "Not another word."

Damn, I need a drink! What I'd give to take out my flask, unscrew the lid, slowly, deliberately put it to my mouth, and tilt my head back, so it could pour right in . . . Then swirl the liquor around and take another swig . . . I tell you, these specsuits are a piece of shit. I've lived for years without a specsuit, Lord knows, and plan to live for many more, but not having a drink at a time like this! Ah, well, enough of that.

The wind seems to have died down and there are no suspicious noises; all we hear is the engine humming steadily and sleepily. Meanwhile the sun is shining, the heat is pressing down . . . There's a haze above the garage. Everything seems fine, the markers are floating by us one by one. Tender's silent, Kirill's silent—they are learning, the novices. *Don't worry, guys, even in the Zone you can breathe if you know how.* Ah, and here's the twenty-seventh marker—a metal pole with a red "27" on it. Kirill looks at me, I nod at him, and our boot stops.

The fun and games are over. Now the most important thing is to stay completely calm. We're in no hurry, there's no wind, and the visibility is good. Over there's the ditch where the Slug kicked the bucket—you can make out something colorful in there, maybe some clothes of his. He was a lousy guy, rest his soul, greedy, stupid, and dirty; that's the only kind that get mixed up with the Vulture, those the Vulture Burbridge spots a mile away and gets his claws into. Although, to be fair, the Zone doesn't give a damn who the good guys and the bad guys are, and it turns out we gotta thank you, Slug: you were an idiot, and no one even remembers your real name, but you did show us smarter folks where not to go . . . OK. The best thing, of course, would be to get to the pavement. The pavement's flat, you can see everything, and I know that crevice in it. Except I don't like those mounds. If we head straight to the pavement, we have to pass right between them. There they stand, smirking and waiting for us. No, I'm not going between the two of you. That's the stalker's second commandment: it has to be clear for a hundred paces either to your left or to your right. Now what we could do is go over the left mound . . . Although I have no idea what's behind it. According to the map there's nothing there, but who trusts maps?

"Listen, Red," whispers Kirill. "Let's jump, eh? Fifty feet up and then right back down, and there we'll be at the garage, eh?"

"Quiet, you," I say. "Just leave me alone right now."

Up, he says. And what if something gets you at that height? They won't even be able to find the pieces. Or maybe there's a bug trap around here—never mind the pieces, there will be nothing left at all. These risk takers really get me: he doesn't like waiting, you see, so let's jump . . . In any case, it's clear how to get to the mound, and we'll figure the rest out from there. I slip my hand into my pocket and pull out a handful of nuts and bolts. I put them on the palm of my hand, show them to Kirill, and say, "Remember the story of Hansel and Gretel? Read it in school? Well, here we'll have that in reverse. Look!"

And I throw the first nut. It flies a short way, like I intended, and lands about twenty-five feet away. The nut goes fine.

"Did you see that?" I ask.

"So?" he says.

"Don't 'so' me. I'm asking you, did you see that?"

"Yeah, I did."

"Now, take our boot over to that nut at low speed and stop six feet in front of it. Got it?"

"Got it. You looking for graviconcentrates?"

"Never you mind what I'm looking for. Give me a second, I want to throw another one. Watch where it falls, then don't take your eyes off it."

I throw another nut. Naturally, this one also goes fine and lands just ahead of the first one.

"Go ahead," I say.

He starts the boot. His face has become completely calm; you can see he's figured everything out. They are all like that, the eggheads. The most important thing for them is to come up with a name. Until he comes up with one, you feel really sorry for him, he looks so lost. But when he finds a label like "graviconcentrate," he thinks he's figured it all out and perks right up.

We pass the first nut, then the second and third. Tender keeps sighing, shifting from one foot to the other and yawning nervously with a slight whimper—he's suffering, the poor guy. It's all right, this will probably do him good. He'll take ten pounds off today, this is better than any diet . . . I throw the fourth nut. It doesn't go quite right. I can't explain it, but I feel it in my gut—something's off. I immediately grab Kirill's hand.

"Stop," I say. "Don't move an inch."

I take the fifth nut and throw it farther and higher. There it is, the bug trap! The nut goes up all right and starts going down fine, but halfway down it looks like someone tugged it off to the side, pulling it so hard that it goes right into the clay and disappears.

"Ever see that?" I whisper.

"Only in the movies," he says, straining forward so far he almost falls off the boot. "Throw one more, eh?"

Jesus. One more! As if one would be enough. Lord, these scientists! Anyway, I throw out eight more nuts, until I figure out the shape of the trap. To be honest, I could have managed with seven, but I throw one especially for him, right into the center, so he can properly admire his graviconcentrate. It smashes into the clay as if it were a ten-pound weight instead of a nut, then goes right out of sight, leaving only a hole in the ground. He even grunts with pleasure.

"All right," I say. "We've had our fun, but that's enough. Look over here. I'm throwing one out to show the way, don't take your eyes off it."

Anyway, we go around the bug trap and climb to the top of the mound. It's a puny little mound, I've never even noticed it until today. Right . . . OK, so we're hanging above the mound, the pavement is a stone's throw away, at most twenty paces from here. Everything's visible—you can make out every blade of grass, every little crack in the ground. It ought to be smooth sailing from here. Just throw the nut and get on with it.

I can't throw the nut.

I don't understand what's happening to me, but I just can't force myself to throw it.

"What is it?" says Kirill. "Why did we stop here?"

"Wait," I say. "Just be quiet, for God's sake."

All right, I think, now I'll throw the nut, nothing to it, we'll glide right by, won't disturb a single blade of grass—half a minute, and there's the pavement . . . And suddenly I break into an awful sweat! Some even gets into my eyes, and I know right then I won't be throwing a nut that direction. To our left—sure, as many as you like. That route is longer, and the stones over there look suspicious, but it'll have to do; I just can't throw a nut in front of us. And so I throw one to our left. Kirill doesn't say a thing, just turns the boot, drives it over to the nut, and only then looks at me. I must look pretty bad, since he immediately looks away.

"Don't worry," I say. "You can't always take the straight path." And I throw the last nut onto the pavement.

Things get easier now. I find my crack in the pavement, which still looks good, isn't overgrown with weeds, and hasn't changed color; I feel happy just looking at it. And it takes us all the way to the gates of the garage better than any markers.

I order Kirill to take us down to five feet, and I lie on my stomach and peer into the open gates. At first, I can't see a thing, just darkness, but then my eyes adjust, and I see that the garage seems unchanged. The dump truck is standing over the pit, just like before—in great shape, without any rust holes or spots—and the stuff on the floor around it also looks the same; that's probably because there isn't much hell slime in the pit, and it hasn't splashed out since my last visit. Only one thing worries me: something silver is sparkling at the back of the garage, near the canisters. That wasn't there before. Well, all right, let it sparkle; we aren't going back because of that! It's not even sparkling in an unusual way, just a tiny bit, mildly and almost gently . . . I get up, dust myself off, and look around. Ah, and here are the trucks parked on the lot, really just like new; since I've last been here, they've gotten even newer, while the gasoline tanker, poor thing, is now completely rusted through and about to fall apart. And there's the tire lying beside the gates, that you can see on their map . . .

I don't like the look of that tire. There's something wrong with its shadow. The sun is at our backs, but the shadow is stretching toward us. Oh well, it's far away from us. Anyway, everything's fine; we'll manage. But still, what could be sparkling there? Or am I imagining things? Now, the thing to do would be to light up, sit down quietly, and think it through—what's that silver stuff above the canisters, why isn't it also beside them? Why is that tire's shadow like that? The Vulture Burbridge was telling us something about the shadows, which sounded strange but harmless . . . The shadows do funny things around here. But what about that silver stuff? It looks just like a cobweb. What sort of spider could have left it behind? I've yet to see a single bug in the Zone. And the worst thing is that my empty is lying right there, two steps away from the canisters. I should have just taken it last time, then I'd have nothing to worry about. But the damn thing is full, so it's heavy—I could have managed to lift it, but to drag it on my back, at night, crawling on all fours . . . Yeah, if you've never carried an empty, go ahead and try: it's like lugging twenty pounds of water without a bucket. Well, should I go in? I guess I should. A drink would sure help . . .

I turn to Tender and say, "Kirill and I are going into the garage now. Stay here with the boot. Don't touch the controls without my permission, no matter what happens, even if the ground below you catches fire. If you chicken out, I'll find you in the afterlife."

He nods at me seriously: *Don't worry, I won't chicken out.* His nose looks like a plum—I really gave it to him. I carefully lower the emergency ropes, take one more look at the silver stuff, wave at Kirill, and start to climb down. I stand on the pavement, waiting for him to go down the other rope. "Take it slow," I say. "Don't rush. Don't raise dust."

We're standing on the pavement, the boot is swaying next to us, the ropes are wriggling under our feet. Tender is sticking his head over the railings, looking at us with despair in his eyes. We have to go in. I tell Kirill, "Walk two steps behind me, keep your eyes on my back, and stay alert."

And I go in. I stop in the doorway and look around. Damn, it sure is easier to work during the day! I remember how I lay in this same doorway. It was pitch black, the hell slime was shooting tongues of flame up from the pit, blue ones, like burning alcohol, and the most frustrating thing was that the damn flames didn't even give off light but only made the garage seem darker. And now it's a breeze. My eyes have gotten used to the gloom, I can see everything, even the dust in the darkest corners. And there really is something sparkling there, silver threads are stretching from the canisters to the floor—looks just like a cobweb. It might in fact be a cobweb, but better to stay away from it.

And here I screw up. I should have Kirill walk next to me, wait until his eyes get used to the dark, and show him this cobweb, point right at it. But I'm used to working alone—my eyes adjust to the light, and I don't think about Kirill.

I step inside and head straight for the canisters. I squat by the empty; there aren't any cobwebs stuck to it. I take one end of it.

"All right, grab hold," I say, "and don't drop it—it's heavy."

I look up at him, and my heart leaps into my throat—I can't say a word. I want to yell *Stop, don't move!* and can't. And there probably isn't enough time, anyway, it all happens so fast: Kirill steps over the empty, turns around, and his back goes right into the silver stuff. The only thing I can do is close my eyes. I feel weak all over, can't hear a thing—just the sound of the cobweb tearing. With a faint crackle, like a regular cobweb, except louder, of course. I'm crouching there with my eyes closed, can't feel my hands or my feet, then Kirill says, "Well, are we picking it up?"

"Let's do it," I say.

We pick up the empty and, walking sideways, carry it to the exit. The damn thing is heavy—it's hard to carry even for the two of us. We go out into the sun and stop near the boot. Tender is reaching his paws toward us already.

"All right," says Kirill, "one, two—"

"No," I say, "wait. Put it down first."

We put it down.

"Turn around," I say.

He turns without a word. I look—there's nothing on his back. I check this way and that. Still nothing. Then I look around and check the canisters. Nothing there either.

"Listen," I say to Kirill, still looking at the canisters. "Did you see the cobweb?"

"What cobweb? Where?"

"Never mind," I say. "The Lord is merciful." Meanwhile, I think, Actually, that remains to be seen. "All right," I say, "grab hold."

We load the empty onto the boot and put it on its side so it won't roll around. It's standing there, looking lovely—spotless, new, the copper gleaming in the sun, the blue filling swirling slowly between the copper disks in cloudy streams. It's now obvious that it isn't an empty but a container, like a glass jar with blue syrup inside. We admire it for a bit, then clamber up onto the boot ourselves and without further ado are on our way back.

These scientists sure have it easy! First of all, they work in the daylight. And second, the only hard part is getting into the Zone—on the way back, the boot drives itself. It has this feature, a route memorizer, I guess, that takes the boot back along the exact same route it took here. We're floating back, repeating each maneuver, stopping, hanging in the air a bit, then continuing; we pass over all the nuts, I could pick them up if I wanted to.

Of course, my novices immediately cheer up. They're looking this way and that, their fear almost gone—only curiosity left, and joy that everything ended well. They begin to chatter. Tender is waving his arms and threatening to come right back into the Zone after dinner, to lay the path to the garage. Kirill takes me by the sleeve and starts explaining his graviconcentrate to me—that is, the bug trap. Well, eventually I have to shut them up. I calmly explain to them how many idiots became careless with relief and kicked the bucket on the way back. Be quiet, I tell them, and keep your eyes open, or you'll meet the fate of Shorty Lyndon. That works. They don't even ask me what happened to Shorty Lyndon. Much better. In the Zone you can easily take a familiar route a hundred times and kick off on the hundred and first. We're floating in silence, and only one thing is on my mind: how I'll twist the cap off the flask. I keep visualizing how I'll take the first sip, but the cobweb occasionally flickers before my mind's eye.

In short, we make it out of the Zone, and they send us, still in our boot, into the delouser, or, as the scientists say, the sanitization hangar. They wash us in three boiling liquids and three alkaline solutions, smear some crap on us, sprinkle us with powder, and wash us again, then dry us and say, "Get going, guys, you're free!" Tender and Kirill drag the empty along. People show up in droves—it's hard to get through, and it's so typical: everyone is staring and shouting greetings, but no one is brave enough to lend a hand to three tired men. Oh well, that's none of my business. Nothing is my business anymore . . .

I pull the specsuit off and throw it on the floor—the sergeant lackeys'll pick it up—then I head for the showers, since I'm soaked from head to toe. I lock myself in the stall, take out the flask, unscrew it, and attach myself to it like a leech. I'm sitting on the bench, my heart is empty, my head is empty, my soul is empty, gulping down the hard stuff like water. Alive. I got out. The Zone let me out. The damned hag. My lifeblood. Traitorous bitch. Alive. The novices can't understand this. No one but a stalker can understand. And tears are pouring down my face—maybe from the booze, maybe from something else. I suck the flask dry; I'm wet, the flask is dry. As usual, I need just one more sip. Oh well, we'll fix that. We can fix anything now. Alive. I light a cigarette and stay seated. I can feel it—I'm coming around. The bonus comes to mind. Here at the Institute that's a given. I could go get the envelope this very minute. Or maybe they'll bring it right to the showers.

I slowly undress. I take off my watch and look at it—my Lord, we were in the Zone for more than five hours! Five hours. I shudder. Yes, my friends, there's no such thing as time in the Zone. Although, really, what's five hours to a stalker? Nothing at all. You want twelve hours instead? Or maybe two whole days? When you don't finish in one night, you stay in the Zone all day long facedown in the dirt; you can't even pray properly but can only rave deliriously, and you don't know if you are dead or alive. And the next night when you finish, you try to get out with the swag, except the guards are patrolling the borders with machine guns. And those toads hate you, they get no pleasure from arresting you, the bastards are scared to death that you might be contagious—they just want to shoot you down . . . And they are holding all the cards: go ahead and prove later that they killed you illegally. So there you are again, facedown in the dirt, praying until dawn, then until dusk, the swag lying beside you, and you don't even know if it's simply lying there or slowly killing you. Or maybe you'll end up like Knuckles Isaac—he got stuck in an open area at dawn, lost his way, and wound up between two ditches—couldn't go left or right. They shot at him for two hours, couldn't hit him. For two hours he played dead. Thank God, they finally got tired of it, figured he was finished, and left. I saw him after that—I didn't recognize him. They broke him, left only a shell of a man.

I wipe away my tears and turn on the water. I take a long shower, first in hot water, then in cold water, then again in hot water. I use up a whole bar of soap. Eventually I get sick of it. I turn the water off and immediately hear rapping on the door, and Kirill yelling cheerfully, "Hey, stalker, come on out! It smells like money out here!"

Money—that's always good news. I open the door, Kirill's standing there wearing only boxer shorts, in great spirits, no sign of melancholy, and he's handing me an envelope.

"Take it," he says, "from grateful humanity."

"Screw grateful humanity! How much is it?"

"For extraordinary courage under danger, just this once—two months' pay!"

Ah. That's real money. If they paid me two months' salary for every empty I brought in, I'd have told Ernest to fuck off a long time ago.

"So, are you happy?" says Kirill, beaming, grinning from ear to ear.

"I'm all right," I say. "How about you?"

He doesn't say anything. He grabs me around the neck, presses me to his sweaty chest, hugs me, then pushes me away and disappears into the next stall.

"Hey!" I shout after him. "Where's Tender? Washing out his undies, I bet."

"No way! Tender is surrounded by reporters, you should see how important he's gotten. He's giving them a real perspicuous account . . ."

"What kind of account?" I say.

"A perspicuous one."

"All right," I say, "sir. Next time I'll bring a dictionary, sir." Then I feel an electric shock go through me. "Wait, Kirill," I say. "Come out here."

"But I'm naked already," he says.

"Come out, I'm not a girl!"

All right, he comes out. I take him by the shoulders and turn his back toward me. No, I imagined it. His back is clean, nothing on it except some rivulets of dried sweat.

"What's with you and my back?" he asks.

I kick his naked ass, dive into my stall, and lock the door. Nerves, God damn it. I keep imagining things: first there, now here. To hell with it all! I'll get plastered tonight. I gotta beat Richard, that's the thing! The bastard sure knows how to play . . . You can't win no matter what you're dealt. I tried cheating, even blessing the cards under the table, nothing worked.

"Kirill!" I yell. "Are you going to the Borscht today?"

"It's pronounced 'borshch,' not 'borsht'—how many times do I have to tell you?"

"Cut it out! The sign says BORSCHT. Don't you try to force your customs on us. Are you coming or not? I'd like to beat Richard."

"I'm not sure, Red. You simple soul, you don't even understand what we found today . . ."

"And you do?"

"To be honest, I don't either. That's fair. But at least we now know what these empties were used for, and if one of my ideas works out . . . I'll write a paper and dedicate it to you personally: 'To Redrick Schuhart, honored stalker, with reverence and gratitude.'"

"And then they'll put me away for two years," I say.

"But you'll go down in science. This thing will forever be known as Schuhart's jar. Sound good?"

While we're joking around, I get dressed. I stuff the empty flask into my pocket, count the money again, and get on my way. "Have a good shower, you complicated soul."

He doesn't reply; the water's very loud.

In the hallway I see Mr. Tender himself, completely red and strutting like a peacock. A crowd has formed around him—coworkers, journalists, even a few sergeants (fresh from dinner, picking their teeth), and he's blathering on: "The technology we command practically guarantees a safe and successful expedition . . ." Here, he notices me and immediately dries up, smiling and waving tentatively. Shit, I think, I need to escape. I take off, but it's too late. I hear footsteps behind me.

"Mr. Schuhart! Mr. Schuhart! A few words about the garage!"

"No comment," I reply, breaking into a run. But I can't get away: a guy with a mike is on my right, and another one, with a camera, is on my left.

"Did you see anything unusual in the garage? Please, just two words!"

"I have no comment!" I repeat, trying to keep the back of my head to the camera. "It's just a garage."

"Thank you. What do you think about the turbo-platforms?"

"They're great," I say, heading straight for the john.

"What's your opinion about the goals of the Visit?"

"Talk to the scientists," I say. And I slide into the bathroom.

I hear them scratching at the door. So I call out, "I highly recommend you ask Mr. Tender why his nose looks like a plum. He's too modest to mention it, but that was our most exciting adventure."

Man, they shoot down the hallway! Just like horses, I swear. I wait a minute—silence. I stick my head out—no one's around. So I walk away, whistling. I go down to the lobby, show my ID to the beefy sergeant, then I see that he's saluting me. Guess I'm the hero of the day.

"At ease, Sergeant," I say. "I'm pleased with you."

He flashes a huge grin at me, as if I paid him the greatest compliment. "Good job, Red," he says. "I'm proud to know you."

"Well," I say, "you'll have something to tell the girls back in Sweden, huh?"

"Hell yeah!" he says. "They'll be all over me!"

Really, the guy is OK. To be honest, I don't like these hale and hearty types. The girls go crazy over them, and for what? It can't just be the height . . . I'm walking along the street, trying to figure out what it could be. The sun is shining, no one's around. And suddenly I want to see Guta real bad. Not for any particular reason. Just to look at her, hold her hand. That's about all you can manage after the Zone: hand holding. Especially when you remember the stories about the children of stalkers—how they turn out . . . No, I shouldn't even be thinking about Guta; first I need a bottle, at least, of the strong stuff.

I pass the parking lot, then I see the checkpoint. Two patrol cars are waiting there in all their glory—wide, yellow, bristling with searchlights and machine guns. And, of course, a whole crowd of cops is blocking the street. I walk along, looking down so I won't see their faces; it's best if I don't look at them in broad daylight. A couple of guys here I'm afraid to recognize;

there'd be one hell of a scene if I did. I swear, they're lucky that Kirill convinced me to work for the Institute, otherwise I'd have found the assholes and finished them off.

I'm pushing my way through the crowd, almost past it, when I hear, "Hey, stalker!" Well, that has nothing to do with me, so I keep walking, pulling a cigarette from the pack. Someone catches up with me and grabs my sleeve. I shake his hand off, turn halfway toward him, and inquire politely, "What the hell are you grabbing my sleeve for, mister?"

"Wait, stalker," he says. "Two questions for you."

I look up at him—it's my old friend Captain Quarterblad. He has completely dried up and turned a shade of yellow. "Hello, Captain," I say. "How's the liver?"

"Don't you try to distract me, stalker," he says angrily, boring his eyes into me. "You better explain to me why you don't stop immediately when called."

And two cops instantly appear behind him, pawing their guns. You can't see their eyes, just their jaws working away below the helmets. Where in the world do they find these guys? Did they send them to Harmont to breed or what? I'm not usually afraid of the guards in the daytime, but the toads could search me, and that wouldn't suit me at all right now.

"I didn't know you meant me, Captain," I say. "You were yelling at some stalker."

"Oh, and you aren't a stalker anymore?"

"I've served my time, thanks to you—and I've given it up since," I say. "I'm done with it. Thank you, Captain, for opening my eyes. If not for you—"

"What were you doing in the restricted area?"

"What do you mean? I work here. For two years now."

And to finish this unpleasant conversation, I take out my ID and show it to Captain Quarterblad. He takes it, examines it, practically sniffs the seals, and seems almost ready to lick it.

He returns my ID, looking satisfied; his eyes have lit up, even his cheeks colored.

"Sorry, Schuhart," he says. "I didn't expect this. That means my advice to you didn't go to waste. Really, that's great. Believe it or not, I always figured you'd make something of yourself. I just couldn't imagine that a guy like you . . ."

And off he goes. Well, I think, just my luck to cure another melancholic. Of course, I listen to him, looking down in embarrassment, nodding, gesturing awkwardly, and even shyly toeing the pavement. The goons behind the captain listen for a while, then get queasy, I bet, and go off somewhere more exciting. Meanwhile, the captain drones on about my future: knowledge is light, ignorance is darkness, God always values and rewards honest labor. Anyway, he tries to feed me the same boring bullshit that the jail priest harassed us with every Sunday. And I need a drink—I just can't wait. All right, I think, Red, you can endure even this. Patience, Red, patience! He can't go on like this for long, he's already out of breath . . . And then, to my relief, one of the patrol cars signals to us. Captain Quarterblad looks around, grunts in annoyance, and extends his hand to me.

"All right," he says. "It was nice to meet you, honest man Schuhart. I would have been happy to drink with you to that. Can't have anything too strong, doctor's orders, but I could have had a beer with you. But you see—duty calls! Well, we'll meet again," he says.

God forbid, I think. But I shake his hand and keep blushing and toeing the pavement—doing everything he wants me to. Then he finally leaves, and I make a beeline for the Borscht.

The Borscht is always empty at this hour. Ernest is standing behind the bar, wiping the glasses and holding them up to the light. This is an amazing thing, by the way: anytime you come in, these barmen are always wiping glasses, as if their salvation depended on it. He'll stand here all day—pick up a glass, squint at it, hold it up to the light, breathe on it, and get wiping; he'll do that for a bit, take another look, this time through the bottom of the glass, and start wiping again . . .

"Hey, Ernie!" I say. "Leave that thing alone, you'll wipe a hole through it!"

He looks at me through the glass, grumbles something indistinct, and without saying a word pours me a shot of vodka. I clamber up onto the stool, take a sip, grimace, shake my head, and take another sip. The fridge is humming, the jukebox is playing something quiet, Ernest is puffing into another glass—it's nice and peaceful. I finish my drink, putting my glass on the bar. Ernest immediately pours me another one. "Feeling better?" he mutters. "Thawing a bit, stalker?"

"You just keep wiping," I say. "You know, one guy wiped for a while, and he finally summoned an evil spirit. He had a great life after that."

"Who was this?" asks Ernest suspiciously.

"He was a barman here," I answer. "Before your time."

"So what happened?"

"Oh, nothing. Why do you think we got a Visit? He just wouldn't stop wiping. Who do you figure visited us, huh?"

"You're full of it today," says Ernie with approval.

He goes to the kitchen and comes back with a plate of fried sausages. He puts the plate in front of me, passes me the ketchup, and returns to his glasses. Ernest knows his stuff. He's got an eye for these things, can instantly tell when a stalker's fresh from the Zone, when he's got swag, and Ernie knows what a stalker needs. Ernie's a good guy. Our benefactor.

After I finish the sausages, I light a cigarette and try to estimate how much money Ernest is making on us. I don't know the going prices in Europe, but I've heard rumors that an empty sells for almost two and a half thousand, while Ernie only gives us four hundred. The batteries go for at least a hundred, and we're lucky to get twenty. That's probably how it is for everything. Of course, getting the swag to Europe must cost a bundle. You gotta grease a lot of palms—even the stationmaster is probably paid off. Anyway, if you think about it, Ernest doesn't pocket that much—fifteen to twenty percent at the most—and if he gets caught, that's ten years of hard labor, guaranteed.

Here my generous meditations are interrupted by some polite type. I don't even hear him come in, but there he is at my right elbow, asking, "May I sit down?"

"Of course!" I reply. "Go right ahead."

It's a skinny little guy with a pointy nose, wearing a bow tie. He looks familiar, I've seen him somewhere before, but I can't remember where. He climbs onto a nearby stool and says to Ernie, "Bourbon, please!" And immediately to me, "Excuse me, I think we've met. You work at the International Institute, right?"

"Yes," I say. "And you?"

He promptly pulls a business card out of his pocket and puts it in front of me. I read "Aloysius Macnaught, Immigration Agent." Right, of course I know him. He pesters people to leave town. Someone must really want us all to leave Harmont. Almost half the population is already gone, but no, they have to get rid of everyone. I push his card away with one finger and tell him, "No, thanks. I'm not interested. I dream of living my entire life in my hometown."

"But why?" he asks eagerly. "I mean no offense, but what's keeping you here?"

Right, like I'll tell him what it really is. "What a question!" I say. "Sweet childhood memories. My first kiss in the park. My mommy and daddy. The first time I got drunk, in this very bar. Our police station, so dear to my heart." I take a heavily used handkerchief out of my pocket and put it to my eyes. "No," I say. "No way!"

He laughs, takes a small sip of bourbon, and says thoughtfully, "I can't understand you people. Life in Harmont is hard. The city is under military control. The provisions are mediocre. The Zone is so close, it's like living on top of a volcano. An epidemic could break out at any moment, or something even worse. I understand the old folks. They're used to this place, they don't want to leave. But someone like you . . . How old are you? Can't be more than twenty-two, twenty-three . . . You have to understand, our agency is a nonprofit, there's no one paying us to do this. We just want people to leave this hellhole, to return to normal life. Look, we even cover the costs of relocation, we find you work after the move . . . For somebody young, like you, we'd pay for your education. No, I don't get it!"

"What," I say, "no one wants to leave?"

"No, not exactly no one. Some do agree, especially people with families. But not the young or the old. What is it about this place? It's just a hole, a provincial town . . ."

And here I give it to him. "Mr. Aloysius Macnaught!" I say. "You are absolutely right. Our little town is a hole. Always was and always will be. Except right now," I say, "it's a hole into the future. And the stuff we fish out of this hole will change your whole stinking world. Life will be different, the way it should be, and no one will want for anything. That's our hole for you. There's knowledge pouring through this hole. And when we figure it out, we'll make everyone rich, and we'll fly to the stars, and we'll go wherever we want. That's the kind of hole we have here . . ."

At this point I trail off, because I notice that Ernie is looking at me in astonishment, and I feel embarrassed. In general, I don't like using other people's words, even if I do happen to like them. Especially since they come out kind of funny. When Kirill's talking, you can't stop listening, you almost forget to close your mouth. And here I'm saying the same stuff, but something seems off. Maybe that's because Kirill never slipped Ernest swag under the counter. Oh well . . .

Here my Ernie comes to and hurriedly pours me a large shot: *Snap out of it, man, what's wrong with you today?* Meanwhile, the pointy-nosed Mr. Macnaught takes another sip of bourbon and says, "Yes, of course. The perpetual batteries, the blue panacea . . . But do you actually think it'll be like you said?"

"What I actually think is none of your business," I say. "I was talking about the town. Now, speaking for myself, I'll say: What's so great about your Europe? The eternal boredom? You work all day, watch TV all night; when that's done, you're off to bed with some bitch, breeding delinquents. The strikes, the demonstrations, the never-ending politics . . . To hell with your Europe!"

"Really, why does it have to be Europe?"

"Oh," I say, "it's the same story all over, and in the Antarctic it's cold, too."

And you know the amazing thing: I'm telling him this, and I completely believe in what I'm saying. And our Zone, the evil bitch, the murderess, is at that moment a hundred times dearer to me than all their Europes and Africas. And I'm not even drunk yet, I simply imagine for a moment how I'd come home strung out after work in a herd of like-minded drones, how I'd get squashed on all sides in their subway, how I'd become jaded and weary of life.

"What do you say?" he asks Ernie.

"I'm a businessman," Ernie replies with authority. "I'm not some young punk! I've invested money in this business. The commandant comes in here sometimes, a general, nothing to sneeze at. Why would I leave?"

Mr. Aloysius Macnaught starts telling him something with numbers, but I'm no longer listening. I take a good swig from my glass, get some change from my pocket, climb down from the stool, and go over to the jukebox to get things going. They have this one song here called "Don't Come Back Unless You're Ready." It does wonders for me after the Zone . . . All right, the jukebox is screeching away, so I pick up my glass and go into the corner to settle scores with the one-armed bandit. And time begins to fly.

Just as I'm losing my last nickel, Gutalin and Richard Noonan barge into our friendly establishment. Gutalin is plastered already—rolling his eyes and looking to pick a fight—while Richard Noonan is tenderly holding on to his elbow and distracting him with jokes. A pretty pair! Gutalin is huge, curly haired, and as black as an officer's boot, with arms down to his knees, while Dick is small, round, pink, and mellow, practically aglow.

"Hey!" yells Dick when he sees me. "Red's here, too! Come here, Red!"

"That's right!" bellows Gutalin. "There are only two people in this town—Red and me! All the others are pigs, spawn of Satan. Red! You also serve Satan, but you're still human."

I come over to them with my glass. Gutalin grabs me by the coat, sits me down at their table, and says, "Sit down, Red! Sit down, servant of Satan! I love you. Let us weep over the sins of humanity—weep in despair!"

"Let us weep," I say. "Swallow the tears of sin."

"Because the day is nigh," proclaims Gutalin. "Because the pale horse has been saddled, and the rider has put a foot in the stirrup. And futile are the prayers of the worshippers of Satan. And only those who renounce him shall be saved. Thou, of human flesh, whom Satan has seduced, who play with his toys and covet his treasures—I tell thee, thou art blind! Awake, fools, before it's too late! Stamp on the devil's baubles!" Here he comes to an abrupt halt, as if forgetting what's next. "Can I get a drink in this place?" he asks in a different voice. "Where am I? You know, Red, I got fired again. An agitator, they said. I was telling them, 'Awake, you're blind, plunging into the abyss and dragging other blind men behind you!' They just laughed. So I socked the boss in the face and left. Now they'll arrest me. And for what?"

Dick comes over and puts a bottle on the table.

"I'm paying today!" I yell to Ernest.

Dick looks sideways at me.

"It's all aboveboard," I say. "We'll be drinking my bonus."

"You went into the Zone?" asks Dick. "Did you bring anything out?"

"A full empty," I say. "For the altar to science. And pocketfuls of joy. Are you gonna pour or not?"

"An empty!" Gutalin rumbles sadly. "You risked your life for some empty! You're still alive, but you brought another work of Satan into this world. And you just don't know, Red, how much sin and grief—"

"Quiet, Gutalin," I tell him sternly. "Eat, drink, and be merry, because I came back alive. A toast to success!"

That toast gets us going. Gutalin becomes completely depressed—sitting there sobbing, liquid gushing from his eyes like water from a faucet. It's OK, I've seen him do this. It's one of his stages—streaming tears and preaching that Satan put the Zone there to tempt us, that you can't take anything out of it, and, if you do, put it back, and live your life as if the Zone didn't exist. Leave Satan's works for Satan. I like him, Gutalin. I like eccentrics in general. When he has enough money, he buys swag from anyone, without haggling, and then he sneaks into the Zone at night and buries it there . . . Lord, is he bawling! Oh well, he'll cheer up yet.

"What's a full empty?" asks Dick. "I've heard of empties, but what's a full one? Never heard of it."

I explain it to him. He nods, smacks his lips. "Yes," he says. "That's interesting. That's something new. Who did you go with? The Russian guy?"

"Yeah," I reply. "I went with Kirill and Tender. You know, our lab assistant."

"You must have had your hands full with them."

"Not at all. They both did pretty well. Especially Kirill, he's a born stalker," I say. "If he had more experience, learned some proper patience, I'd go into the Zone with him every day."

"And every night?" he asks with a drunken laugh.

"Stop that," I say. "Enough with the jokes."

"I know," he says. "Enough with the jokes, or I might get a punch in the face. Let's say you can take a couple swings at me sometime . . ."

"Who's getting punched?" Gutalin comes to life. "Which one of you?"

We grab his arms, barely getting him into his seat. Dick sticks a cigarette in his teeth and lights it. We calm him down. Meanwhile, people keep coming in. There's no room left at the bar, and most tables are taken. Ernest has called up his girls, and they're running around, fetching drinks—beer for some, cocktails or vodka for others. Lately I've been noticing a lot of new faces in town—young punks with colorful scarves down to the floor. I mention this to Dick, and he nods.

"That's right," he says. "They're starting a lot of construction. The Institute's putting up three new buildings, and they're also going to wall off the Zone from the cemetery to the old ranch. The good times for stalkers are coming to an end."

"Like we stalkers ever had them," I say. At the same time, I think, What the hell is this? That means I won't be able to work on the side. Oh well, might be for the best—less temptation. I'll go into the Zone during the day, like an honest man; the money isn't as good, of course, but it's much safer. There's the boot, the specsuits, and all that crap, and I won't give a damn about patrols. I can live on my salary, and I'll drink my bonuses.

Now I get really depressed. I'll have to count every cent again: This I can afford, this I can't. I'll have to pinch pennies for Guta's gifts . . . No more bars, only cheap movies . . . And everything's gray, all gray. Gray every day, and every evening, and every night.

I sit there thinking this while Dick keeps buzzing in my ear. "Last night I go to the hotel bar for a late-night drink, and I see some new faces in there. I didn't like them from the start. One of them comes over and starts working up to something, tells me he knows about me, knows who I am and what I do, and hints that he'll pay good money for certain services . . ."

"An informer," I say. I'm not too interested in all this, I've seen my share of informers and heard plenty of talk about services.

"No, my friend, not an informer. You listen. I talked to him for a bit—being careful, of course, playing the fool. He's interested in certain items from the Zone, and these items are no joke. Trinkets like batteries, shriekers, and black sparks aren't for him. And he only hinted at what he does need."

"So what exactly does he need?" I ask.

"Hell slime, if I understood correctly," Dick says, and gives me a strange look.

"Ah, so he needs hell slime!" I say. "Maybe he'd like a death lamp as well?"

"I asked him about that, too."

"Well?"

"Believe it or not, he does."

"Yeah?" I say. "Then he can go get them himself. It's easy as pie! We have basements full of hell slime, he can take a bucket and dip right in. It's his funeral."

Dick stays silent, looks at me from beneath his brows, and doesn't even smile. What the hell, is he trying to hire me or something? And then it clicks.

"Wait," I say. "Who could that have been? We aren't even allowed to study the hell slime at the Institute."

"Exactly," says Dick deliberately, keeping his eyes on me. "It's research that might pose a danger to humanity. Now do you understand who that was?"

I don't understand a thing. "An alien?" I say.

He bursts out laughing and pats me on the arm. "Why don't we have a drink, you simple soul?"

"Why don't we?" I reply, although I feel mad. Screw this—enough of this "simple soul" business, bastards! "Hey, Gutalin!" I say. "Wake up, let's have a drink."

No, Gutalin's asleep. He's put his black face down on the black table and is asleep, arms hanging to the floor. Dick and I have a drink without Gutalin.

"All right," I say. "I might be a simple or a complicated soul, but I'd report this guy. I have no love for the police, but I'd go and report him myself."

"Yeah," says Dick. "And the police would ask you: why, exactly, did this fellow come to you with his offers? Hmm?"

I shake my head. "It doesn't matter. You fat pig, you've spent three years in town, but you haven't been in the Zone, and you've only seen the hell slime in movies. And if you saw it in real life—saw what it does to a man—you'd shit your pants right there. This is awful stuff, my friend, you shouldn't take it out of the Zone . . . As you know, stalkers are crude men, they only care about the money, the more the better, but even the late Slug wouldn't go for this. The Vulture Burbridge wouldn't do it. I can't even imagine who would want hell slime and what they'd want it for."

"Well," says Dick, "that's all very admirable. But you see, I don't want to be found dead in bed one morning with a suicide note beside me. I'm not a stalker, but I'm also a crude and practical man, and I happen to like life. I've been alive for a while, I'm used to it . . ."

Here Ernest suddenly hollers from behind the bar, "Mr. Noonan! Phone for you!"

"Damn it," says Dick viciously. "It's probably the claims department again. They always track me down. Give me a minute, Red."

He gets up and goes to the phone. I stay with Gutalin and the bottle, and since Gutalin is of no use, I get real chummy with the bottle. Damn that Zone, there's no getting away from it. Wherever you go, whoever you talk to—it's always the Zone, the Zone, the Zone . . . It's very nice for Kirill to argue that the Zone will help bring about world peace and eternal sunshine. Kirill is a great guy, no one would call him dumb—in fact, he's as smart as they come—but he doesn't know shit about life. He can't even imagine the scum that gathers around the Zone. Here, take a look: someone wants hell slime. No, Gutalin might be a drunk and a religious fanatic, but sometimes you think about it and you wonder: maybe we really should leave Satan's works for Satan? Hands off the shit . . .

Here some punk wearing a colorful scarf sits down in Dick's seat. "Mr. Schuhart?" he asks.

"Yes?" I say.

"My name's Creon," he says. "I'm from Malta."

"OK," I say. "And how are things in Malta?"

"Things in Malta are all right, but that's not why I'm here. Ernest referred me to you."

Ah, I think. Ernest is a bastard after all. He's got no pity, none at all. Look at this kid—dark skinned, innocent, good-looking, he's probably never shaved and has never kissed a girl, but what's that to Ernie? He just wants to herd us all into the Zone—if one out of three returns with swag, that's a profit already. "Well, and how's old Ernest doing?" I ask.

He turns around to look at the bar and says, "As far as I can tell, he's doing pretty well. I'd trade with him."

"I wouldn't," I say. "Want a drink?"

"Thank you, I don't drink."

"How about a smoke?"

"Sorry, I don't smoke either."

"God damn it!" I say. "Then what do you need money for?"

He reddens, stops smiling, and says softly, "That's probably my own business, right, Mr. Schuhart?"

"Can't argue with that," I say, and pour myself a shot. By now my head is buzzing, and my limbs feel pleasantly relaxed; the Zone has completely let go. "Right now I'm drunk," I say. "Celebrating, as you see. Went into the Zone, came back alive and with money. It's not often that you come back alive, and the money is real rare. So let's postpone the serious discussion."

He jumps up, says he's sorry, and I see that Dick is back. He's standing next to his chair, and from his face I can tell that something happened.

"Well," I ask, "are your containers leaking again?"

"Yeah," he says, "them again."

He sits down, pours himself a drink, and tops mine off, and I see that this isn't about the claims department. To be honest, he doesn't give a damn about them—a real hard worker.

"Let's have a drink, Red," he says. And without waiting for me, he gulps down his drink and pours another one. "You know," he says, "Kirill Panov died."

I don't even understand through the stupor. So someone's dead, that's too bad. "All right," I say, "let's drink to the departed . . ."

He stares at me wide eyed, and only then do I feel my insides turn to mush. I get up, lean on my hands, and look down at him.

"Kirill!" And the silver cobweb is in front of me, and again I hear it crackle as it tears. And through this terrible sound, I hear Dick's voice as if coming from another room.

"A heart attack, they found him in the shower, naked. No one understands a thing. They asked about you, and I said you were perfectly fine."

"What's there to understand?" I say. "It's the Zone . . ."

"Sit down," says Dick. "Sit down and have a drink."

"The Zone . . ." I repeat, and I can't stop. "The Zone . . . The Zone . . ."

I see nothing but the silver cobweb. The whole bar is tangled in the cobweb, people are moving around, and the web crackles softly as they touch it. And at the center of it is the Maltese boy, his face childlike and surprised—he doesn't understand a thing.

"Kid," I tell him tenderly, "how much money do you need? Is a thousand enough? Take it, take it!" I shove the money at him and shout, "Go to Ernest and tell him that he's an asshole and a bastard, don't be afraid, tell him! He's nothing but a coward . . . Tell him and then go straight to the station, buy yourself a ticket back to Malta. Don't stop anywhere!"

I don't know what else I'm shouting. The next thing I know I'm in front of the bar. Ernest puts a drink in front of me and asks, "You got money today?"

"Yeah, I got money," I say.

"Can you pay your tab? I have to pay taxes tomorrow."

And now I see that I'm holding a wad of cash. I'm looking at this dough and mumbling, "Oh, I guess he didn't take it, Creon from Malta . . . Too proud, probably. Well, the rest is fate."

"What's wrong with you?" asks my buddy Ernie. "Drank a bit much?"

"No," I say. "I'm totally fine. Up for anything."

"You should go home," says Ernie. "You drank too much."

"Kirill died," I tell him.

"Which Kirill? The mangy one?"

"You're mangy yourself, bastard," I tell him. "You couldn't make one Kirill out of a thousand of you. You're an asshole," I say. "A stinking hustler. You're dealing in death, you jerk. You bought us all with your money. You want me to take this place apart for you?"

And just as I take a swing, someone suddenly grabs me and drags me away. And I'm no longer thinking and don't even want to try. I'm screaming, punching, kicking someone, then finally I come to. I'm sitting in the bathroom, completely wet, and my face is bloody. I look in the mirror and don't recognize myself, and there's a tic in my cheek—that's never happened before. And there are noises coming from the barroom, crashes and the sound of dishes breaking, girls are squealing, and I hear Gutalin roaring, like a polar bear in heat, "Get away, bastards! Where's Red? What did you do with Red, Satan's spawn?" Then the wail of a police siren.

And as soon as I hear it, everything becomes clear. I remember, know, and understand everything. And there's nothing left in my soul except icy fury. *All right,* I think, *now I'll get even with you. You stinking hustler, I'll show you what a stalker can do.* I take a shrieker out of my pocket, a nice new unused one, squeeze it a few times to get it going, open the door to the barroom, and quietly throw it in. Then I open the window and climb out to the street. Of course, I really want to stay and watch the show, but I have to take off. I can't stand shriekers; they give me nosebleeds.

As I run away, I hear my shrieker going at full blast. First, every dog in the neighborhood starts barking and howling—they always sense it first. Then an awful scream comes from the bar, loud enough to make my ears ring even at that distance. I can just imagine the people running to and fro—some becoming melancholy, some violent, some scared out of their wits . . . A shrieker is a terrible thing. It'll be a while before Ernest gets a full bar again. Of course, the bastard will figure out who did it to him, but I don't give a shit. I'm done. No more stalker Red—I've had enough. I'm finished going to my death and teaching other idiots to do the same. *You were wrong, Kirill, my friend. I'm sorry, but it turns out that Gutalin was right, not you.* We don't belong here. There's no good in the Zone.

I climb over the fence and slowly shuffle home. I'm biting my lip—I want to cry, but I can't. And there's nothing but emptiness ahead. Only boredom, melancholy, routine. Kirill, my only friend, how did we get here? What will I do without you? You painted the future for me, showed me a new world, a changed world. And now what? Someone in far-off Russia will cry for you, but I can't cry. And this is all my fault, no one else's! How could I, the damn fool, dare take him into the garage before his eyes got used to the dark? I've always been a lone wolf, never thought of anyone but myself. For once in my life I decided to help someone, to give someone a gift . . . Why the hell did I even tell him about this empty? And when I realize this, something grabs me by the throat, enough to make me actually want to howl like a wolf. I probably really start howling—people begin to shy away from me, and then I suddenly feel a little better: I see Guta coming.

She's coming toward me, my beauty, my girl, showing her lovely legs, her skirt swaying above her knees as she walks; all the men ogle her as she passes by, while she keeps walking straight, without looking around, and for some reason I immediately figure out she's looking for me.

"Hey, Guta," I say. "Where are you heading?"

She looks me over and quickly takes everything in—my bloody face and my wet jacket and my bruised knuckles. She doesn't mention any of this but says instead, "Hey, Red. Actually, I was looking for you."

"I know," I say. "Let's go to my place."

She stays silent, turns away, and looks to the side. Ah, what a head she has, what a neck—like a spirited young filly, proud but already loyal to her master. Then she says, "I don't know, Red. Maybe you won't want to see me anymore."

My heart skips a beat—what does this mean? But I say calmly, "I don't understand you, Guta. I'm sorry, I've had a bit much today, maybe I'm not thinking straight. Why wouldn't I want to see you anymore?"

I take her arm, and we slowly walk to my house, and all the guys who were ogling her quickly hide their faces. I've lived on this street my entire life, and they all know Red Schuhart real well. And the ones who don't know him would soon get a lesson, and they can feel it.

"My mom told me to get an abortion," Guta says suddenly. "But I don't want to."

I have to walk another couple of steps before I get it.

Meanwhile, Guta keeps going. "I don't want any abortions, I want to have your child. And you can do as you like. Take off if you want, I won't keep you."

I'm listening to her as she's slowly getting mad, working herself up, listening then gradually tuning out. I can't think straight at all. Only one stupid thought is spinning in my head: one person less in the world—one person more.

"She's been telling me," says Guta, "'It's a stalker's child, why breed freaks? He's a criminal,' she says. 'You two won't have a family, nothing. Today he's free—tomorrow he's in jail.' Except I don't care, I'll manage. I can handle everything myself. I'll give birth myself, I'll raise him myself, I'll make him human myself. I don't need you. Only don't you come near me—I won't let you in the door . . ."

"Guta," I say, "my love! Just wait a minute . . ." And I can't go on, I'm breaking into stupid, nervous laughter. "Honey," I say, "why are you chasing me away, really?"

I'm shouting with laughter like a total idiot, while she stops, sticks her face into my chest, and starts bawling.

"What are we going to do now, Red?" she says through her tears. "What are we going to do now?"

2.

REDRICK SCHUHART, 28 YEARS OLD, MARRIED, NO KNOWN OCCUPATION.

Redrick Schuhart lay behind a tombstone and, holding a tree branch out of the way, looked at the road. The patrol car's searchlights darted around the cemetery, and when they flashed into his eyes, he squinted and held his breath.

Two hours had already passed, but the situation on the road hadn't changed. The car, motor rumbling steadily as it idled, stood in the same place and continued to probe with its searchlights, combing the unkempt, neglected graves, the slanted rusty crosses, the overgrown ash trees, and the crest of the nine-foot wall that ended to the left. The patrols were afraid of the Zone. They never got out of the car. Here, near the cemetery, they didn't even have the guts to fire. Occasionally, Redrick heard muffled voices; sometimes he'd see the flash of a cigarette butt fly out of the car and roll along the road, bouncing up and down and scattering dim reddish sparks. It was very damp—it had rained recently—and despite his waterproof coat, Redrick felt the wet chill.

He carefully let go of the branch, turned his head, and listened. To his right, not very far but not close, he heard a noise—there was someone else in the cemetery. Over there, the leaves were rustling, soil was trickling down, and then something hard and heavy hit the ground with a soft thud. Redrick carefully crawled backward without turning around, flattening himself against the wet grass. Once again, a beam of light glided over his head. Redrick froze, following it with his eyes; he thought that on a grave between the crosses he saw a motionless man in black. The man sat there without concealing himself, leaning against the marble obelisk, turning a white face with sunken black eyes toward Redrick. Actually, Redrick didn't see him that clearly—he couldn't have in that instant—but he could imagine how it must look. He crawled for another few feet, felt the flask under his jacket, took it out, and lay there for some time, pressing the warm metal to his cheek. Then, without letting go of the flask, he crawled on. He no longer listened or looked around.

There was a gap in the wall, and right next to it, on a spread-out lead-lined jacket, lay Burbridge. He was on his back, tugging at his collar with both hands, and was quietly, painfully groaning, the groans often turning into moans of agony. Redrick sat down next to him and unscrewed the flask. He carefully put his hand under Burbridge's head, feeling the hot, sweaty bald pate with his entire palm, and put the mouth of the flask to the old man's lips. It was dark, but in the dim reflected glow of the searchlights Redrick could see Burbridge's wide-open, glassy eyes and the black stubble that covered his cheeks. Burbridge took a few greedy gulps and started fidgeting anxiously, groping the bag of swag.

"Came back . . ." he said. "Good man . . . Red . . . Won't leave an old man . . . to die . . ."

Redrick tilted his head back and took a big gulp. "Not moving, the damn thing," he said. "Like it's glued to the road."

"That's . . . no accident . . ." said Burbridge. He was talking intermittently as he exhaled. "Someone squealed on us. They're waiting."

"Maybe," said Redrick. "Want any more?"

"No. That's enough. Don't leave me. If you stay—I'll make it. You won't be sorry. You won't leave, Red?"

Redrick didn't answer. He was looking toward the road at the blue beams of the searchlights. From here, you could see the marble obelisk, but you couldn't tell whether *that* one was still sitting there or had vanished.

"Listen, Red. I'm not kidding. You won't be sorry. Do you know why old Burbridge is still alive? Do you? Bob the Gorilla is dead, the Pharaoh Banker is no more. He was a real stalker! But still, he croaked. And the Slug, too. Norman Four-Eyes. Kallogen. Scabby Pete. All of them. Only I'm left. Why? Do you know why?"

"You were always a piece of scum," said Redrick, without taking his eyes off the road. "A vulture."

"Scum. That's right. You gotta be like that. But they were all the same. The Pharaoh. The Slug. But I'm the only one left. Do you know why?"

"Yes," said Redrick, to shut him up.

"You're lying. You don't know. Have you heard of the Golden Sphere?"

"Yes."

"You think it's a fairy tale?"

"You should be quiet," advised Redrick. "You're wasting your strength!"

"It's all right, you'll get me out. We've done so much together! You wouldn't actually leave me? You were this tall when we first met. Knew your father."

Redrick stayed silent. He badly needed a smoke, so he took out a cigarette, crumbled some tobacco onto his palm, and tried smelling it. It didn't help.

"You have to get me out," said Burbridge. "It's your fault I'm here. You wouldn't take the Maltese."

The Maltese really wanted to go with them. He paid for their drinks, offered a good deposit, and swore that he could get specsuits. Burbridge, who sat next to the Maltese, shielding his face with a heavy leathery hand, had winked furiously at Redrick: *Take him, we won't regret it.* Maybe that was precisely why Redrick had said no. "Your own greed got you here," Redrick said coldly. "Nothing to do with me. Just be quiet."

For a while, Burbridge only groaned. He tugged on his collar again and threw his head all the way back. "You can keep everything," he muttered. "Just don't leave me."

Redrick looked at his watch. It was now almost dawn, but the patrol car still wasn't leaving; it continued to comb the bushes with its searchlights. Their camouflaged Jeep was hidden somewhere there, very near the patrols, and any moment now it might be discovered.

"The Golden Sphere," said Burbridge. "I found it. Lots of stories told about it. Told some myself. That it'll grant any wish. Yeah, right—any wish! If it granted any wish, I wouldn't be here anymore. I'd be living it up in Europe. Swimming in cash."

Redrick looked at him from above. In the flickering blue light, Burbridge's upturned face looked dead. But his glassy eyes were wide open, and they followed Redrick intently, without looking away.

"Eternal youth—like hell I got that. Money—hell with that, too. But I have my health. And I got good kids. And I'm alive. You couldn't even dream of the places I've been. And I'm still alive." He licked his lips. "That's all I'm asking it for. To let me live. And my health. And my kids."

"Shut up," Redrick finally said. "You sound like an old woman. If I can, I'll drag you out. I feel sorry for your Dina—the girl will be out on the street."

"Dina . . ." croaked Burbridge. "My baby. A beauty. You know, I've spoiled them, Red. Never denied them a thing. They'll be lost. Arthur. My Archie. You know what he's like, Red. Where else have you seen kids like that?"

"I told you. If I can, I'll get you out."

"No," Burbridge said stubbornly. "You'll get me out either way. The Golden Sphere. Want me to tell you where it is?"

"Fine, tell me."

Burbridge moaned and shifted. "My legs . . ." he groaned. "Can you feel them?"

Redrick stretched out his arm and, examining, ran his hand along the leg below the knee.

"Bones . . ." wheezed Burbridge. "Are there still bones?"

"Yes, yes," lied Redrick. "Don't worry."

Actually, he could only feel the kneecap. Below there, all the way down to the heel, the leg felt like a rubber stick—you could tie it in knots.

"You're lying," said Burbridge. "Why are you lying? What, you think I don't know, you think I've never seen this before?"

"The knees are OK," said Redrick.

"You're probably lying again," Burbridge said miserably. "Forget it. Just get me out of here. I'll give you everything. The Golden Sphere. Draw you a map. Show you all the traps. Tell you everything."

He kept talking and promising things, but Redrick was no longer listening. He was looking toward the road. The searchlights had stopped darting through the bushes; they had frozen, converging on that same marble obelisk, and in the bright blue fog Redrick distinctly saw a hunched figure wandering between the crosses. The figure seemed to be moving blindly, heading right toward the searchlights. Redrick saw it crash into a huge cross, stagger back, bump into the cross again, and only then go around it and keep going, stretching long arms with fingers spread wide in front of it. Then it suddenly disappeared, as if falling through the ground, and in a few seconds appeared again, farther and to the right, walking with an absurd, inhuman persistence, like a windup toy.

And the searchlights abruptly went off. The clutch started grinding, the motor roared to life, red and blue signal lights flashed through the bushes, and the patrol car took off. It sped up furiously, flew toward town, and disappeared behind the wall. Redrick swallowed hard and unzipped his jumpsuit.

"They left . . ." Burbridge muttered feverishly. "Let's go, Red. Hurry up!" He fidgeted, groped around him, grabbed the bag of swag, and tried to sit up. "Come on, what are you waiting for?"

Redrick kept looking toward the road. It was now dark and he couldn't see a thing, but *that* one was out there somewhere—marching like a windup toy, stumbling, falling, crashing into crosses, getting tangled in bushes. "All right," Redrick said aloud. "Let's go."

He picked Burbridge up. The old man clutched his neck with a pincerlike grip, and Redrick, unable to get up, dragged him on all fours through the gap in the wall, gripping the wet grass with his hands. "Keep going, keep going . . ." Burbridge pleaded. "Don't worry, I got the swag, I won't let go. Keep going!"

He knew the way, but the wet grass was slippery, the branches whipped his face, and the corpulent old man was impossibly heavy, like a corpse; and then there was the bag of swag, which, knocking and clanging, kept getting caught, and he was terrified of stumbling on *that* one, who might be roaming here in the dark.

When they came out onto the road, it was still completely dark, but dawn was palpably near. In the grove across the highway, the birds were beginning to chirp sleepily; the night sky over the distant black houses and sparse yellow streetlights of the outskirts had already turned blue, and there was a damp chilly breeze. Redrick lay Burbridge down on the side of the road, glanced around, and, looking like a gigantic black spider, ran across it. He quickly found their Jeep, swept the masking branches off the hood and trunk, got behind the wheel, and carefully, without turning on the headlights, drove onto the pavement. Burbridge was sitting up, holding the bag with one hand, and with the other feeling his legs. "Hurry up!" he rasped. "Hurry up and go! My knees, I still have my knees . . . If I could save my knees!"

Redrick picked him up and, gritting his teeth from the effort, threw him into the car. Burbridge collapsed onto the backseat with a thud and moaned. He still hadn't let go of the bag. Redrick picked the lead-lined jacket up off the ground and threw it over him. Burbridge had even managed to drag the jacket along.

Redrick took out a flashlight and went back and forth along the side of the road, looking for tracks. There were almost none. As it rolled onto the road, the Jeep had flattened the tall, thick grass, but in a couple of hours this grass would stand up. The area around the spot where the patrol car had been was littered with cigarette butts. Redrick remembered that he'd long wanted a smoke, took out a cigarette, and lit up, even though what he most wanted right now was to jump in the car and speed away. But he couldn't do that yet. Everything had to be carefully thought through.

"What's going on?" whined Burbridge from the car. "You haven't poured out the water, the fishing gear is dry . . . Why are you standing there? Hide the swag!"

"Shut up!" said Redrick. "Get off my back." He took a drag on his cigarette. "We'll drive through the southern outskirts," he said.

"The outskirts? Are you nuts? You'll ruin my knees, asshole! My knees!"

Redrick took a last drag and stuffed the butt into a matchbox. "Calm down, Vulture," he said. "We can't go through town. There are three checkpoints on the way, we'll get stopped at one of them, at least."

"So what?"

"So they'll take one look at your legs—and we're finished."

"What about my legs? We were fishing with dynamite, my legs got blasted, that's all!"

"And if someone touches them?"

"Touches them . . . I'll scream so loud, they'll never touch a leg again."

But Redrick had already decided. He turned on the flashlight, lifted the driver's seat, opened the secret hatch, and said, "Give me the swag."

The spare fuel tank under the seat was fake. Redrick took the bag and shoved it inside, listening to the clanging, rolling sounds coming from within.

"I can't risk it," he mumbled. "Got no right."

He closed the hatch, sprinkled some garbage on top, threw some rags over it, and lowered the seat. Burbridge was grunting, moaning, plaintively demanding he hurry up; then he was again promising the Golden Sphere, the entire time fidgeting in his seat, staring anxiously into the lightening sky. Redrick paid no attention. He ripped open the plastic bag of water with the fish, poured out the water onto the fishing gear piled on the bottom of the trunk, and threw the wriggling fish into a canvas bag. After that, he folded the plastic bag and stuffed it into his pocket. Now everything was in order: two fishermen were returning from a moderately successful expedition. He got behind the wheel and started the car.

He drove all the way to the turn without switching on his headlights. To their left stretched the immense nine-foot wall that guarded the Zone, while to their right were bushes, thin groves, and the occasional abandoned cottage with boarded-up windows and peeling paint. Redrick had good night vision, and in any case, the darkness was no longer that thick; besides, he knew what was coming, so when the steadily walking, bent figure appeared ahead, he didn't even slow down. He only hunched over the wheel. *That* one was marching right in the middle of the road—like the rest of them, he was walking to town. Redrick passed him, driving on the shoulder, and then pressed hard on the gas.

"My God!" mumbled Burbridge from the back. "Red, did you see that?"

"Yeah," said Redrick.

"Jesus. That's all we need . . ." Burbridge muttered, and then immediately began reciting a loud prayer.

"Shut up!" snapped Redrick.

The turn had to be here somewhere. Redrick slowed down, examining the row of lopsided houses and fences stretching to their right. An old transformer booth . . . an electric pole . . . a rotting bridge over a ditch. Redrick turned the wheel. The car bounced over a pothole.

"Where are you going?" Burbridge shrieked wildly. "You'll ruin my legs, bastard!"

Redrick quickly turned around and slapped him, feeling the old man's stubbly cheek with the back of his hand. Burbridge sputtered and shut up. The car bounced up and down, and the wheels constantly skidded in the fresh dirt left by the night's rain. Redrick turned on the headlights. The dancing white light illuminated the old overgrown tire tracks, the giant puddles, and the rotting, slanted fences by the side. Burbridge was crying, sniffling and blowing his nose. He no longer promised things, he threatened and complained, but very quietly and indistinctly, so Redrick could only make out single words. Something about legs, about knees, about beautiful Archie . . . Then he quieted down.

The village stretched beside the western border of town. Once upon a time, there were cottages here, gardens, fruit orchards, and the summer residences of city officials and factory administrators. There were lovely green spaces, small lakes with clean sandy banks, transparent birch groves, and ponds stocked with carp. The factory stench and acrid factory smoke never reached here, although neither did the city sewer system. Now, everything was deserted and abandoned, and throughout the drive they only saw one occupied house—the curtained window was yellow with light, rain-soaked laundry hung on the line, and a giant dog had rushed out of the yard, barking furiously, and chased the car in the clouds of dirt thrown up by the wheels.

Redrick carefully drove over another old crooked bridge, and, when the turn to the western highway appeared ahead, stopped the car and turned off the engine. He climbed out onto the road, without looking at Burbridge, and walked forward, shivering and stuffing his hands into his damp jumpsuit pockets. It was now light out. The world was wet, quiet, and sleepy. He reached the highway and cautiously looked out from behind the bushes. From here, it was easy to see the police outpost: a little trailer on wheels, three windows shining with light, and smoke rising from the tall narrow chimney. A patrol car was parked nearby, with no one inside. For some time Redrick stood there and watched. The outpost was completely still; the patrols were probably cold and weary from the night's vigil and were now warming up in their trailer—nodding off, with cigarettes stuck to their lower lips.

"Toads," Redrick said quietly.

He felt the brass knuckles in his pocket, put his fingers through the rings, gripped the cold metal in his fist, and walked back, still shivering and keeping his hands in his pockets. The Jeep was standing between the bushes, tilting slightly. They were in a remote, deserted place; it had probably been a decade since anyone had been there.

When Redrick approached the car, Burbridge sat up and looked at him, mouth agape. Right now, he seemed even older than usual—wrinkled, bald, covered in dirty stubble, rotten toothed. For some time they silently looked at each other, and suddenly Burbridge mumbled, "Give you a map . . . all the traps, all of them . . . Find it yourself, won't be sorry . . ."

Redrick listened to him, motionless, then he unclenched his fingers, let go of the brass knuckles in his pocket, and said, "Fine. You gotta be unconscious, OK? Moan and don't let them touch you."

He got into the car, started the engine, and drove forward.

And everything turned out OK. No one left the trailer when the Jeep, in strict accordance with the road signs and instructions, slowly rolled by and then, quickly picking up speed, flew toward town through the southern outskirts. It was 6 AM, the streets were empty, the pavement was wet and black, and the traffic lights at the intersections kept a lonely and pointless vigil. They passed a bakery with tall, brightly lit windows, and Redrick let the warm, incredibly delicious aroma wash over him.

"I'm starving," said Redrick and, kneading his muscles, which were stiff from the tension, stretched, pushing his hands into the wheel.

"What?" said Burbridge in alarm.

"I said I'm starving. Where are we going? Your house or straight to the Butcher?"

"To the Butcher, to the Butcher, quick!" Burbridge babbled impatiently, his whole body leaning forward, his hot, feverish breath on Redrick's neck. "Go straight there! Right now! He still owes me seven hundred. Go, go, quickly, why are you crawling like an injured snail?" And then he suddenly began to curse, impotently and spitefully, using vile, dirty words, showering Redrick with spittle, gasping and coughing in fits.

Redrick didn't answer. He didn't have the time or the energy to soothe the raging Vulture. He had to quickly finish with all this and catch at least an hour, a half hour, of sleep before the meeting at the Metropole. He turned onto Sixteenth Street, drove two blocks, and parked the car in front of the gray two-story house.

The Butcher opened the door himself—he probably had just gotten up and was going to the bathroom. He was wearing a splendid robe with gold tassels and holding a glass with dentures in his hand. His hair was tousled and there were dark circles under his dull eyes.

"Oh!" he said, "Red, it'sh you? What ish it?"

"Put in your teeth and let's go," said Redrick.

"Uh-huh," replied the Butcher, nodding invitingly toward the foyer, and then, shuffling his feet in Persian slippers and moving with surprising speed, he headed to the bathroom. "Who?" he asked from within.

"Burbridge," answered Redrick.

"What?"

"Legs."

In the bathroom, water started running, he heard snorting and splashing, and then something fell and rolled along the tiled floor. Redrick wearily sat down in an armchair, took out a cigarette, and, looking around, lit up. Yeah, this was quite the foyer. The Butcher must have spent a bundle. He was a very skilled and very fashionable surgeon, renowned in the medical community not only of the city but of the state, and, of course, the reason he got mixed up with stalkers wasn't the money. Like many others, he profited from the Zone: by receiving swag and then applying it in his practice; by treating crippled stalkers, in the process investigating mysterious new injuries, diseases, and deformities of the human body; and by becoming famous as the first doctor on the planet to specialize in nonhuman illnesses of man. Although, to be honest, he also eagerly took the money.

"What exactly is wrong with his legs?" he asked, emerging from the bathroom with a huge towel draped over his shoulder. He was carefully wiping his long nervous fingers with a corner of the towel.

"Got into the slime," said Redrick.

The Butcher whistled. "So, that's the end of Burbridge," he muttered. "Too bad, he was a famous stalker."

"Nah," said Redrick, leaning back in his chair. "You'll make prostheses for him. He'll hop through the Zone on prostheses yet."

"Well, OK," said the Butcher. His face became completely professional. "Give me a second, I'll get dressed."

While he got dressed and talked on the phone, probably instructing his clinic to prepare for the surgery, Redrick lounged motionless in the armchair and smoked. He only moved once, to take out his flask. He drank in small sips, since the flask was almost empty, and tried not to think about anything. He simply waited.

Then they both walked to the car, Redrick got behind the wheel, and the Butcher sat down next to him, immediately leaning over the seat and feeling Burbridge's legs. Burbridge, hushed and deflated, mumbled something plaintive, promised untold riches, constantly mentioned his children and dead wife, and begged him to at least save his knees. When they drove up to the clinic, the Butcher cursed at not finding the orderlies outside, jumped out of the still-moving car, and disappeared behind the door. Redrick lit another cigarette, and Burbridge suddenly spoke, clearly and distinctly, as if he was completely calm: "You wanted to kill me. I'll remember that."

"But I didn't," said Redrick indifferently.

"No, you didn't." Burbridge was quiet. "I'll remember that, too."

"You do that," said Redrick. "You, of course, wouldn't have killed me . . ."

He turned around and looked at Burbridge. The old man was grimacing uncertainly, twisting his parched lips.

"You would have just abandoned me," said Redrick. "Left me in the Zone, and that would be that. Like Four-Eyes."

"Four-Eyes died on his own," Burbridge sullenly disagreed. "I had nothing to do with it. He got stuck."

"You're scum," said Redrick dispassionately, turning away. "A vulture."

Two disheveled, sleepy orderlies jumped out of the door and, unfolding the stretcher as they ran, rushed up to the car. Redrick, taking occasional drags of his cigarette, watched as they dexterously pulled Burbridge from the backseat, laid him down on the stretcher, and carried him to the door. Burbridge was lying motionless, crossing his arms on his chest and staring remotely into the sky. His huge feet, cruelly damaged by the slime, were strangely and unnaturally bent.

He was the last of the old stalkers, the ones that began the search for alien treasures immediately after the Visit, when the Zone wasn't yet called the Zone, and there was no Institute, no wall, and no UN police force; when the town was paralyzed by terror, and the world giggled over the latest newspaper hoax. At the time, Redrick was ten years old, and Burbridge was still a strong and agile man—he loved drinking on someone else's dime, brawling, and chasing girls. Back then, he had absolutely no interest in his children, but he was already a piece of scum: when drunk, he got some vile pleasure out of beating his wife, loudly, so everyone could hear . . . Eventually, he beat her to death.

Redrick turned the Jeep around and, paying no attention to the traffic lights, cutting corners and honking at the rare pedestrians, sped straight home.

He stopped in front of the garage and, getting out of the car, saw the superintendent walking toward him from the park. As usual, the superintendent was in a foul mood, and his flabby, puffy-eyed face expressed extreme distaste, as if he weren't walking on solid earth but wading through a field of manure.

"Good morning," said Redrick politely.

The superintendent stopped two steps away and jabbed his thumb over his shoulder. "Did you do that?" he asked indistinctly. It was clear these were his first words of the day.

"Do what?"

"That swing. Did you put it up?"

"I did."

"What for?"

Redrick didn't answer, went up to the gates of the garage, and unlocked them. The superintendent followed and stopped right behind him.

"I'm asking you, why did you put up the swing? Who asked you to do that?"

"My daughter asked," said Redrick very calmly. He rolled the gates open.

"I'm not talking about your daughter!" The superintendent raised his voice. "Your daughter is a separate topic. I'm asking, who gave you permission? Who, exactly, said you could rearrange the park?"

Redrick turned toward him and for a while stood motionless, gazing fixedly at the man's pale, veined nose. The superintendent took a step back and said in a lower tone, "And you don't repaint the balcony. How many times do I have to—"

"Don't waste your breath," said Redrick. "I'm not going to leave."

He went back to the car and turned on the engine. As he put his hands on the steering wheel, he noticed that his knuckles had turned white. Then he leaned out of the car and, no longer controlling himself, said, "But if you do make me leave, asshole, you better say a prayer."

He drove the car into the garage, turned on the light, and closed the gates. He pulled the bag of swag out of the false gas tank, cleaned up the car, stuffed the bag into an old wicker basket, and put the fishing gear—still damp and covered in leaves—on top; finally, he dumped in the fish, which Burbridge had bought in the outskirts last night. Then he again examined the car from every side, just out of habit. He found a flattened cigarette stuck to the rear right tire. Redrick peeled it off—the cigarette was Swedish. Redrick thought about it, then stuffed it into a matchbox. The box already contained three butts.

He didn't meet anyone on the stairs. He stopped in front of his door, and it opened before he could take out his key. He walked in sideways, with the heavy basket under his arm, and soaked in the familiar warmth, the familiar smells of his home; Guta hugged him around the neck and stayed still, her face pressed into his chest. Even through the thick layers of his clothing, he felt the frantic beating of her heart. He didn't get in her way—he stood there patiently and waited until she came around, although that was precisely the moment he realized how exhausted and drained he was.

"All right," she said eventually in a low husky voice. She let go of him, turned on the light in the corridor, and, without turning around, went to the kitchen. "I'll make you coffee," she called out.

"I brought you some fish," he said in a deliberately cheerful voice. "Fry them up, every one, I'm dying of hunger!"

She returned, hiding her face in her hair; he put the basket on the floor and helped her take out the bag of fish, then they carried the bag together into the kitchen and dumped the fish into the sink. "Go wash up," she said. "By the time you're done, the food will be ready."

"How's the Monkey?" said Redrick, sitting down and pulling off his boots.

"Oh, she chattered all evening," replied Guta. "Barely managed to put her to bed. Wouldn't leave me alone: 'Where's Daddy, where's Daddy?' Give her Daddy right then and there . . ."

She moved silently and gracefully through the kitchen—so capable and lovely—and water was already boiling on the stove, and fish scales were flying from under the knife, and oil sputtered in their biggest frying pan, and the incredible smell of fresh coffee spread through the air.

Redrick got up and, walking barefoot, came back to the front door, picked up the basket, and carried it to the den. On the way, he glanced into the bedroom. The Monkey was dozing peacefully: her blanket hung to the floor, her nightie was riding up, and he could see her whole body—she was a small sleeping animal. Redrick couldn't resist it and stroked her back, covered in warm golden fur, and for the hundredth time marveled at how silky and long it was. He really wanted to pick her up, but he was worried he'd wake her, and besides, he was dirty as hell, drenched in the Zone and death. He came back to the kitchen, sat down at the table, and said, "Pour me a cup of coffee? I'll shower in a bit."

There was a stack of evening mail on the table: the *Harmont Times*, an *Athlete*, a *Playboy*—a whole bunch of magazines had arrived—and there were also the thick, gray-covered *Reports of the International Institute of Extraterrestrial Cultures*. Redrick took a steaming mug of coffee from Guta and pulled the *Reports* toward him. Squiggles, weird symbols, diagrams . . . The photos depicted familiar objects from strange angles. Another one of Kirill's posthumous papers had been published: "A Surprising Property of Magnetic Traps of Type 77b." The name "Panov" was framed in black, and there was a note in small print: "Dr. Kirill A. Panov, USSR, tragically perished while conducting an experiment in April of 19—." Redrick tossed the magazine away, gulped down some burning hot coffee, and asked, "Did anyone come by?"

"Gutalin dropped by," said Guta after a slight pause. She was standing next to the stove and looking at him. "He was totally drunk, I threw him out."

"How did the Monkey take it?"

"Didn't want him to go, of course. Almost started bawling. But I told her that Uncle Gutalin wasn't feeling well. And she replied understandingly, 'Uncle Gutalin is sloshed again.'"

Redrick chuckled and took another sip. Then he asked, "How about the neighbors?"

And again Guta hesitated a bit before answering. "Same as usual," she said eventually.

"Fine, don't tell me."

"Oh!" she said, waving her hand in disgust. "That hag from downstairs knocked during the night. Eyes bulging, foaming at the mouth. Why the hell are we sawing in the bathroom at night?"

"Bitch," said Redrick through his teeth. "Listen, maybe we really should move? Buy a house in the outskirts, where no one lives, get some abandoned cottage . . ."

"What about the Monkey?"

"My God," said Redrick. "Don't you think the two of us could figure out how to make her happy?"

Guta shook her head. "She loves children. And they love her. It's not their fault, that—"

"Yes," said Redrick. "It's definitely not their fault."

"No use talking about it," said Guta. "Oh, someone called for you. Didn't leave a name. I said you were out fishing."

Redrick put the cup down and stood up. "All right," he said. "I really should go shower. I still have a lot to do."

He locked the bathroom, threw his clothes into a tub, and put the brass knuckles, remaining screws, and other odds and ends on a shelf. He spent a long time under the hot, almost-boiling water, groaning and scrubbing his body with a coarse sponge until his skin turned red; then he turned off the shower, sat on the side of the tub, and lit a cigarette. Water was gurgling through the pipes, Guta was clinking dishes in the kitchen; he smelled fried fish, then Guta knocked on the door and handed him clean underwear. "Hurry up," she commanded. "The fish is getting cold."

She had completely recovered and was issuing orders again. Chuckling, Redrick got dressed; that is, he pulled on boxers and a T-shirt and, wearing this outfit, came back to the kitchen. "Now I can have some food," he said, sitting down.

"Did you put the clothes in the tub?" asked Guta.

"Uh-huh," he said with his mouth full. "Great fish!"

"Did you pour water over them?"

"No . . . My fault, sir, won't happen again, sir. Come on, do that later, have a seat!"

He caught her hand and tried to put her on his knees, but she slipped away and sat across from him.

"Neglecting your husband, huh?" said Redrick, filling his mouth again. "Giving him the cold shoulder."

"Some husband you are right now," said Guta. "An empty sack instead of a husband. First, you have to be stuffed."

"Hey, anything's possible!" said Redrick. "Don't you believe in miracles?"

"That would be quite the miracle. Want a drink?"

Redrick played indecisively with his fork. "N-no, probably not," he said. He looked at his watch and got up. "I should go now. Could you prepare a suit for me? Make it first rate, with a dress shirt and tie."

Enjoying the sensation of the cool floor on his bare feet, he walked to the den and barred the door. He put on a rubber apron, pulled on elbow-high rubber gloves, and started unloading the items in the bag onto the table. Two empties. A box of pins. Nine batteries. Three bracelets. And another hoop—resembling a bracelet but made from a white metal, lighter and about an inch larger in diameter. Sixteen black sparks in a plastic bag. Two perfectly preserved sponges close to a fist in size. Three shrickers. A jar of carbonated clay. There was still a heavy porcelain container, packed carefully in fiberglass, remaining in the bag, but Redrick left it alone. He took out his cigarettes and lit up, looking over the swag laid out on the table.

Then he pulled out a drawer and took out a piece of paper, a pencil stub, and his balance sheet. Holding the cigarette in the corner of his mouth and squinting from the smoke, he wrote down number after number, lining them up in three columns, and adding the first two. The sums turned out to be impressive. He crushed the cigarette in the ashtray, carefully opened the box, and poured the pins out onto the paper. In the electric light the pins looked shot with blue and would on rare occasion burst into pure spectral colors—red, yellow, green. He picked up one pin and, being careful not to prick himself, squeezed it between his finger and thumb. He turned off the light and waited a little, getting used to the dark. But the pin was silent. He put it aside, groped for another one, and also squeezed it between his fingers. Nothing. He squeezed harder, risking a prick, and the pin starting talking: weak reddish sparks ran along it and changed all at once to rarer green ones. For a couple of seconds Redrick admired this strange light show, which, as he learned from the *Reports*, had to mean something, possibly something very significant, then he put the pin down separately from the first one and picked up a new one.

Overall, there were seventy-three pins, out of which twelve talked and the rest were silent. Actually, these would also talk, but fingers weren't enough; you needed a special machine the size of a table. Redrick turned on the light and added two numbers to those already on the page. And only after this did he make up his mind.

He shoved both hands into the bag and, holding his breath, took out the package and put it on the table. He stared at it for some time, pensively scratching his chin with the back of his hand. Then he finally picked up a pencil, spun it in his clumsy rubber fingers, and threw it down again. He took out another cigarette and, without lifting his eyes from the package, smoked it whole.

"To hell with this!" he said loudly, resolutely picked up the package, and stuffed it back into the bag. "That's it. That's enough."

He quickly poured the pins back into the box and rose from the table. It was time to go. He could probably nap for half an hour to clear his head, but on the other hand, it might be smarter to arrive early and get a sense of things. He took off his gloves, hung up the apron, and, without turning off the light, left the den.

The suit was already laid out on the bed, and Redrick began to dress. He was tying his tie in front of a mirror, when the floorboards squeaked softly behind him, he heard agitated breathing, and he had to make a serious face to avoid laughing.

"Boo!" a high voice suddenly yelled beside him, and he felt someone grab his leg.

"Aah!" exclaimed Redrick, collapsing on the bed.

The Monkey, squealing and shouting with laughter, immediately climbed on top of him. She stepped on him, pulled his hair, and showered him with important information. The neighbor kid Willy tore dolly's leg off. There was a new kitten on the third floor, all white and with red eyes—he probably didn't listen to his mommy and went in the Zone. There was oatmeal and jam for supper. Uncle Gutalin was sloshed again and felt sick, he even cried. Why don't fish drown, if they're in water? Why wasn't Mommy sleeping at night? Why do we have five fingers, but only two arms, and one nose? Redrick carefully hugged the warm creature crawling all over him, looked into the huge, entirely black eyes with no whites, pressed his face to the chubby little cheek covered in silky golden fur, and repeated, "My Monkey . . . Oh, you Monkey . . . What a little Monkey . . ."

The phone rang sharply in his ear. He stretched out a hand and picked up the receiver. "Yes?"

There was no response.

"Hello?" said Redrick. "Hello?"

No one answered. Then there was a click, and he heard a series of short beeps. After this, Redrick stood up, put the Monkey down on the floor, and, no longer listening to her, put on his jacket and pants. The Monkey chattered without pause, but he only smiled absentmindedly, and so it was eventually announced that Daddy must have bitten then swallowed his tongue, and he was left alone.

He came back to the den, put the items on the table into his briefcase, stopped by the bathroom to get the brass knuckles, again returned to the den, took the briefcase in one hand and the wicker basket in the other, and went out, carefully locking the den door and shouting to Guta, "I'm leaving!"

"When are you coming back?" said Guta, coming in from the kitchen. She had already brushed her hair and put makeup on, and she was no longer wearing a bathrobe but had changed into a dress—his favorite one, bright blue and low cut.

"I'll call you," he said, looking at her, then came up to her, bent down, and kissed her cleavage.

"Well, go on . . ." said Guta quietly.

"And me? What about me?" hollered the Monkey, climbing between them. He had to bend down even farther. Guta was looking at him with frozen eyes.

"It's nothing," he said. "Don't worry. I'll call you."

In the stairwell on the floor below, Redrick met a heavy man in striped pajamas who stood in front of his door, fiddling with his lock. From the dark recesses of his apartment wafted a warm smell of sour cooking. Redrick stopped and said, "Good morning."

The heavy man looked warily at him over his huge shoulder and mumbled something.

"Your wife came by last night," said Redrick. "Thought we were sawing something. There must have been a mistake."

"What's it to me?" grumbled the man in pajamas.

"My wife was doing the laundry last night," continued Redrick. "If we bothered you, I apologize."

"I didn't say anything," said the man in pajamas. "Feel free."

"Well, I'm very glad," said Redrick.

He went downstairs, stopped by the garage, put the basket down in the corner, covered it with an old seat cushion, took one last look, and came out onto the street.

It wasn't a long walk—two blocks to the square, a bit through the park, and another block until Central Avenue. As usual, the street in front of the Metropole gleamed with the chrome and lacquer of a colorful collection of cars, doormen in raspberry uniforms lugged suitcases toward the entrance, and some respectable foreign-looking men congregated in groups of two or three on the marble staircase, chatting and smoking cigars. Redrick decided not to go there yet. He settled under the awning of a small café across the street, ordered coffee, and lit up. At a table two steps away, he saw three undercover members of the international police force, sitting silently, hastily stuffing themselves with fried sausages à la Harmont, and drinking dark beer from tall glass steins. On his other side, about ten steps away, some sergeant was gloomily scarfing down fried potatoes, holding his fork in his fist. His blue helmet was upside down on the floor beside him, and his holster was hanging on the back of his chair. No one else was in the café. The waitress, an unfamiliar middle-aged woman, stood off to the side and yawned occasionally, tactfully covering her painted mouth with her hand. It was twenty minutes to nine.

Redrick watched as Richard Noonan came out of the hotel, munching on something and pulling a soft hat over his ears. He briskly marched down the stairs—small, fat, and pink, the picture of prosperity and good health, freshly washed and cheerful, completely convinced that the day would be a good one. He waved to someone, threw his rolled-up jacket over his right shoulder, and walked to his Peugeot. Dick's Peugeot was itself round, short, and freshly washed and somehow also gave the impression of total optimism.

Hiding his face behind his hand, Redrick watched Noonan fussily and industriously settle in behind the wheel, moving an item from the front seat to the back, bending down to pick up something, and adjusting the rearview mirror. The Peugeot coughed out a puff of bluish smoke, beeped at some African in a burnoose, and briskly rolled onto the street. From the looks of things, Noonan was heading to the Institute and therefore would go around the fountain and drive past the café. It was now too late to get up and go, so Redrick just covered his whole face with his hand and hunched over his cup. Unfortunately, this didn't help. The Peugeot beeped right in his ear, the brakes squealed, and Noonan's cheerful voice called out, "Hey! Schuhart! Red!"

Cursing under his breath, Redrick lifted his head. Noonan was already walking toward him, stretching out his hand. He was beaming.

"What are you doing here this early?" he asked when he came closer. "Thanks, dear," he called to the waitress, "I don't need anything." And then, again addressing Redrick, "Haven't seen you in ages. Where have you been hiding? What have you been doing with yourself?"

"Not much . . ." said Redrick without enthusiasm. "This and that."

He watched as Noonan, fussy and meticulous as always, settled on the chair across from him, his plump little hands pushing the napkin holder to one side and the sandwich plate to the other; and he listened as he chattered amicably. "You look kind of beat—not getting enough sleep? You know, I've been run off my feet myself with the new machinery, but sleep—no, my friend, sleep's the first thing, screw the machinery . . ." He suddenly looked around. "Pardon me, maybe you're waiting for someone? Am I bothering you?"

"No, no . . ." said Redrick listlessly. "I just had a bit of time, thought I'd at least have a cup of coffee."

"All right, I won't keep you long," Dick said and looked at his watch. "Listen, Red, why don't you drop your this and your that and come back to the Institute? You know they'd take you back in a second. They just got a new Russian, want to work with him?"

Redrick shook his head. "No," he said, "the next Kirill hasn't been born yet. Besides, there's nothing for me to do at your Institute. It's all automated now, the robots go into the Zone, the robots, I suppose, also get the bonuses. And lab assistant salary—that won't even cover my tobacco . . ."

Noonan disagreed. "Come on, that could all be sorted out."

"And I don't like it when other people sort things out for me," said Redrick. "I've been sorting things out myself my whole life and plan to continue that way."

"You've gotten proud," Noonan said reproachfully.

"I'm not proud. I just don't like counting pennies, that's all."

"Well, you've got a point," said Noonan absentmindedly. He glanced casually at Redrick's briefcase sitting on the nearby chair and rubbed his finger over the silver plating with the Cyrillic engraving. "That's exactly right. A man needs money in order to never think about it . . . A present from Kirill?" he asked, nodding at the briefcase.

"My inheritance," said Redrick. "Why haven't I seen you at the Borscht lately?"

"More like I haven't seen you," said Noonan. "I almost always eat dinner there; here at the Metropole everything costs an arm and a leg . . . Listen," he said suddenly, "how are you doing for money?"

"Want to borrow some?" asked Redrick.

"On the contrary."

"Then you want to lend some."

"There's work," said Noonan.

"Oh God!" said Redrick. "Not you, too!"

"Who else?" Noonan asked immediately.

"Oh, there are a lot of you . . . employers."

Noonan, as if he just understood, started laughing. "No, no, this isn't related to your primary career."

"Then what?"

Noonan checked his watch again. "Listen," he said, getting up. "Drop by the Borscht today at lunchtime, around one. We'll talk."

"I might not make it by one," said Redrick.

"Then in the evening, around six. All right?"

"We'll see," said Redrick and also checked his watch. It was five to nine.

Noonan waved and toddled off to his Peugeot. Redrick watched him leave, called the waitress, asked for a pack of Lucky Strikes, paid the bill, and, picking up his briefcase, walked leisurely across the street to the hotel. The sun was already hot, the street was rapidly becoming muggy, and Redrick's eyes were starting to sting. He squeezed them shut, regretting that he didn't have the chance to nap before this important deal. And then it happened.

He had never felt this outside of the Zone, and even in the Zone it had only happened two or three times. Suddenly, he seemed to be in another world. A million smells assaulted him at once—smells that were sharp, sweet, metallic; dangerous, caressing, disturbing; as immense as houses, as tiny as dust particles, as rough as cobblestones, and as delicate and intricate as watch gears. The air turned hard, it appeared to have surfaces, corners, edges, as if space had been filled with huge coarse spheres, polished pyramids, and gigantic prickly crystals, and he was forced to make his way through all this, as if in a dream, pushing through a dark antique shop full of ancient misshapen furniture . . . This only lasted a moment. He opened his eyes, and everything disappeared. This wasn't another world—it was his same old world turning an unfamiliar side toward him, revealing it for an instant, then immediately sealing it off, before he even had the chance to investigate.

An irritated horn blared in his ear; Redrick sped up, then broke into a run, only stopping next to the hotel wall. His heart was racing, so he put down his briefcase, impatiently tore open a pack of cigarettes, and lit up. He was inhaling deeply, resting, as if after a fight, and the policeman on beat walked up and asked anxiously, "Mister, would you like some help?"

"N-no," Redrick forced out the word, then coughed. "It's a bit stuffy . . ."

"Would you like me to walk with you?"

Redrick bent down and picked up his briefcase. "I'm fine now," he said. "Nothing to worry about, buddy. Thank you."

He quickly walked toward the door, went up the stairs, and came into the lobby. It was cool, dim, and full of echoes. He would have liked to sit in one of the gigantic leather armchairs, come to his senses, and catch his breath, but he was already late. He only let himself finish his cigarette, watching the people around him through half-closed eyes. Bony was already here, looking irritated and rifling through the magazines at the newsstand. Redrick threw the cigarette butt into a trash can and got into the elevator.

He didn't close the door in time, and a few people squeezed in next to him: a fat man breathing asthmatically, an overperfumed woman with a sullen boy munching a chocolate bar, and a heavy old lady with a badly shaved chin. Redrick was squished into a corner. He closed his eyes so he wouldn't have to see the boy, whose mouth was dripping with chocolate saliva but whose face was fresh, pure, without a single hair; so he wouldn't have to see his mother, whose meager bust was adorned with a necklace of black sparks, set in silver; and so he wouldn't have to see the bulging sclerotic eyes of the fat man and the repulsive warts on the old woman's bloated mug. The fat man tried to light a cigarette, but the old lady tore into him and continued berating him until the fifth floor, where she got off; and as soon as she got off, the fat man finally lit up, looking like a man who had defended his rights, and then immediately began to cough, wheezing and gasping, extending his lips like a camel, and jabbing Redrick in the ribs with his elbow.

On the eighth floor Redrick got off and, in order to let off some steam, loudly and emphatically declared, "Screw you,

you old unshaven hag, and same to you, coughing cretin, and you, you reeking broad with your snotty, chocolate-covered punk, go to hell!"

Then he walked on the plush carpet along the hallway, which was bathed in the cozy light of hidden lamps. Here, it smelled like fancy tobacco, Parisian perfumes, gleaming leather wallets overstuffed with banknotes, expensive call girls worth five hundred a night, and massive gold cigar cases. It stank of vulgarity, of the foul scum that had grown on the Zone, gotten rich by the Zone, fed, drank, and fattened from the Zone, and didn't give a damn—and especially didn't give a damn about what would happen when it gorged itself to its heart's content, and all that used to be in the Zone settled in the outside world. Redrick quietly pushed open the door of suite 874.

Raspy was sitting on a chair by the window and making a cigar. He was still wearing pajamas, and his thinning hair was damp—but it was already carefully combed over, and his sallow, puffy face was clean shaven. "Aha," he said, "punctuality is the courtesy of kings. Hello, my boy!"

He finished snipping the end of the cigar, picked it up with both hands, brought it to his nose, and sniffed it from end to end.

"And where is our old friend Burbridge?" he asked, and lifted his eyes. His eyes were clear, blue, and angelic.

Redrick put his briefcase on the couch, sat down, and took out his cigarettes. "Burbridge isn't coming," he said.

"Good old Burbridge," said Raspy, holding the cigar with two fingers and carefully bringing it to his mouth. "Good old Burbridge had a case of nerves . . ." He continued to stare at Redrick with his innocent blue eyes and didn't blink. He never blinked.

The door opened slightly, and Bony squeezed into the room. "Who was that man you were talking to?" he asked straight from the doorway.

"Oh, hello," said Redrick amiably, flicking his cigarette ashes onto the floor.

Bony stuffed his hands into his pockets and walked toward him, taking long strides with his giant, pigeon-toed feet, and stopped in front of Redrick. "We've told you a hundred times," he said reproachfully. "No get-togethers before the meeting. And what do you do?"

"Me—I greet you," said Redrick. "And you?"

Raspy laughed, and Bony said irritably, "Hello, hello." He stopped glaring at Redrick reproachfully and collapsed on the couch next to him. "You can't do that," he said. "Got it? You can't!"

"Then name a meeting place where I don't have any friends," said Redrick.

"The boy is right," noted Raspy. "Our mistake. So who was that man?"

"That was Richard Noonan," said Redrick. "He represents some firms that supply equipment to the Institute. He lives here, in the hotel."

"You see how simple it is!" said Raspy to Bony, picking up an enormous lighter, shaped like the Statue of Liberty, from the table. He looked at it doubtfully, then put it back.

"And where's Burbridge?" said Bony, sounding completely mollified.

"Burbridge is out," said Redrick.

The other two quickly exchanged glances. "May he rest in peace," said Raspy warily. "Or maybe he got arrested?"

For some time, Redrick didn't reply, leisurely puffing on his cigarette. Then he threw the butt on the floor and said, "Don't worry, everything's fine. He's in the hospital."

"That's what you call 'fine'?" Bony said nervously, jumping up and walking to the window. "In which hospital?"

"Don't worry," repeated Redrick. "In the right hospital. Let's get down to business, I need to sleep."

"In which hospital, exactly?" asked Bony, already sounding irritated.

"I just told you," answered Redrick. He picked up his briefcase. "Are we going to do business or not?"

"We are, we are, my boy," Raspy said cheerfully. Showing unexpected agility, he jumped to his feet, briskly pushed a coffee table toward Redrick, and in a single motion swept the pile of newspapers and magazines onto the carpet. He sat down across from Redrick, putting his hairy pink hands on his knees. "Show us," he said.

Redrick opened the briefcase, took out the list of prices, and laid it on the table in front of Raspy. Raspy looked at it and pushed it away with one finger. Bony, standing behind his back, stared at the list over his shoulder.

"That's the bill," said Redrick.

"I see that," replied Raspy. "Show us, show us!"

"The money?" said Redrick.

"What is this 'ring'?" Bony demanded suspiciously, jabbing his finger at the list over Raspy's shoulder.

Redrick was silent. He held the open briefcase on his knees and kept staring into the angelic blue eyes. Finally, Raspy chuckled.

"Why do I love you so much, my boy?" he cooed. "And they say there's no love at first sight!" He sighed theatrically. "Phil, buddy, how do they say it around here? Pay the man, give him some moola . . . and pass me a match, already! As you can see . . ." And he shook the cigar still gripped between his fingers.

Bony grumbled something unintelligible, threw him a matchbox, and went into the neighboring room through a curtain-covered doorway. Redrick heard him speaking, irritably and indistinctly, saying something about a pig in a poke. Meanwhile, Raspy, having finally lit his cigar, kept examining Redrick with a fixed smile on his pale, thin lips and seemed to be considering something—so Redrick put his chin on his briefcase and stared back, also trying not to blink, although his eyes were burning and he was tearing up. Then Bony returned, threw two bundles of cash down on the table, and, looking sullen, sat next to Redrick. Redrick lazily reached for the money, but Raspy gestured him to stop, unwrapped the cash, and stuffed the wrappers into his pocket.

"Now you're welcome to it," he said.

Redrick took the money and, without counting, shoved it into an inner pocket of his jacket. After that, he spread out the swag. He did this slowly, giving them both a chance to examine each item and check it against the list. The room was silent, except for Raspy's laborious breathing and a barely audible clinking coming from behind the curtain—probably a spoon tapping a glass.

When Redrick finally closed and locked his briefcase, Raspy looked up at him and asked, "All right, and our main object?"

"Nothing," answered Redrick. He paused and added, "Yet."

"I like that 'yet,'" said Raspy affectionately. "And you, Phil?"

"You're muddling things, Schuhart," said Bony with distaste. "Why the secrecy, I ask?"

"This business is full of secrets," said Redrick. "It's a difficult business."

"Well, all right," said Raspy. "And where's the camera?"

"Oh, shit!" Redrick rubbed his cheek with his hand, feeling his face turn red. "I'm sorry," he said. "I totally forgot."

"Over there?" asked Raspy, gesturing vaguely with his cigar.

"I'm not sure . . . Probably over there . . ." Redrick closed his eyes and leaned back on the couch. "No. I really can't remember."

"Too bad," said Raspy, "But did you at least see it?"

"No, we didn't," said Redrick with vexation. "That's the thing. We didn't even make it to the furnaces. Burbridge got into the slime, and we turned right back. You can be sure that if I saw it, I wouldn't have forgotten."

"My God, Hugh, take a look!" Bony suddenly said in a frightened whisper. "What the hell is this?"

He was sitting with his right index finger extended tensely in front of him. Spinning around his finger was that same white metal bracelet, and Bony was staring at it wild-eyed.

"It won't stop!" Bony said loudly, moving his astonished eyes from the bracelet to Raspy and back again.

"What do you mean, 'won't stop'?" Raspy said cautiously, and drew back slightly.

"I put it on my finger and spun it once, just for fun. And it's now been spinning a whole minute!"

Bony bolted up and, holding his extended finger before him, ran through the curtained doorway. The bracelet, shimmering with silver, continued to rotate steadily in front of him, like an airplane propeller.

"What's this you brought us?" asked Raspy.

"Hell if I know!" said Redrick. "I had no idea. If I did, I would have charged more."

Raspy looked at him for some time, then got up and also disappeared through the doorway. Redrick immediately heard the murmur of voices. He took out a cigarette, lit up, picked up a magazine from the floor, and absentmindedly flipped through it. The magazine was full of tight-bodied beauties, but for some reason looking at them right now nauseated him. Redrick flung the magazine down and scanned the suite, searching for a drink. Then he pulled the money out of his pocket and counted the bills. Everything was fine, but in order to stay awake, he also counted the second pack. As he was putting it back in his pocket, Raspy returned.

"You're in luck, my boy," he announced, again sitting down across from Redrick. "Have you heard of perpetual motion?"

"Nope," said Redrick. "Didn't do that in school."

"Just as well," said Raspy. He pulled out another bundle of cash. "That's the payment for the first specimen," he declared, unwrapping the cash. "For every new specimen of this ring of yours, you'll get two such bundles. You got it, my boy? Two bundles. But only under the condition that no one but us ever finds out about these rings. Deal?"

Redrick silently put the money in his pocket and got up. "I'm going," he said. "When and where next time?"

Raspy also got up. "You'll get a call," he said. "Wait by the phone every Friday from nine to nine thirty in the morning. They'll send regards from Phil and Hugh and arrange a meeting."

Redrick nodded and headed for the door. Raspy followed him, laying his hand on Redrick's shoulder.

"There's something I want you to understand," he continued. "This is all very nice, really quite charming, and the ring—that's just lovely. But what we need most of all are two things: the photos and a full container. Bring us back our camera, but with the film exposed, and our porcelain container, but full instead of empty, and you'll never need to enter the Zone again . . ."

Redrick shifted his shoulder, shook off the hand, unlocked the door, and left. He walked along the soft carpet, not looking back, the entire time feeling the angelic unblinking gaze on the back of this head. He didn't wait for the elevator and instead walked down from the eighth floor.

After leaving the Metropole, he hailed a cab and took it to the other side of town. He didn't know the driver, a new guy, some pimply beaked kid, one of the thousands who had recently flocked to Harmont looking for hair-raising adventures, untold riches, international fame, or some special religion; they came in droves but ended up as taxi drivers, waiters, construction workers, and bouncers in brothels—yearning, untalented, tormented by nebulous desires, angry at the whole world, horribly disappointed, and convinced that here, too, they'd been cheated. Half of them, after lingering for a month or two, returned home cursing, spreading news of their great disappointment to almost every corner of the globe; a rare few became stalkers and quickly perished, never having made any sense of things and turning posthumously into legendary heroes; some managed to get jobs at the Institute, the brightest and best-educated ones, capable at least of becoming lab assistants; the rest founded political parties, religious sects, and self-help groups and idled away their evenings in bars, brawling over differences of opinion, over girls, or just for the hell of it. From time to time they organized protests and petitions, staged demonstrations, went on strike—sit-down strikes, stand-up strikes, and even lie-down strikes—enraging the city police, administrators, and established residents; but the longer they stayed, the more thoroughly they calmed down and resigned themselves to things, and the less they worried about what exactly they were doing in Harmont.

The pimply driver reeked of alcohol, and his eyes were red like a rabbit's, but he was extremely agitated and immediately started telling Redrick how a corpse from the cemetery showed up this morning on his street. "He came to his old house, except this house, it's been boarded up for years, everyone has left—the old lady, his widow, and his daughter with her husband, and his grandkids. He passed away, the neighbors say, about thirty years ago, before the Visit, and now here you go—hello!—he's turned up. He walked around and around the house, rattled the door, then sat down by the fence and just stayed there. A crowd gathered—the whole neighborhood had come to gawk—but, of course, no one had the guts to go near. Eventually, someone figured it out: broke down the door to his house, gave him a way in. And what do you know, he stood up and walked in and closed the door behind him. I had to get to work, don't know how it turned out, all I know is that they were planning to call the Institute, so they'd take him the hell away from us. You know what they say? They say the military has been drafting an order, that these corpses, if their relatives have moved out, should be sent to them at their new place of residence. Won't the family be delighted! And the stench of him . . . Well, he's not a corpse for nothing."

"Stop," said Redrick. "Drop me off here."

He rummaged in his pocket. He didn't find any change and had to break a hundred. Then he stood by the gates, waiting for the taxi to leave. Burbridge's cottage wasn't bad: two floors, a glass-enclosed wing with a billiards room, a well-kept garden, a hothouse, and a white gazebo among the apple trees. And all this was surrounded by a carved iron fence, painted light green. Redrick rang the doorbell a couple of times, the gate opened with a slight squeak, and Redrick started slowly walking along a sandy path lined with rosebushes. The Gopher—gnarled, dark crimson, and quivering with enthusiasm from the desire to be of service—was already waiting on the cottage porch. Seized with impatience, he turned sideways, lowered his foot down a step, groped convulsively for support, steadied himself, then reached for the bottom step with his other foot, the entire time jerking his healthy arm in Redrick's direction: *Wait, wait, I'm coming.*

"Hey, Red!" called a female voice from the garden.

Redrick turned his head and, in the greenery next to the carved white roof of the gazebo, saw bare, tanned shoulders, a bright red mouth, and a waving hand. He nodded to the Gopher, turned off the path, cut through the rosebushes, and, walking on the soft green grass, headed toward the gazebo.

A huge red mat was spread on the lawn, and on it, holding a glass in her hand, Dina Burbridge lounged regally in a minuscule bathing suit; a book with a colorful cover lay nearby, and right there, in the shadow of the bush, stood a metal ice bucket with a slender bottle neck peeking out from inside.

"What's up, Red?" said Dina Burbridge, making a welcoming gesture with her glass. "And where's the old man? Did he get caught again?"

Redrick came up to her and, placing his briefcase behind his back, stopped, admiring her from above. Yes, the children Burbridge had wished up in the Zone were magnificent. She was silky, luscious, sensuously curvy, without a single flaw, a single extra ounce—a hundred and twenty pounds of twenty-year-old delectable flesh—and then there were the emerald eyes, which shone from within, and the full moist lips and the even white teeth and the jet-black hair that gleamed in the sun, carelessly thrown over one shoulder; the sunlight flowed over her body, drifting from her shoulders to her stomach and hips, throwing shadows between her almost-bare breasts. He was standing over her and openly checking her out while she looked up at him, smiling knowingly; then she brought her glass to her lips and took a few sips.

"Want some?" she said, licking her lips, and, waiting just long enough for him to appreciate the double entendre, offered him the glass.

He turned away, looked around, and, finding a lounge chair in the shade, sat down and stretched his legs. "Burbridge is in the hospital," he said. "They'll cut off his legs."

Still smiling, she looked at him with one eye, the other hidden behind a thick mass of hair falling over her shoulder, except her smile had frozen—it was a fixed grin on a tan face. She mechanically shook her drink, as if listening to the tinkling of the ice against the glass, and asked, "Both legs?"

"Both of them. Maybe up to the knee, and maybe higher."

She put down the glass and swept the hair off her face. She was no longer smiling. "A pity," she said. "That means that you, then . . ."

To her, Dina Burbridge, and her alone, he could have described exactly what happened and how it all was. He could have probably even described how he came back to the car, gripping the brass knuckles, and how Burbridge had begged—not even for himself, but for the kids, for her and for Archie, and how he promised the Golden Sphere. But he didn't describe it. He silently reached into his pocket, pulled out a bundle of cash, and threw it on the red mat, next to Dina's long bare legs. The bills spread into a colorful fan. Dina absentmindedly picked up a few and began to examine them, as if she had never seen one before but wasn't all that interested.

"The last pay, then," she said.

Redrick bent down from the lounge chair, reached for the bucket, and, taking out the bottle, glanced at the label. Water was trickling down the dark glass, and Redrick held the bottle off to the side so it wouldn't drip on his pants. He didn't like expensive whiskey, but right now it would do. And he was about to chug some straight from the bottle, but was stopped by inarticulate protesting sounds coming from behind his back. He turned around and saw the Gopher hurrying across the lawn, painfully moving his twisted legs, holding a tall glass with a clear mixture in front of him with both hands. He was sweating from the strain, perspiration poured down his dark crimson face, and his bloodshot eyes were almost popping out of their sockets; then, when he saw that Redrick was looking at him, he almost desperately held the glass out in front of him, making the same pitiful mewling sound, opening his toothless mouth wide in helpless frustration.

"I'm waiting, I'm waiting," Redrick told him and stuck the bottle back into the ice.

The Gopher finally limped up, gave Redrick the glass, and with a timid familiarity patted his shoulder with a clawlike hand.

"Thank you, Dixon," said Redrick seriously. "That's exactly what I needed right now. As usual, you're on top of your game, Dixon."

And while the Gopher in embarrassment and delight shook his head and spasmodically beat his hip with his healthy hand, Redrick solemnly raised the glass, nodded to him, and drank half in one gulp. He looked at Dina. "Want some?" he said, showing her the glass.

She wasn't answering. She was folding a banknote in half, then again, and again.

"Stop that," he said. "You'll manage. Your father—"

She interrupted him. "So you carried him out, then," she said. She wasn't asking, but stating. "Hauled him, the moron, through the whole Zone, carried that piece of scum on your back—you redheaded idiot, what a chance you blew!"

He looked at her, forgetting his drink, while she got up, came closer, stepping over the scattered banknotes, and stopped in front of him; she put her fists on her hips, blocking the whole world from him with her incredible body, smelling of sweet sweat and perfume.

"He has all you idiots wrapped around his finger . . . Dancing on your bones, on your skulls . . . You just wait, you just wait, he'll be dancing on your bones on crutches, he'll still show you brotherly love and mercy!" She was now almost shrieking.

"Promised you the Golden Sphere, huh? Maps and traps, huh? Moron! I can tell from your freckled mug that he promised. You just wait, he'll still show you a map, may the foolish soul of redheaded idiot Redrick Schuhart rest in peace . . ."

Then Redrick slowly stood up and slapped her, and she stopped midsentence, sank down as if her legs had given way, and buried her face in her hands.

"Idiot . . . redhead." she said indistinctly. "What a chance you blew. What a chance!"

Redrick, looking at her from above, finished his drink and, without turning around, shoved it at the Gopher. There was nothing else to say. Burbridge sure finagled some great kids out of the Zone. Loving and respectful ones.

He went out onto the street, flagged a cab, and ordered the driver to take him to the Borscht. He needed to finish with all this business, he was unbearably sleepy, the world was swimming before his eyes—and he did in fact fall asleep, slumping heavily on his briefcase, and only woke up when the driver shook his shoulder.

"We're here, mister."

"Where are we?" he asked, sleepily looking around. "I told you to drive to the bank."

"No way, mister." The driver scowled. "You said the Borscht. This is the Borscht."

"All right," grumbled Redrick. "Must have dreamed it."

He paid the fare and climbed out, painfully moving his stiff legs. It was very hot, and the pavement was already baking. Redrick noticed he was soaked through, that his mouth tasted vile, and that his eyes were tearing up. Before coming in, he took a look around. As was usual at this hour, the street in front of the Borscht was deserted. The businesses across the street weren't open yet, even the Borscht was technically closed, but Ernest was already on duty—wiping glasses, sullenly glancing from behind the bar at the three goons lapping up beer at a corner table. The remaining tables still had chairs on top of them, an unfamiliar black man in a white jacket was industriously scrubbing the floor, and another black man was struggling with a case of beer behind Ernest's back. Redrick came up to the bar, put his briefcase on top, and said hello. Ernest grumbled something unfriendly.

"Pour me some beer," said Redrick, yawning uncontrollably.

Ernest slammed an empty stein down on the bar, grabbed a bottle from the fridge, opened it, and tilted it over the stein. Redrick, covering his mouth, gaped at Ernest's hand. The hand was shaking. The neck of the bottle kept clattering against the stein. Redrick looked Ernest in the face. Ernest's heavy lids were lowered, his small mouth was twisted, his fat cheeks drooped. One of the men was swinging a mop right under Redrick's feet, the goons in the corner were viciously arguing about the races, and the man handling the beer bumped into Ernest so hard he wobbled. He began mumbling apologies. In a strained voice, Ernest asked, "You got it?"

"Got what?" Redrick looked over his shoulder.

One of the goons lazily got up from the table, walked to the entrance, and stood in the doorway, lighting a cigarette.

"Let's go have a talk," said Ernest.

The man with the mop was now also standing between Redrick and the door. An enormous black man, like Gutalin, only twice as broad. "Let's go," said Redrick, grabbing his briefcase. He was now wide awake.

He walked behind the bar and squeezed past the black man with the beer. The guy must have crushed his finger—he was licking his nail, scowling at Redrick from beneath his brows: another powerfully built black man, with a broken nose and cauliflower ears. Ernest went into the back room, and Redrick followed, because by now, all three goons were standing by the entrance, and the man with the mop blocked the way to the storeroom.

In the back room Ernest stepped aside and, hunching over, sat on a chair next to the wall while Captain Quarterblad, mournful and yellow, got up from behind the desk; a huge UN soldier, with his helmet pulled over his eyes, materialized from the left and quickly patted Redrick down, going over his pockets with enormous hands. He paused at the right side pocket, removed the brass knuckles, and softly nudged Redrick toward the captain. Redrick approached the desk and placed his briefcase in front of Captain Quarterblad.

"Good job, bastard," he told Ernest.

Ernest gave him a dejected look and shrugged one shoulder. Everything was clear. The two black men were already standing, smirking, in the door, and there were no other exits, and the window was shut and grated with thick iron bars.

Captain Quarterblad, grimacing in disgust, was digging with both hands through the briefcase, laying the contents out on the table: two extra-small empties; sixteen sparks of various sizes in a plastic bag; two beautifully preserved sponges; and a single jar of carbonated clay.

"Is there anything in your pockets?" Captain Quarterblad asked softly. "Take it all out . . ."

"Assholes," said Redrick. "Idiots."

He stuck his hand in his pocket and hurled a bundle of cash down on the table. The bills flew in all directions.

"Wow!" said Captain Quarterblad. "Anything else?"

"You stinking toads!" shrieked Redrick, grabbed the second bundle from his pocket, and hurled it forcefully at his feet. "Take it! Choke on it!"

"Very interesting," Captain Quarterblad said calmly. "And now pick it up."

"Screw you!" said Redrick, putting his hands behind his back. "Your lackeys will pick it up. You'll pick it up yourself!"

"Pick up the money, stalker," said Captain Quarterblad without raising his voice, digging his fists into the table and leaning forward with his whole body.

For a few seconds they silently looked each other in the eye, then Redrick, muttering curses, squatted down on the floor and started reluctantly collecting the money. The guys behind his back snickered, and the UN soldier snorted spitefully. "Don't snort!" said Redrick. "What are you, a horse?"

He was already crawling on his knees, collecting bills one by one, getting closer and closer to the dark copper ring, lying peacefully in a dirt-filled groove in the floor; he turned to position himself, continuing to shout dirty words, all the ones that he knew, and a few he made up along the way, and when the moment came, he shut up, strained, grabbed the ring, and pulled on it with all his might: the thrown-open trapdoor hadn't even clattered onto the floor when he was diving headfirst, arms outstretched, into the cool dank darkness of the wine cellar.

He landed on his hands, rolled over, jumped up, and, crouching, relying only on memory and on luck, blindly threw himself into a narrow passage between the rows of boxes; he bumped into the boxes as he ran, listening to them clang and clatter into the passage behind him, and, stumbling, ran up the invisible steps, rammed his whole body into a rusty tin-plated door, and burst into Ernest's garage. He was shaking and breathing heavily, red spots swam in front of his eyes, and his heart thumped loudly and painfully in his throat, but he didn't even stop for a second. He immediately threw himself into a corner and, skinning his hands, started to tear down the mountain of junk that hid the missing planks in the garage wall. Then he lay on his stomach and crawled through the hole, listening to something tear in his jacket. Out in the yard—as narrow as a well—he crouched by the garbage bins, pulled off his jacket, and tore off his tie; he quickly looked himself over, dusted off his pants, stood up, and, running across the yard, ducked into a low foul-smelling tunnel that led to an identical adjacent yard. As he ran, he pricked up his ears, but the wail of the police sirens wasn't audible yet; then he ran even faster, scattering recoiling children, diving under hanging laundry, and crawling through holes in rotten fences—trying to quickly flee this district while Captain Quarterblad still hadn't cordoned it off. He knew these places like the back of his hand. In these yards, these cellars, and these abandoned laundries he had played as a boy, everywhere around here he had acquaintances and even friends, and under different circumstances it would be child's play to hide here and sit it out, even for a whole week; but that wasn't why he had made a "daring escape from custody" right under Captain Quarterblad's nose, instantly adding a year to his sentence.

He had a stroke of luck. Yet another procession of some league swarmed down Seventh Street, hollering and raising dust—some two hundred long-haired idiot men and short-haired idiot women, waving stupid signs, as filthy and tattered as himself and even worse, as if they'd all been crawling through holes in fences, spilling garbage cans on themselves, and on top of that had recently spent a wild night in a coal bin. He jumped out of the doorway, burst into the crowd, and, zigzagging, shoving, stepping on toes, getting the occasional fist in the face and returning the favor, forced his way through to the other side and ducked into another doorway—right at the moment when the familiar repulsive wail of the police sirens sounded ahead, and the procession stopped, folding like an accordion. But he was now in a different district, and Captain Quarterblad had no way of knowing which one.

He approached his garage from the direction of the electronics warehouse and had to wait for a while as the workers loaded their cart with gigantic cardboard boxes with television sets. He made himself comfortable in the stunted lilac bushes in front of a windowless wall of a neighboring house, caught his breath, and smoked a cigarette. He smoked greedily, crouching down, leaning his back against the rough plaster of the wall, occasionally touching his cheek to still the nervous tic, and thought and thought and thought; then when the cart with the workers rolled, honking, into the yard, he laughed and softly said in its direction, "Thanks, boys, you slowed an idiot down . . . gave him time to think." From that moment on, he was quick without being rash, his motions deft and deliberate, as if he were working in the Zone.

He crept into his garage through a secret passage, silently removed the old seat cushion, stuck a hand into the basket, carefully took the package out of the bag, and placed it under his shirt. He grabbed an old threadbare leather jacket from the hook, found a grease-stained cap in the corner, and, using both hands, pulled it low over his forehead. Narrow strips of sunlight, full of dancing dust particles, entered the gloom of the garage through the cracks in the door; the kids in the yard shrieked in excitement and glee, and just as he was getting ready to leave, he suddenly recognized his daughter's voice. Then he pressed his eye to the widest crack and watched for a bit as the Monkey, waving two balloons, ran around the new swings while three old ladies with knitting in their laps sat on a bench nearby and stared at her, grimly pursing their lips. Exchanging their lousy opinions, the old hags. But the kids, they're just fine, playing with her like everything's all right, it wasn't for nothing he bribed them as best he could—the wooden slide he made them, and the dollhouse, and the swing . . . And that bench, on which the old hags were assembled—he made that, too. All right, he said, only moving his lips as he tore himself away from the crack, took one last look at the garage, and ran into the passage.

In the southwestern outskirts, by the abandoned gas station at the end of Miner Street, there was a telephone booth. Lord knows who used it now—the surrounding houses were all boarded up, and farther south stretched the endless vacant lot of the old town dump. Redrick sat right on the ground in the shadow of the booth and stuck his hand into the space beneath it. He groped around and felt the dusty wax paper and the handle of the gun that was wrapped in the paper; the zinc-coated cartridge box was also in its place, as was the bag of bracelets and the old wallet with fake documents—the cache was intact. Then he took off his leather jacket and cap and felt under his shirt. He sat there for an entire minute, weighing in his hand the porcelain container with inevitable and inexorable death within. He felt his cheek twitch again.

"Schuhart," he muttered, not hearing his voice. "What are you doing, bastard? You lowlife, with this thing they'll squash us all . . ." He pressed his fingers to his twitching cheek, but it didn't help. "Those jerks," he said about the workers loading televisions onto the cart. "Had to get in my way . . . I'd have tossed the wretched stuff back in the Zone, no one would have been the wiser."

He looked around in despair. The hot air was quivering over the cracked pavement, the boarded-up windows stared sullenly, dust clouds were wandering over the plain. He was all alone.

"Fine," he said with decision. "All for one, only the Lord for all. In our age it'll do . . ."

Hurrying so he wouldn't change his mind again, he stuffed the container in the cap and wrapped the cap in his leather jacket. He stood on his knees and, pushing with all his strength, slightly tilted the booth. The thick package fit in the bottom of the pit, still leaving a lot of free space. He carefully put the booth down, rocked it with both hands, and stood up, dusting off his palms.

"That's that," he said. "It's done."

He climbed into the oppressively hot booth, inserted a coin, and dialed a number.

"Guta," he said. "Don't worry, please. I got caught again." He could hear her shuddering sigh and hurriedly said, "This is all peanuts, six to eight months . . . with visits . . . We'll manage. And you won't be left without money, they'll send you money." She was still silent. "Tomorrow morning they'll summon you to headquarters, we'll meet there. Bring the Monkey."

"Will there be a search?" she said tonelessly.

"Let them search if they like. The place is clean. All right, stay strong. Hang in there and don't worry. Married a stalker, now don't complain. Well, till tomorrow . . . Keep in mind, I never called you. Kisses."

He abruptly hung up and stood still for a few seconds, squeezing his eyes tightly shut and clenching his teeth so hard his ears rang. Then he again inserted a coin and dialed another number.

"Hello?" said Raspy.

"This is Schuhart speaking," said Redrick. "Listen carefully and don't interrupt."

"Schuhart?" said Raspy with very genuine surprise. "Which Schuhart?"

"Don't interrupt, I said! I got caught, escaped, and am now going to give myself up. They'll give me two and a half or three years. My wife will be left penniless. You will provide for her. Make sure she has everything she needs, you understand? Do you understand, I'm asking?"

"Go on," said Raspy.

"Near the place where we first met, there's a telephone booth. There's only one here, you'll find it. The porcelain container is lying underneath. If you want it, take it; if you don't, don't take it—but make sure my wife has everything she needs. You and I still have a lot of work to do. And if I come back and find that you've double-crossed me . . . I don't suggest you double-cross me. Got it?"

"I got it all," said Raspy. "Thank you." After hesitating a little, he asked, "Maybe a lawyer?"

"No," said Redrick. "All the money, to the last penny—to my wife. Bye."

He hung up the phone, looked around, stuffed his hands deep into his pockets, and leisurely walked up Miner Street between the abandoned, boarded-up buildings.

3.

RICHARD H. NOONAN, 51 YEARS OLD, A REPRESENTATIVE OF ELECTRONIC EQUIPMENT SUPPLIERS TO THE HARMONT BRANCH OF THE IIEC.

Richard H. Noonan was sitting behind his office desk and doodling in an enormous notebook. At the same time, he was smiling sympathetically, nodding his bald head, and not listening to his visitor. He was simply waiting for a phone call while his visitor, Dr. Pillman, was lazily reprimanding him. Or imagining that he was reprimanding him. Or trying to convince himself that he was reprimanding him.

"We'll keep all that in mind, Valentine," Noonan said finally, finishing his tenth doodle for an even count and slamming his notebook shut. "You're right, this is a disgrace."

Valentine stretched out a slender hand and carefully flicked the ashes into the ashtray. "And what exactly will you be keeping in mind?" he inquired politely.

"Oh, everything you said," replied Noonan cheerfully, leaning back in his armchair. "Every last word."

"And what did I say?"

"That's irrelevant," said Noonan. "Whatever you said, we'll keep it all in mind."

Valentine (Dr. Valentine Pillman, Nobel laureate, etc., etc.) was sitting in front of him in a deep armchair—small, neat, and elegant, his suede jacket spotless, and his pulled-up trousers ironed to perfection. He was wearing a blindingly white shirt, a severe solid-colored tie, and gleaming shoes; there was a sardonic smile on his pale thin lips, enormous sunglasses hid his eyes, and his black hair bristled in a crew cut over a broad low forehead. "In my opinion, they pay you your incredible salary for nothing," he said. "And on top of that, Dick, I think you're also a saboteur."

"Shh!" said Noonan in a whisper. "For God's sake, not so loud."

"As a matter of fact," continued Valentine, "I've been watching you for some time. As far as I can tell, you do no work at all."

"Wait a minute!" interrupted Noonan, wagging a fat pink finger at him in protest. "What do you mean, 'no work'? Has a single claim been without consequences?"

"No idea," said Valentine, flicking his ashes again. "We get good equipment, and we get bad equipment. We get the good stuff more often, but what you have to do with it—I don't have a clue."

"And if it wasn't for me," objected Noonan, "the good stuff would be rarer. Besides, you scientists keep damaging good equipment, you file claims, and who covers for you then? Take, for example, what you've done with the bloodhound. An outstanding machine, made a brilliant showing during the geological surveys—reliable, autonomous. And you were running it at ridiculous settings, rode the mechanism too hard, like a racehorse . . ."

"Didn't give it enough water and didn't feed it oats," commented Valentine. "You're a stablemaster, Dick, not a manufacturer!"

"A stablemaster," Noonan repeated thoughtfully. "That's more like it. Now a few years ago we had a Dr. Panov working here—you probably knew him, he later perished . . . Anyway, he figured that my true calling is breeding crocodiles."

"I've read his papers," said Valentine. "A very serious-minded and thoughtful man. If I were you, I'd consider his words carefully."

"All right. I'll mull them over sometime. Why don't you tell me instead what happened at yesterday's experimental SK-3 launch?"

"SK-3?" repeated Valentine, furrowing his pale forehead. "Oh . . . The minstrel! Nothing in particular. It followed the route well and brought back a few bracelets and a strange disk." He paused. "And a buckle from a pair of Lux-brand suspenders."

"What kind of disk?"

"An alloy of vanadium, hard to say more right now. No unusual attributes."

"Then why did the SK grab it?"

"Ask the company. That's more in your line."

Noonan pensively tapped his notebook with his pencil. "After all, it was an experimental launch," he mused. "Or maybe the disk lost charge. You know what I'd advise you to do? Throw it back into the Zone, and after a day or two send the bloodhound after it. I remember, the year before last—"

The phone rang, and Noonan, immediately forgetting Valentine, grabbed the receiver.

"Mr. Noonan?" asked the secretary. "General Lemchen calling for you again."

"Put him through."

Valentine stood up, placed his extinguished cigarette in the ashtray, twirled two fingers near his temple as a sign of farewell, and went out—small, straight backed, well built.

"Mr. Noonan?" said the familiar drawl.

"Speaking."

"It's hard to find you at work, Mr. Noonan."

"A new shipment has arrived . . ."

"Yes, I already know that. Mr. Noonan, I'm in town for a short time. There are a couple of issues that need to be discussed in person. I'm referring to the latest contracts for Mitsubishi Denshi. The legal aspects."

"I'm at your service."

"Then, if you don't mind, we'll meet in half an hour in our department. Is that convenient for you?"

"That's fine. See you in half an hour."

Richard Noonan put down the receiver, got up, and, rubbing his plump hands, walked around his office. He even started singing a pop song but immediately hit a sour note and laughed genially at himself. Then he took his hat, threw his raincoat over his arm, and went into the waiting room.

"My dear," he said to the secretary, "I have to go make my rounds. You're now in charge of the troops. Hold the fort, as they say, and I'll bring you back some chocolates."

The secretary perked up. Noonan blew her an air kiss and walked briskly along the Institute's corridors. A few times people tried to waylay him; he dodged them, put them off with jokes, urged them to hold the fort without him, to take it easy, not to overwork themselves; finally, having successfully avoided everyone, he strode out of the building, waving his unopened pass in the guard's face with his usual motion.

Heavy clouds were hanging over the city, it was muggy, and the first hesitant raindrops were spreading into little black stars on the pavement. Throwing his raincoat over his head and shoulders, Noonan trotted along the long row of cars to his Peugeot, dived inside, and, tearing his raincoat off his head, threw it into the backseat. He took a round black spacell out of a side pocket of his jacket, inserted it into a jack on the dashboard, and pushed it in with his thumb until it clicked. Finally, wriggling his rear, he made himself comfortable behind the wheel and pressed on the gas. The Peugeot silently rolled into the middle of the street and raced toward the exit from the restricted area.

The rain gushed down all at once, as if a gigantic bucket of water had been tipped over in the sky. The road became slippery, and the car started skidding on turns. Noonan turned on his windshield wipers and slowed down. So they've received the report, he thought. Now they'll praise me. Well, I'm all for that. I like being praised. Especially by General Lemchen, in spite of himself. It's funny, I wonder why we like being praised. There's no money in it. Fame? How famous could we get? *He became famous: now he's known to three.* Maybe four, if you count Bayliss. Aren't humans absurd? I suppose we like praise for its own sake. The way children like ice cream. It's an inferiority complex, that's what it is. Praise assuages our insecurities. And ridiculously so. How could I rise in my own opinion? Don't I know myself—fat old Richard H. Noonan? By the way, what does that *H* stand for? What a thing! And there's no one to ask. Not like I can ask General Lemchen . . . Oh, I got it! Herbert. Richard Herbert Noonan. Boy, is it pouring.

He turned onto Central Avenue, and a thought popped into his head. How our little town has grown in recent years! Skyscrapers all around . . . There's another one under construction. And what will we have here? Oh yes, the Luna Complex—featuring the world's best jazz and a variety show and the brothel that'll hold a thousand—all for our valiant troops and brave tourists, especially the wealthy ones, and for our noble knights of science. Meanwhile, the suburbs are emptying out. And there's no longer anywhere for the returning dead to go.

"The risen dead have no place to return," he enunciated, "and that is why they're sorrowful and stern."

Yes, I'd like to know how all this will end. By the way, about ten years ago I knew with absolute certainty what would happen. Impenetrable police lines. A belt of empty land fifty miles wide. Scientists and soldiers, no one else. A hideous sore on the face of the planet permanently sealed off . . . And the funny thing is, it seemed like everybody thought this, not just me. The speeches that were made, the bills that were proposed! And now you can't even remember how all this unanimous steely resolve suddenly evaporated into thin air. *On the one hand, we are forced to admit, on the other hand, we can't dispute.* And it all seems to have started when the stalkers brought the first spacells out of the Zone. The batteries . . . Yes, I think that's really how it started. Especially when it was discovered that spacells multiply. It turned out that the sore wasn't such a sore; maybe it wasn't a sore at all but, instead, a treasure trove . . . And now no one has a clue what it is—a sore, a treasure trove, an evil temptation, Pandora's box, a monster, a demon . . . We're using it bit by bit. We've struggled for twenty years, wasted billions, but we still haven't stamped out the organized theft. Everyone makes a buck on the side, while the learned men pompously hold forth: *On the one hand, we are forced to admit; on the other hand, we can't dispute, because object so-and-so, when irradiated with X-rays at an eighteen-degree angle, emits quasiheated electrons at a twenty-two-degree angle.* The hell with it! One way or another, I won't live till the end.

The car was rolling past the Vulture Burbridge's mansion. Because of the torrential rain, the whole house was lit up—in the second-story windows, in gorgeous Dina's rooms, you could see dancing pairs moving to the music. Either they've been up since dawn, or they're still going strong from last night, he thought. That's the fashion in town nowadays—parties around the clock. A vigorous generation we've raised, hardworking and untiring in their pursuits . . .

Noonan stopped the car in front of an unprepossessing building with a modest sign—LAW FIRM OF CORSH, CORSH, AND SAYMACK. He took the spacell out and put it in his pocket, pulled his raincoat over his head again, grabbed his hat, and made a headlong rush inside—past the porter, absorbed in his newspaper, and up the stairs, covered with threadbare carpet—then he ran, heels tapping on the floor, along a dark second-story hallway permeated with a distinctive odor he had long ago stopped trying to identify. He opened the door at the end of the hallway and entered the waiting room. Behind the secretary's desk sat an unfamiliar, very tan young man. He wasn't wearing his jacket, and his shirtsleeves were rolled up. He was rummaging in the guts of some complicated electronic device that had replaced the typewriter on top of the desk. Richard Noonan hung his raincoat and hat on a hook, smoothed down the remnants of his hair with both hands, and looked inquiringly at the young man. He nodded. Noonan opened the door to the office.

General Lemchen rose heavily from the large leather armchair by the curtained window to greet him. His square-jawed soldierly face was gathered into creases, representing either a welcoming smile or displeasure with the weather, or possibly a barely suppressed desire to sneeze. "Oh, there you are," he drawled. "Come in, take a seat."

Noonan looked around for a place to sit and couldn't find anything except a hard straight-backed chair tucked behind the desk. He sat on the desk's edge. His cheerful mood was dissipating for some reason—he himself didn't yet understand why. Suddenly, he realized that there would be no praise today.

Quite the contrary. The day of wrath, he thought philosophically, and prepared for the worst.

"Feel free to smoke," offered General Lemchen, lowering himself back into the armchair.

"No thanks, I don't smoke."

General Lemchen nodded his head with a look that suggested his worst suspicions had been confirmed, pressed his fingertips together in front of his face, and spent some time intently examining the resulting shape.

"I suppose the legal affairs of the Mitsubishi Denshi Company will not be under discussion today," he said finally.

This was a joke. Richard Noonan smiled readily and answered, "As you wish!" Sitting on the desk was incredibly uncomfortable; his feet didn't reach the floor, and the edge bit into his ass.

"I regret to inform you, Richard," said General Lemchen, "that your report created an extremely favorable impression higher up."

"Hmm," said Noonan. Here it comes, he thought.

"They were even planning to present you with a medal," continued General Lemchen, "but I suggested they wait. And I was right." He finally tore himself away from contemplating the configuration of his fingers and glowered at Noonan from beneath his brows. "You will ask why I displayed such seemingly excessive caution."

"You probably had your reasons," said Noonan in a dull voice.

"Yes, I did. What do we learn from your report, Richard? The Metropole gang has been liquidated. Through your efforts. The entire Green Flower gang has been caught red-handed. Brilliant work. Also yours. The Varr, Quasimodo, and Traveling Musicians gangs and the rest, I don't remember their names, have closed up shop, realizing that sooner or later they'd get nabbed. All this really did happen, everything has been verified by other sources. The battlefield is empty. Your victory, Richard. The enemy has retreated in disarray, having sustained heavy losses. Have I given a correct account of the situation?"

"At any rate," Noonan said carefully, "in the last three months, the flow of materials from the Zone through Harmont has stopped . . . At least according to my sources," he added.

"The enemy has retreated, right?"

"Well, if you insist on that particular expression, yes."

"No!" said General Lemchen. "The thing is, this enemy never retreats. I know this for a fact. By hastily submitting a victorious report, Richard, you have demonstrated immaturity. That is precisely why I suggested we abstain from immediately presenting you with an award."

To hell with you and your awards, thought Noonan, swinging his leg and sullenly staring at his shiny toe. *Your medal isn't worth the metal it's made of. And please skip the preaching and condescension—I know perfectly well without you who I'm dealing with, and I don't need a damn sermon about the enemy. Just tell me straight out: when, where, and how I've messed up . . . what else these bastards managed to pull . . . when and where they've found a crack. And stop beating around the bush, I'm not some green kid, I'm over half a century old, and I'm not sitting here because of your damn medals.*

"What have you heard about the Golden Sphere?" asked General Lemchen abruptly.

My Lord, thought Noonan in annoyance, what does the Golden Sphere have to do with it? *To hell with you and your manner of talking.* "The Golden Sphere is a legend," he reported in a flat tone. "A mythical object in the Zone, which appears in the form of a certain golden sphere and which is rumored to grant human wishes."

"Any wishes?"

"According to the canonical text of the legend—any wishes. However, there exist variants."

"All right," said General Lemchen. "And what have you heard about the death lamp?"

"Eight years ago," Noonan droned dully, "a stalker by the name of Stephen Norman, nicknamed Four-Eyes, brought out of the Zone a device that, as far as anyone could tell, consisted of a ray-emitting system fatal to Earth organisms. The aforementioned Four-Eyes was attempting to sell this instrument to the Institute. They couldn't agree on the price. Four-Eyes left for the Zone and never came back. The current whereabouts of the instrument are unknown—the guys at the Institute are still tearing out their hair about it. Hugh, from the Metropole, who is well known to you, had offered to buy it for any sum that could fit on a check."

"Is that all?" asked General Lemchen.

"That's all," answered Noonan. He looked around the room with an exaggerated motion. The room was boring; there was nothing to look at.

"OK," said Lemchen. "And what have you heard about lobster eyes?"

"About what eyes?"

"Lobster eyes. Lobster. You know?" General Lemchen made a snipping motion with his fingers. "With claws."

"First time I've heard of them," said Noonan, frowning.

"Well, what do you know about rattling napkins?"

Noonan climbed off the desk and faced Lemchen, his hands stuffed into his pockets. "I don't know anything," he said. "How about you?"

"Unfortunately, I also don't know anything. Neither about lobster eyes nor about rattling napkins. And yet they exist."

"In my Zone?" asked Noonan.

"Sit down, sit down," said General Lemchen, waving his hand. "Our conversation has just started. Sit down."

Noonan walked around the desk and sat down on the hard straight-backed chair. What's he getting at, he thought feverishly. What the hell is going on? They probably found some things in the other Zones, and he's playing tricks on me, the bastard, may he go to hell. He's always disliked me, the old ass, he can't forget the limerick.

"Let us continue our little examination," announced Lemchen, pulling back the curtain and looking out the window. "It's pouring," he reported. "I like it." He let go of the curtain, leaned back in his armchair, and, staring at the ceiling, asked, "How is old Burbridge doing?"

"Burbridge? The Vulture Burbridge is under surveillance. He's crippled, well-to-do. No connections to the Zone. He owns four bars, a dance studio, and organizes picnics for the garrison officers and tourists. His daughter, Dina, is leading a dissipated life. His son, Arthur, just finished law school."

General Lemchen gave a contented nod. "Very concise," he complimented. "And how is Creon the Maltese?"

"One of the few active stalkers. He was connected to the Quasimodo group and is now peddling his swag to the Institute through me. I let him roam free; someday someone might take the bait. Unfortunately, he's been drinking a lot lately, and I'm afraid he won't last long."

"Connections to Burbridge?"

"Courting Dina. No luck."

"Very good," said General Lemchen. "And what's going on with Red Schuhart?"

"He got out of jail a month ago. No financial difficulties. He's trying to emigrate, but he has—" Noonan hesitated. "Anyway, he has family troubles. He has no time for the Zone."

"That's all?"

"That's all."

"It's not much," said General Lemchen. "And how is Lucky Carter?"

"He hasn't been a stalker for years. He sells used cars, and he also owns a shop that rejiggers vehicles to run on spacells. He has four kids; his wife died a year ago. There's a mother-in-law."

Lemchen nodded. "So, which of the old-timers have I forgotten?" he inquired amiably.

"You've forgotten Jonathan Miles, nicknamed the Cactus. He's currently in the hospital, dying of cancer. And you've forgotten Gutalin—"

"Yes, yes, what about Gutalin?"

"Gutalin's the same as always," said Noonan. "He has a gang of three men. They disappear into the Zone for weeks; everything they find, they destroy. But his Warring Angels society has collapsed."

"Why?"

"Well, as you remember, they would buy up swag, then Gutalin would haul it back into the Zone. Returning Satan's works to Satan. Nowadays there's nothing to buy, and besides, the new director of the Institute has set the police on them."

"I understand," said General Lemchen. "And the young ones?"

"Oh, the young ones . . . They come and go; there are five or six with some experience, but lately they've had no one to sell the swag to, and they've become confused. I'm taming them bit by bit. I would say, chief, that my Zone is practically free of stalkers. The old-timers are gone, the young ones are clueless, and on top of that, the prestige of the craft isn't what it once was. The coming thing is technology, robot-stalkers."

"Yes, yes, I've heard of this," said General Lemchen. "However, these robots aren't even worth the energy they consume. Or am I mistaken?"

"That's just a matter of time. They'll soon be worth it."

"How soon?"

"In five or six years."

General Lemchen nodded again. "By the way, you might not have heard this yet, but the enemy has also started using robot-stalkers."

"In my Zone?" asked Noonan again, pricking up his ears.

"In yours as well. In your case, they set up base in Rexopolis and use a helicopter to convey the equipment over the mountains to Serpent's Gorge, to the Black Lake, and to the foothills of Boulder's Peak."

"But that's all on the periphery," said Noonan suspiciously. "It's empty, what could they possibly find?"

"Little, very little. But they do find it. However, that's just for reference, it's not your concern . . . Let us recap. There are almost no professional stalkers left in Harmont. Those who are left have no connection to the Zone. The young ones are confused and are currently in the process of being tamed. The enemy has been defeated, repulsed, and is holed up somewhere licking his wounds. Swag is scarce, and when it does appear, there's nobody to sell it to. The illegal flow of materials from the Harmont Zone has now been over for three months. Correct?"

Noonan stayed silent. Now's the time, he thought. Now he'll let me have it. But what could I have missed? And it must be quite the oversight. Well, go on, go on, bastard! Don't drag it out . . .

"I don't hear an answer," said General Lemchen, cupping a hand to his hairy, wrinkled ear.

"All right, chief," said Noonan gloomily. "That's enough. You've already boiled me and fried me, now you can serve me up."

General Lemchen vaguely harrumphed. "You have absolutely nothing to say for yourself," he said with unexpected bitterness. "Here you stand, looking dumb before authority, but imagine how I felt, when two days ago—" He cut himself off, stood up, and plodded toward his safe. "In short, during the last two months, according to our sources alone, the enemy forces have received more than six thousand units of material from various Zones." He stopped near the safe, stroked its painted side, and whirled toward Noonan. "Don't kid yourself!" he roared. "The fingerprints of Burbridge! The fingerprints of the Maltese! The fingerprints of Ben-Halevy the Nose, whom you didn't even bother to mention! The fingerprints of Nasal Haresh and Midget Zmig! This is how you tame your youths! Bracelets! Needles! White whirligigs! And if that wasn't enough—we've got lobster eyes, bitches' rattles, and rattling napkins, whatever the hell they are! Damn them all!"

He cut himself off again, returned to the armchair, joined his fingertips, and inquired politely, "What do you think about this, Richard?"

Noonan took out a handkerchief and wiped his neck and the back of his head. "I don't think anything," he croaked honestly. "I'm sorry, chief, right now I'm just . . . Let me catch my breath . . . Burbridge! I'd bet a whole month's salary that Burbridge has no connection to the Zone! I know his every move! He organizes picnics and drinking parties at the lakes, he's raking it in, and he simply doesn't need . . . I'm sorry, I'm babbling nonsense of course, but I swear I haven't lost sight of Burbridge since he got out of the hospital."

"I won't detain you any longer," said General Lemchen. "You have a week. Provide an explanation for how material from your Zone falls into the hands of Burbridge and the rest of that scum. Good-bye!"

Noonan stood up, awkwardly nodded to General Lemchen's profile, and, continuing to wipe his profusely sweating neck, fled to the reception area. The tan young man was smoking, staring thoughtfully into the entrails of the disassembled machine. He cast a cursory glance in Noonan's direction—his eyes were blank, focused inward.

Richard Noonan clumsily pulled on his hat, grabbed his raincoat, tucked it under his arm, and beat a hasty retreat. Nothing like this has ever happened to me before, he fumed, his thoughts confused and disjointed. Give me a break—Ben-Halevy the Nose! He's already earned a nickname . . . When? That twerp—a strong wind could snap him in half . . . That snot-nosed kid . . . No, something's not right. Damn you, Vulture, you legless bastard! You've really fucked me this time! Caught me with my pants down, fed me a load of bullshit. How in the world did this happen? This simply couldn't have happened! Just like that time in Singapore—face slammed against the table, head slammed against the wall . . .

He got into his car and, unable to think straight, spent a while groping under the dashboard in search of the ignition. His hat was dripping onto his knees, so he took it off and blindly hurled it into the back. Rain was flooding the windshield, and for some reason Richard Noonan kept imagining that this was why he had no idea what to do next. Realizing this, he banged his bald forehead with his fist. That helped. He immediately remembered that there was no ignition and there couldn't possibly be and that in his pocket was a spacell. A perpetual battery. And he had to take the damn thing out of his pocket and stick it into the jack, and then he could at least drive away—drive as far as possible from this place, where that old ass was certainly watching him from the window . . .

Noonan's hand, which was holding the spacell, froze halfway. All right. At least I know where to start. I'll start with him. Boy, how I'll start with him! He won't even know what hit him. And the fun I'll have! He turned on the windshield wipers and sped along the boulevard, seeing almost nothing in front of him but already calming down. Fine. Let it be like Singapore. After all, Singapore turned out OK. Big deal—your face got slammed against the table. It might have been worse. It might not have been your face, and it might not have been a table, but something nail studded . . . My God, this could all be so simple! We could round up these scum and put them away for a decade . . . or send them the hell away! Now, in Russia they've never even heard of stalkers. Over there, they really have an empty belt around the Zone—a hundred miles wide, no one around, none of these stinking tourists, and no Burbridges. *Think simple, gentlemen! I swear this doesn't need to be so complicated. No business in the Zone—good-bye, off you go to the hundred and first mile.* All right, let's not get sidetracked. Where's my little establishment? Can't see a damn thing . . . Oh, there it is.

It wasn't a busy hour, but Five Minutes was blazing with lights fit for the Metropole. Shaking off like a dog after a swim, Richard Noonan stepped into a brightly lit hall that reeked of tobacco, perfume, and stale champagne. Old Benny, not yet in his uniform, was sitting at a table across from the entrance and gobbling something, his fork in his fist. In front of him, resting her enormous breasts between the empty glasses, towered the Madam, dolefully watching him eat. The hall still hadn't been cleaned from last night. When Noonan came in, the Madam immediately turned her broad painted face toward him, at first looking displeased but quickly dissolving into a professional smile. "Ha!" she boomed. "Mr. Noonan himself! Missed the girls?"

Benny continued to gobble; he was as deaf as a post.

"Hello, old lady!" replied Noonan, approaching. "What do I need with girls, when I have a real woman in front of me?"

Benny finally noticed him. His hideous mug, crisscrossed with red and blue scars, contorted with effort into a welcoming smile. "Hello, boss!" he wheezed. "Come in to dry off?"

Noonan smiled in response and waved his hand. He didn't like talking to Benny; he always had to holler. "Where's my manager, guys?" he asked.

"In his office," replied the Madam. "Tomorrow is tax day."

"Oh, those taxes!" said Noonan. "All right. Madam, fix me my favorite drink, I'll be right back."

Silently stepping on the thick synthetic carpet, he walked along the hallway past the curtain-covered stalls—the walls by the stalls were decorated with pictures of various flowers—turned into an unremarkable cul-de-sac, and, without knocking, opened the leather-covered door.

Hamfist Kitty was sitting behind the desk and examining an evil-looking sore on his nose in a mirror. He couldn't care less that tomorrow was tax day. The surface in front of him held only a jar of mercury ointment and a glass of some see-through liquid. Hamfist Kitty raised his bloodshot eyes at Noonan and leaped up, dropping the mirror. Without saying a word, Noonan lowered himself into the armchair across from him and spent a while silently scrutinizing the rascal and listening as he mumbled something incoherent about the damn rain and his rheumatism. Then Noonan said, "Please lock the door, pal."

Hamfist, stomping his huge flat feet, ran to the door, turned the key, and came back to the desk. He towered like a hairy mountain over Noonan, staring devotedly at his mouth. Noonan kept examining him through screwed-up eyes. For some reason he suddenly remembered that Hamfist Kitty's real name was Raphael. The nickname Hamfist came from his monstrous bony fists, bluish red and bare, that protruded from the thick fur covering his arms as if from a pair of sleeves. And he named himself Kitty in complete confidence that this was the traditional name of the great Mongolian kings. Raphael. *Well, Raphael, let us begin.*

"How are things?" Noonan asked affectionately.

"In perfect order, boss," Raphael-Hamfist answered hastily.

"Did you patch up the scandal at headquarters?"

"Put down a hundred fifty bucks. Everyone is happy."

"That's a hundred fifty from your pocket," said Noonan. "That was your fault, pal. Should have kept an eye on it."

Hamfist made a miserable face and spread his huge hands in submission.

"The hardwood floor in the lobby should be replaced," said Noonan.

"Will do."

Noonan paused, pursing his lips. "Any swag?" he asked, lowering his voice.

"There's some," said Hamfist, also lowering his voice.

"Show me."

Hamfist darted to the safe, took out a package, placed it on the desk in front of Noonan, and unwrapped it. Noonan poked a finger into the pile of black sparks, picked up a bracelet, examined it from every side, and put it back.

"Is that it?" he asked.

"They don't bring any," Hamfist said guiltily.

"'They don't bring any,'" repeated Noonan.

He took careful aim and kicked Hamfist's shin as hard as he could with the toe of his shoe. Hamfist moaned and started to bend over to grab the injured leg but immediately drew himself up and stood at attention. Then Noonan leaped up, as if someone had jabbed him in the ass, kicked aside the armchair, grabbed Hamfist by the collar of his shirt, and went at him, kicking, rolling his eyes, and whispering obscenities. Hamfist, gasping and moaning and rearing his head like a frightened horse, backed away from him until he collapsed onto the couch.

"Working both sides, bastard?" hissed Noonan right into his eyes, which were white with terror. "Burbridge is swimming in swag, and you bring me little beads wrapped in paper?" He turned around and smacked Hamfist in the face, taking care to hit the sore on his nose. "I'll have you rot in jail! You'll be living in shit . . . Eating shit . . . You'll curse the day you were born!" He took another hard jab at the sore. "How is Burbridge getting swag? Why do they bring it to him but not to you? Who brings it? Why don't I know anything? Who are you working for, you hairy pig? Tell me!"

Hamfist opened and closed his mouth like a fish. Noonan let him go, returned to the armchair, and put his feet up on the desk.

"Well?" he said.

Hamfist noisily sucked the blood in through his nose and said, "Really, boss . . . What's going on? What swag does the Vulture have? He doesn't have any swag. Nowadays no one has swag."

"You're going to argue with me?" Noonan asked with seeming affection, taking his feet off the desk.

"No, no, boss . . . I swear," said Hamfist hastily. "Honest to God! Argue with you? I never even considered it."

"I'll get rid of you," said Noonan gloomily. "Because either you've sold out, or you don't know how to work. What the hell do I need you for, you lazy bum? I could get dozens like you. I need a real man for the job, and all you do is ruin the girls and guzzle beer."

"Wait a minute, boss," argued Hamfist, smearing blood around his face. "Why attack me all of a sudden? Let's try to get this straight." He gingerly felt the sore with his fingertips. "Burbridge has lots of swag, you say? I don't know about that. I apologize, of course, but someone's been pulling your leg. No one has any swag nowadays. It's only the raw kids that go into the Zone, and they almost never come back . . . No, boss, I swear someone's pulling your leg."

Noonan was watching him out of the corner of his eye. It seemed that Hamfist really didn't know a thing. Anyway, it wasn't worth his while to lie—the Vulture didn't pay well. "Those picnics of his—are they profitable?" he asked.

"The picnics? Not very. He isn't shoveling it in . . . But then there's no profitable work left in town."

"Where are these picnics held?"

"Where are they held? At various places. At the White Mountain, at the Hot Springs, by the Rainbow Lakes . . ."

"And who are his clients?"

"His clients?" Hamfist felt his sore again, glanced at his fingers, and spoke confidentially, "Boss, if you're thinking of getting into that business, I'd advise against it. You can't compete with the Vulture."

"Why not?"

"It's his clients; he has the police—that's one." Hamfist was counting on his fingers. "The officers from headquarters—that's two. Tourists from the Metropole, White Lily, and the Alien—that's three. And his advertising is good, the locals use him, too. I swear, boss, it wouldn't be worth it to get involved. And he pays us for the girls—if not that generously."

"The locals use him, too?"

"Young men, mostly."

"And what do you do there, at the picnics?"

"What do we do? We go there by bus, see? They already have tents, food, and music set up. Then everyone amuses themselves. The officers mostly enjoy the girls, the tourists troop off to see the Zone—when it's at the Hot Springs, the Zone is a stone's throw away, right over the Sulfur Gorge. The Vulture has scattered horse bones over there for them, so they look at them through binoculars."

"And the locals?"

"The locals? The locals, of course, aren't interested in that. They amuse themselves."

"And Burbridge?"

"What about Burbridge? Burbridge is like everyone else."

"And you?"

"What about me? I'm like everyone else. I make sure no one's bothering the girls, and . . . uh . . . well . . . Anyway, I'm like everyone else . . ."

"And how long do these things last?"

"It varies. Sometimes three days, sometimes a whole week."

"And how much does this pleasure trip cost?" asked Noonan, now thinking about something else entirely.

Hamfist said something, but Noonan didn't hear him. There it is, my oversight, he thought. A couple of days . . . A couple of nights. Under these circumstances, it would be simply impossible to keep track of Burbridge, even if you were completely focused on doing so and weren't busy cavorting with the girls and guzzling beer like my Mongolian king. But I'm still missing something. He's legless, and there's a gorge . . . No, something's off.

"Which locals come frequently?"

"Locals? As I said—mostly young men. The hoodlums of the town. Like, say, Halevy, Rajba, Zapfa the Chicken, and what's his name . . . Zmig. Sometimes the Maltese. A tight-knit crowd. They call it Sunday school. 'Let's go to Sunday school,' they say. They're mostly in it for the women tourists—that's easy money for them. Say an old lady from Europe shows up—"

"'Sunday school' . . ." Noonan repeated.

A strange thought suddenly occurred to him. School. He got up.

"All right," he said. "To hell with these picnics. That's not for us. What you do need to know is that the Vulture has swag—

that's our business, pal. That we simply can't allow. Keep looking, Hamfist, keep looking, or you'll be out on your ass. Figure out where he gets the swag and who supplies it to him—then beat him by twenty percent. Got it?"

"Got it, boss," Hamfist was already standing at attention, devotion on his blood-smeared mug.

"And stop ruining the girls, you animal!" Noonan roared, and left.

Standing by the bar in the hall, he leisurely sipped his aperitif, chatted with the Madam about the decline in morality, and hinted that in the very near future he was planning to expand the establishment. Lowering his voice for effect, he consulted her on what to do about Benny: the guy is getting old, his hearing is almost gone, his reaction time is shot, he can't manage like before . . . It was already six o'clock, he was getting hungry, but that same unexpected thought kept boring and twisting through his brain—a strange, incongruous thought that nonetheless explained a lot. But in any case, much had already been explained, the business had been stripped of its irritating and frightening aura of mysticism, and all that remained was chagrin that he didn't think of this before; but that wasn't the important thing, the important thing was the thought that kept spinning and twisting through his brain and wouldn't let him rest.

After he said good-bye to the Madam and shook Benny's hand, Noonan drove straight to the Borscht. The problem is we don't notice the years pass, he thought. Screw the years—we don't notice things change. We know that things change, we've been told since childhood that things change, we've witnessed things change ourselves many a time, and yet we're still utterly incapable of noticing the moment that change comes—or we search for change in all the wrong places. A new breed of stalker has appeared—armed with technology. The old stalker was a sullen, dirty man, stubborn as a mule, crawling through the Zone inch by inch on his stomach, earning his keep. The new stalker is a tie-wearing dandy, an engineer, somewhere a mile away from the Zone, a cigarette in his teeth, a cocktail by his elbow—sitting and watching the monitors. A salaried gentleman. A very logical picture. So logical that other possibilities don't even occur. And yet there are other possibilities—Sunday school, for one.

Suddenly, for no apparent reason, he felt a wave of despair. Everything was useless. Everything was pointless. My God, he thought, we can't do a thing! We can't stop it, we can't slow it down! No force in the world could contain this blight, he thought in horror. It's not because we do bad work. And it's not because they are more clever and cunning than we are. The world is just like that. Man is like that. If it wasn't the Visit, it would have been something else. Pigs can always find mud.

The Borscht was brightly lit and full of delicious smells. The Borscht had also changed—no more boozing and no more merrymaking. Gutalin didn't come here anymore, turned up his nose, and Redrick Schuhart had probably stuck his freckled mug inside, scowled, and went off. Ernest was still in jail; his old lady was enjoying being in charge: there was a steady respectable clientele, the whole Institute came here for lunch, as did the senior officers. The booths were cozy, the food was tasty, the prices were moderate, the beer was always fresh. A good old-fashioned pub.

Noonan saw Valentine Pillman sitting in one of the booths. The Nobel laureate was drinking coffee and reading a magazine folded in half. Noonan approached. "May I join you?" he asked.

Valentine raised his dark glasses at him. "Ah," he said. "Feel free."

"One second, let me wash my hands," said Noonan, remembering the sore.

He was well known here. When he came back and sat down across from Valentine, there was already a small grill with sizzling barbecue and a tall stein of beer on the table—neither warm nor cold, just the way he liked it. Valentine put the magazine down and took a sip of coffee.

"Listen, Valentine," said Noonan, cutting a piece of meat and dipping it in the sauce. "How do you think it's all going to end?"

"What are you talking about?"

"The Visit. Zones, stalkers, military-industrial complexes—the whole stinking mess. How could it all end?"

For a long time, Valentine stared at him through his opaque black lenses. Then he lit up a cigarette and said, "For whom? Be more specific."

"Well, say, for humanity as a whole."

"That depends on our luck," said Valentine. "We now know that for humanity as a whole, the Visit has largely passed without a trace. For humanity everything passes without a trace. Of course, it's possible that by randomly pulling chestnuts out of this fire, we'll eventually stumble on something that will make life on Earth completely unbearable. That would be bad luck. But you have to admit, that's a danger humanity has always faced." He waved away the cigarette smoke and smiled wryly. "You see, I've long since become unused to discussing humanity as a whole. Humanity as a whole is too stable a system, nothing upsets it."

"You think so?" said Noonan with disappointment. "Well, that may be . . ."

"Tell me the truth, Richard," said Valentine, obviously amusing himself. "What changed for you, a businessman, after the Visit? So you've learned that the universe contains at least one intelligent species other than man. So what?"

"How can I put it?" mumbled Richard. He was already sorry that he started the subject. There was nothing to say here. "What changed for me? For example, for many years now I've been feeling a bit uneasy, apprehensive. All right, so they came and left immediately. And what if they come back and decide to stay? For me, a businessman, these aren't idle questions, you know: who they are, how they live, what they need. In the most primitive case, I'm forced to consider how to modify my product. I have to be ready. And what if I turn out to be completely superfluous in their society?" He became more animated. "What if we're all superfluous? Listen, Valentine, since we're on the subject, are there answers to these questions? Who they are, what they wanted, if they'll come back . . ."

"There are answers," said Valentine with an ironic smile. "Lots of them, pick any you like."

"And what do you think?"

"To be honest, I've never let myself seriously consider it. For me, the Visit is first and foremost a unique event that could potentially allow us to skip a few rungs in the ladder of progress. Like a trip into the future of technology. Say, like Isaac Newton finding a modern microwave emitter in his laboratory."

"Newton wouldn't have understood a thing."

"You'd be surprised! Newton was a very smart man."

"Oh yeah? Anyway, never mind Newton. What do you actually think about the Visit? Even if not seriously."

"Fine, I'll tell you. But I have to warn you, Richard, that your question falls under the umbrella of a pseudoscience called xenology. Xenology is an unnatural mixture of science fiction and formal logic. At its core is a flawed assumption—that an alien race would be psychologically human."

"Why flawed?" asked Noonan.

"Because biologists have already been burned attempting to apply human psychology to animals. Earth animals, I note."

"Just a second," said Noonan. "That's totally different. We're talking about the psychology of *intelligent* beings."

"True. And that would be just fine, if we knew what intelligence was."

"And we don't?" asked Noonan in surprise.

"Believe it or not, we don't. We usually proceed from a trivial definition: intelligence is the attribute of man that separates his activity from that of the animals. It's a kind of attempt to distinguish the master from his dog, who seems to understand everything but can't speak. However, this trivial definition does lead to wittier ones. They are based on depressing observations of the aforementioned human activity. For example: intelligence is the ability of a living creature to perform pointless or unnatural acts."

"Yes, that's us," agreed Noonan.

"Unfortunately. Or here's a definition-hypothesis. Intelligence is a complex instinct which hasn't yet fully matured. The idea is that instinctive activity is always natural and useful. A million years will pass, the instinct will mature, and we will cease making the mistakes which are probably an integral part of intelligence. And then, if anything in the universe changes, we will happily become extinct—again, precisely because we've lost the art of making mistakes, that is, trying various things not prescribed by a rigid code."

"Somehow this all sounds so . . . demeaning."

"All right, then here's another definition—a very lofty and noble one. Intelligence is the ability to harness the powers of the surrounding world without destroying the said world."

Noonan grimaced and shook his head. "No," he said. "That's a bit much . . . That's not us. Well, how about the idea that humans, unlike animals, have an overpowering need for knowledge? I've read that somewhere."

"So have I," said Valentine. "But the issue is that man, at least the average man, can easily overcome this need. In my opinion, the need doesn't exist at all. There's a need to understand, but that doesn't require knowledge. The God hypothesis, for example, allows you to have an unparalleled understanding of absolutely everything while knowing absolutely nothing . . . Give a man a highly simplified model of the world and interpret every event on the basis of this simple model. This approach requires no knowledge. A few rote formulas, plus some so-called intuition, some so-called practical acumen, and some so-called common sense."

"Wait," said Noonan. He finished his beer and banged the empty stein down on the table. "Don't get off track. Let's put it this way. A man meets an alien. How does each figure out that the other is intelligent?"

"No idea," Valentine said merrily. "All I've read on the subject reduces to a vicious circle. If they are capable of contact, then they are intelligent. And conversely, if they are intelligent, then they are capable of contact. And in general: if an alien creature has the honor of being psychologically human, then it's intelligent. That's how it is, Richard. Read Vonnegut?"

"Damn it," said Noonan. "And here I thought you'd sorted everything out."

"Even a monkey can sort things," observed Valentine.

"No, wait," said Noonan. For some reason, he felt cheated. "But if you don't even know such simple things . . . All right, never mind intelligence. Looks like there's no making heads or tails of it. But about the Visit? What do you think about the Visit?"

"Certainly," said Valentine. "Imagine a picnic—"

Noonan jumped. "What did you say?"

"A picnic. Imagine: a forest, a country road, a meadow. A car pulls off the road into the meadow and unloads young men, bottles, picnic baskets, girls, transistor radios, cameras . . . A fire is lit, tents are pitched, music is played. And in the morning they leave. The animals, birds, and insects that were watching the whole night in horror crawl out of their shelters. And what do they see? An oil spill, a gasoline puddle, old spark plugs and oil filters strewn about . . . Scattered rags, burnt-out bulbs, someone has dropped a monkey wrench. The wheels have tracked mud from some godforsaken swamp . . . and, of course, there are the remains of the campfire, apple cores, candy wrappers, tins, bottles, someone's handkerchief, someone's penknife, old ragged newspapers, coins, wilted flowers from another meadow . . ."

"I get it," said Noonan. "A roadside picnic."

"Exactly. A picnic by the side of some space road. And you ask me whether they'll come back . . ."

"Let me have a smoke," said Noonan. "Damn your pseudoscience! Somehow this isn't at all how I envisioned it."

"That's your right," observed Valentine.

"What, you mean they never even noticed us?"

"Why?"

"Or at least they paid no attention."

"I wouldn't get too disappointed if I were you," advised Valentine.

Noonan took a drag, coughed, and threw the cigarette down. "All the same," he said stubbornly. "It couldn't be . . . Damn you scientists! Where do you get this disdain for man? Why do you constantly need to put him down?"

"Wait," said Valentine. "Listen. 'You ask: what makes man great?'" he quoted. "'Is it that he re-created nature? That he harnessed forces of almost-cosmic proportions? That in a brief time he has conquered the planet and opened a window onto the universe? No! It is that despite all this, he has survived, and intends to continue doing so.'"

There was silence. Noonan was thinking. "Maybe," he said uncertainly. "Of course, from that point of view . . ."

"Don't get so upset," Valentine said kindly. "The picnic is only my hypothesis. And not even a hypothesis, really, but an impression. So-called serious xenologists try to justify interpretations that are much more respectable and flattering to human vanity. For example, that the Visit hasn't happened yet, that the real Visit is yet to come. Some higher intelligence came to Earth and left us containers with samples of their material culture. They expect us to study these samples and make a technological leap, enabling us to send back a signal indicating we're truly ready for contact. How's that?"

"That's much better," said Noonan. "I see that even among the scientists there are decent men."

"Or here's another one. The Visit did take place, but it is by no means over. We're actually in contact as we speak, we just don't know it. The aliens are holed up in the Zones and are carefully studying us, simultaneously preparing us for the 'time of cruel miracles.'"

"Now *that* I understand!" said Noonan. "At least it explains the mysterious bustle in the ruins of the factory. By the way, your picnic doesn't account for that."

"Why not?" disagreed Valentine. "Some little girl might have dropped her favorite windup doll."

"Now cut that out," said Noonan emphatically. "Some doll—the ground is shaking. Then again, of course, it could be a doll . . . Want some beer? Rosalie! Come here, old lady! Two beers for the xenologists! It really is a pleasure to talk to you," he told Valentine. "A real brain cleansing—like someone poured Epsom salts under my skull. Otherwise, you work and work, but you never think about why or what for, grapple with what might happen, try to lighten your load . . ."

They brought the beer. Noonan took a sip and, looking over the foam, saw Valentine with an expression of fastidious skepticism, examining his stein.

"What, you don't like it?" he asked, licking his lips.

"To be honest, I don't drink," said Valentine with hesitation.

"Oh yeah?" said Noonan in astonishment.

"Damn it!" said Valentine. "There has to be one nondrinker in the world." He decisively pushed the stein away. "Order me a cognac, then," he said.

"Rosalie!" Noonan shouted immediately, now completely mellow.

When they brought the cognac, Noonan said, "Still, it's not right. I won't even mention your picnic—that's a complete disgrace—but even accepting the hypothesis that this is, say, a prelude to contact, it's still no good. Bracelets, empties—those I could understand. But why the slime? Or the bug traps or that disgusting fuzz?"

"Excuse me," said Valentine, choosing a slice of lemon. "I don't exactly understand your terminology. What traps?"

Noonan laughed. "That's folklore," he explained. "Stalkers' jargon. Bug traps—those are the areas of increased gravity."

"Oh, the graviconcentrates . . . Directed gravity. Now that's something I would enjoy discussing, but you wouldn't understand a thing."

"Why not? I'm an engineer, after all."

"Because I don't understand a thing myself. I have a system of equations, but I haven't a notion about how to interpret it. And the slime—that's probably the colloidal gas?"

"The very same. You heard about the catastrophe in the Carrigan Labs?"

"I've heard something," Valentine replied reluctantly.

"Those idiots placed a porcelain container with the slime into a special, maximally insulated chamber. That is, they thought that it was maximally insulated, but when they opened the container with the mechanical arm, the slime went through the metal and plastic like water through a sieve, escaped, and turned everything it touched into the same slime. The tally: thirty-five dead, more than a hundred injured, and the entire laboratory is completely unusable. Have you ever been there? It's a gorgeous building! And now slime has seeped into the basement and lower floors . . . That's a prelude to contact for you."

Valentine made a face. "Yes, I know all that," he said. "But you have to admit, Richard, that the aliens had nothing to do with this. How could they have known about the existence of military-industrial complexes?"

"Well, they should have known!" said Noonan didactically.

"And here's what they'd say in reply: *You should have long since gotten rid of military-industrial complexes.*"

"That's fair," agreed Noonan. "Maybe that's what they should have worked on, if they are so powerful."

"So you're suggesting interference with the internal affairs of mankind?"

"Hmm," said Noonan. "That, of course, could lead us all sorts of places. Forget about it. Let's return to the beginning of the conversation. How is it all going to end? Say, take you scientists. Are you hoping to acquire something fundamental from the Zone, something that could really revolutionize our science, technology, way of life?"

Valentine finished his drink and shrugged his shoulders. "You're talking to the wrong man, Richard. I don't like empty fantasies. When it comes to such a serious subject, I prefer cautious skepticism. Judging from what we've already acquired, there is a whole spectrum of possibilities, and nothing definite can be said."

"Rosalie, more cognac!" yelled Noonan. "Well, all right,

let's try another tack. What, in your opinion, have we already acquired?"

"Amusingly enough, relatively little. We've found many marvels. In a number of cases, we've even learned how to adapt these marvels to our needs. We've even gotten used to them. A lab monkey presses a red button and gets a banana, presses a white button and gets an orange, but has no idea how to obtain bananas or oranges without buttons. Nor does it understand the relationship between buttons and oranges and bananas. Take, say, the spacells. We've learned to apply them. We've even discovered conditions under which they multiply by division. But we have yet to create a single spacell, have no idea how they work, and, as far as I can tell, won't figure it out anytime soon. Here's what I'd say. There are a number of objects for which we have found applications. We use them, although almost certainly not in the ways that the aliens intended. I'm absolutely convinced that in the vast majority of cases we're using sledgehammers to crack nuts. Nevertheless, some things we do apply: spacells, bracelets that stimulate vital processes . . . all sorts of quasibiological masses, which caused such a revolution in medicine . . . We've gained new tranquilizers, new mineral fertilizers, we've revolutionized astronomy. In any case, why am I listing them? You know it all better than I do—I see you wear a bracelet yourself. Let us call this group of objects useful. You could say that, to a certain extent, these objects have benefited humanity, although we can never forget that in our Euclidean world every stick has two ends . . ."

"Undesirable applications?" inserted Noonan.

"Exactly. For example, applications of spacells in the defense industry . . . Let's not get off track. The behavior of each useful object has been more or less studied and more or less explained. Right now we're held back by technology, but in fifty years or so we will learn how to manufacture these sledgehammers ourselves, and then we'll crack nuts with them to our hearts' content. The story's more complicated with another group of objects—more complicated precisely because we can't find any application for them, and yet their properties, given our current theories, are completely inexplicable. For example, take the magnetic traps of various types. We know they are magnetic traps, Panov gave a very witty proof of that. But we don't know where the generator of such a strong magnetic field could be nor understand the reason for its amazing stability; we don't understand a thing. We can only make up fantastic conjectures about properties of space which we've never even suspected before. Or the K-twenty-three . . . What do you call those pretty black beads that are used for jewelry?"

"Black sparks," said Noonan.

"Right, right, black sparks. Good name. Well, you know their properties. If you shine a light at such a bead, the light will be emitted after a pause, and the length of the pause depends on the weight of the ball, its size, and a number of other parameters, while the frequency of the emitted light is always less than its original frequency. What does this mean? Why? There's an insane idea that these black sparks are actually vast expanses of space—space with different properties from our own, which curled up into this form under the influence of our space . . ." Valentine took out a cigarette and lit it. "In short, the objects in this group are currently completely useless for human purposes, yet from a purely scientific point of view they have fundamental significance. These are miraculously received answers to questions we don't yet know how to pose. The aforementioned Sir Isaac mightn't have made sense of the microwave emitter, but he would have at any rate realized that such a thing was possible, and that would have had a very strong effect on his scientific worldview. I won't get into details, but the existence of such objects as the magnetic traps, the K-twenty-three, and the white ring instantly disproved a number of recently thriving theories and gave rise to some entirely new ideas. And then there's also a third group . . ."

"Yes," said Noonan. "Hell slime and other shit."

"No, no. All those belong either to the first or the second group. I meant objects about which we either know nothing or have only hearsay information, objects which we've never held in our hands. Ones that were carried off by stalkers from under our noses—sold to God knows who, hidden. The ones they don't talk about. The legends and semilegends: the wish machine, Dick the Tramp, happy ghosts . . ."

"Wait, wait," said Noonan. "What's all this? I understand the wish machine."

Valentine laughed. "You see, we also have our work jargon. Dick the Tramp—that's the same hypothetical windup doll which is causing havoc in the ruins of the factory. And happy ghosts are a kind of dangerous turbulence that can happen in certain regions of the Zone."

"First time I've heard of them," said Noonan.

"You see, Richard," said Valentine, "we've been digging through the Zone for two decades, but we don't even know a thousandth part of what it contains. And if you count the Zone's effect on man . . . By the way, we're going to have to add another, fourth group to our classification. Not of objects, but of effects. This group has been outrageously badly studied, even though, in my opinion, we've gathered more than enough data. And you know, Richard, I'm a physicist and therefore a skeptic. But sometimes even I get goose bumps when I think about this data."

"Living corpses . . ." muttered Noonan.

"What? Oh . . . No, that's mysterious, but nothing more. How can I put it? It's conceivable, maybe. But when, for no reason at all, a person becomes surrounded by extraphysical, extrabiological phenomena—"

"Oh, you mean the emigrants?"

"Exactly. You know, statistics is a very precise science, despite the fact that it deals with random variables. And furthermore, it's a very eloquent science, very visual . . ."

Valentine had apparently become tipsy. He was speaking louder, his cheeks had turned rosy, and the eyebrows above the dark glasses had risen high in his forehead, wrinkling his brow. "Rosalie!" he barked. "More cognac! A large shot!"

"I like nondrinkers," said Noonan with respect.

"Don't get distracted!" said Valentine strictly. "Listen to what I'm telling you. It's very strange." He picked up his glass, drank off half in one gulp, and continued, "We don't know what happened to the poor people of Harmont at the very moment of the Visit. But now one of them has decided to emigrate. Some ordinary resident. A barber. The son of a barber and the grandson of a barber. He moves to, say, Detroit. Opens a barbershop, and all hell breaks loose. More than ninety percent of his clients die in the course of a year; they die in car accidents, fall out of windows, are cut down by gangsters and hooligans, drown in shallow places, and so on and so forth. Furthermore. The number of municipal disasters in Detroit increases sharply. The number of gas pump explosions jumps by a factor of two. The number of fires caused by faulty wiring jumps by a factor of three and a half. The number of car accidents jumps by a factor of three. The number of deaths from flu epidemics jumps by a factor of two. Furthermore. The number of natural disasters in Detroit and its environs also increases. Tornadoes and typhoons, the likes of which haven't been seen in the area since the 1700s, make an appearance. The heavens open, and Lake Ontario or Michigan, or wherever Detroit is, bursts its banks. Well, and more to that effect. And the same cataclysms happen in any town, any region, where an emigrant from the neighborhood of a Zone settles down, and the number of cataclysms is directly proportional to the number of emigrants that settle in that particular place. And note that this effect is only observed with emigrants who lived through the Visit. Those who were born after the Visit have no impact on the accident statistics. You've lived in Harmont for ten years, but you moved here after the Visit, and you could safely move to the Vatican itself. How do we explain this? What do we have to give up—statistics? Or common sense?" Valentine grabbed the shot glass and drained it in one gulp.

Richard Noonan scratched behind his ear. "Hmm," he said. "I've actually heard a lot about these things, but frankly, I've always assumed this was all, to put it mildly, a bit exaggerated. Someone just needed a pretext for banning emigration."

Valentine smiled bitterly. "That's quite the pretext! Who would believe this lunacy? No, they'd make up an epidemic, a danger of spreading subversive rumors, anything but this!" He put his elbows on the table and looked unhappy, burying his face in his hands.

"I do sympathize," said Noonan. "You're right, from the point of view of our mighty positivist science—"

"Or, say, the mutations caused by the Zone," interrupted Valentine. He took off his glasses and stared at Noonan with nearsighted dark eyes. "All people in contact with the Zone for a sufficiently long time undergo changes—both in phenotype and in genotype. You know what stalkers' children are like, you know what happens with stalkers themselves. Why? What causes the mutations? There's no radiation in the Zone. The chemical structure of the air and soil in the Zone, though peculiar, poses no mutation risk. What am I supposed to do under these circumstances—start to believe in witchcraft? In the evil eye? Listen, Richard, let's order another round. I've really gotten a taste for it, damn it . . ."

Richard Noonan, smirking, ordered another shot of cognac for the laureate and another beer for himself. Then he said, "All right. I am, of course, sympathetic to your turmoil. But to be honest, I personally find the reanimated corpses much more disturbing than your statistical data. Especially since I've never seen the data, but the corpses I've seen, and smelled them, too."

Valentine gave a careless wave. "Oh, you and your corpses . . ." he said. "Listen, Richard, aren't you ashamed of yourself? After all, you're an educated man. Do you really not see that from the perspective of fundamental principles, these corpses of yours are neither more nor less astonishing than the perpetual batteries? It's just that the spacells violate the first principle of thermodynamics, and the corpses, the second; that's the only difference. In some sense, we're all cavemen—we can't imagine anything more frightening than a ghost or a vampire. But the violation of the principle of causality—that's actually much scarier than a whole herd of ghosts . . . or Rubinstein's monsters . . . or is that Wallenstein?"

"Frankenstein."

"Yes, of course. Mrs. Shelley. The poet's wife. Or daughter." He suddenly laughed. "These corpses of yours do have one curious property—autonomous viability. For example, you can cut off their leg, and the leg will keep walking. Well, not actually walking but, in any case, living. Separately. Without any physiological salt solutions. Anyway, the Institute recently had a delivery of one of these . . . unclaimed ones. So they prepared him. Boyd's lab assistant told me about it. They cut off his right hand for some experiments, came in the next morning, and saw—it's giving them the finger!" Valentine laughed uproariously. "Hmm? And it's still at it! It just keeps making a fist, then flipping them off. What do you figure it's trying to say?"

"I'd say the gesture is pretty transparent. Isn't it time for us go home, Valentine?" said Noonan, looking at his watch. "I have another important errand to run."

"All right," Valentine agreed enthusiastically, vainly attempting to stick his face into the frame of his glasses. "Ugh, Richard, you've really gotten me drunk . . ." He picked up his glasses with both hands and carefully hoisted them in place. "You drove?"

"Yes, I'll drop you off."

They paid and headed toward the exit. Valentine held himself even straighter than usual and kept smacking his temple with his finger—greeting familiar lab assistants, who were watching one of the leading lights of world science with curiosity and wonder. Right by the exit, greeting the grinning doorman, he knocked off his glasses, and all three of them quickly rushed to catch them.

"Ugh, Richard," Valentine kept repeating, climbing into the Peugeot. "You've gotten me shame-less-ly drunk. Not right, damn it. Awkward. I have an experiment tomorrow. You know, it's curious . . ."

And he launched into a description of the next day's experiment, constantly getting sidetracked by jokes and repeating, "Got me drunk . . . what a thing! Totally wasted . . ." Noonan dropped him off in the science district, having decisively put down the laureate's sudden desire to top things off ("What damn experiment? You know what I'm going to do with your experiment? I'm going to postpone it!") and handed him over to his wife, who, upon observing her husband's condition, became highly indignant.

"Guests?" rumbled the husband. "Who? Ah, Professor Boyd? Excellent! Now we'll hit the bottle. No more shots, damn it—we'll drink by the cup. Richard! Where are you, Richard?"

Noonan heard this already running down the stairs. So they are scared, too, he thought, again getting into his Peugeot. Scared, the eggheads. And maybe that's how it should be. They should be even more scared than the rest of us ordinary folks put together. Because we merely don't understand a thing, but they at least understand how much they don't understand. They gaze into this bottomless pit and know that they will inevitably have to climb down—their hearts are racing, but they'll have to do it—except they don't know how or what awaits them at the bottom or, most important, whether they'll be able to get back out. Meanwhile, we sinners look the other way, so to speak . . . Listen, maybe that's how it should be? Let things take their course, and we'll muddle through somehow. He was right about that: mankind's most impressive achievement is that it has survived and intends to continue doing so. *Still, I hope you go to hell,* he told the aliens. *You couldn't have had your picnic somewhere else. On the moon, say. Or on Mars. You are just callous assholes like the rest of them, even if you have learned to curl up space.* Had to have a picnic here, you see. A picnic . . .

How can I best deal with my picnics, he thought, slowly navigating the Peugeot along the brightly lit streets. What would be the most clever way to go about it? Using the principle of least action. Like in mechanics. What's the damn point of my engineering degree if I can't even figure out a cunning way to catch that legless bastard . . .

He parked the car in front of Redrick Schuhart's building and sat behind the wheel for a bit, thinking about how to conduct the conversation. He took out the spacell, climbed out of the car, and only then noticed that the building looked abandoned. Almost all the windows were dark, and there was no one in the park—even the lights there weren't lit. That reminded him of *what* he was about to see, and he shuddered uncomfortably. It even crossed his mind that it might make sense to call Redrick up and ask him to meet in the car or in some quiet bar, but he chased the thought away. For a number of reasons. Besides, he told himself, let me not become like those pitiful scum who have fled this place like rats from a sinking ship.

He entered the building and slowly walked up the long-unswept stairs. All around him was a vacant silence. Most of the doors on the landings were ajar or even open wide—the dark entryways beyond them gave off a stale odor of dampness and dust. He stopped in front of the door to Redrick's apartment, smoothed down the hair behind his ears, sighed deeply, and rang the doorbell. For a while there was no sound behind the door, then the floorboards squeaked, the lock clicked, and the door softly opened. He never did hear footsteps.

In the doorway stood the Monkey, Redrick Schuhart's daughter. Bright light fell from the foyer into the dimly lit landing, and for a second Noonan only saw the girl's dark silhouette and thought how much she had grown in the past few months. But then she stepped farther back into the apartment, and he saw her face. His mouth immediately became dry.

"Hello, Maria," he said, trying to speak as gently as possible. "How are you, Monkey?"

She didn't reply. She stayed quiet and silently backed up toward the door of the living room, glaring at him from beneath her brows. It looked like she didn't recognize him. But then, to be honest, he didn't recognize her either. The Zone, he thought. Shit.

"Who's there?" asked Guta, peering out of the kitchen. "My God, Dick! Where have you been hiding? You know, Redrick came back!"

She hurried toward him, wiping her hands on a towel thrown over her shoulder—the same good-looking, strong, energetic woman, except she seemed more haggard somehow:

her face had become drawn, and her eyes were . . . feverish, maybe?

He kissed her cheek, handed her his raincoat and hat, and said, "I've heard, I've heard. Just couldn't pick a time to drop by. Is he home?"

"Yeah," said Guta. "There's someone over. He'll probably leave soon, they've been in there awhile . . . Come in, Dick."

He took a few steps along the hallway and stopped in the living room doorway. The old man was sitting behind the table. Alone. Motionless and listing slightly to one side. The pink light from the lamp shade fell on the dark, wide face—as if carved from old wood—on the sunken lipless mouth, and on the fixed vacant eyes. And immediately Noonan sensed the smell. He knew that it was just a freak of the imagination, that the smell only lasted the first few days and then disappeared without a trace, but Richard Noonan could sense it as if with his memory—a damp, heavy smell of fresh earth.

"Why don't we go to the kitchen," Guta said hastily. "I'm cooking dinner; we can talk at the same time."

"Of course," Noonan said brightly. "Haven't seen each other in ages! Do you still remember what I like to drink before dinner?"

They went to the kitchen, Guta immediately opened the fridge, and Noonan sat down at the table and looked around. As usual, everything in here was tidy, everything sparkled, and there was steam rising from the pots. The stove was a new electric one, which meant there was money in the house. "Well, how is he?"

"Same as always," answered Guta. "He lost weight in jail, but he's already gained it back."

"Redheaded?"

"I'll say!"

"Mean?"

"Of course! He'll take that to the grave."

Guta put a Bloody Mary in front of him—a clear layer of Russian vodka seemed to be suspended above a layer of tomato juice.

"Too much?" she asked.

"Just the right amount." Noonan gathered air into his lungs and, screwing up his eyes, poured the mixture into his mouth. He remembered that this was basically the first real drink he'd had today. "That's much better," he said. "Now life is good."

"Everything OK with you?" asked Guta. "Why haven't you come by in so long?"

"I've been damned busy," said Noonan. "Every week I was planning to drop by or at least call, but first there was the trip to Rexopolis, then I had to deal with a scandal, then they told me 'Redrick came back'—all right, I think, why get in the way . . . Anyway, Guta, I've been run off my feet. Sometimes I ask myself, Why the hell are we always in such a whirl? For the money? But why in the world do we need money, if all we ever do is keep working?"

Guta clanged the pot lids, took a pack of cigarettes from the shelf, and sat across from Noonan. Her eyes were lowered. Noonan quickly snatched out a lighter and lit her cigarette, and for the second time in his life saw her hands shake—like that time when Redrick had just been convicted, and Noonan came by to bring her money: at first, she was completely destitute, and the assholes in the building refused to lend her a cent. Eventually, the money did appear and, in all likelihood, a considerable sum, and Noonan could guess where it was from, but he continued to drop by—bringing the Monkey toys and candy, spending whole evenings drinking coffee with Guta, helping her plan Redrick's successful future life. Finally, getting his fill of her stories, he would go to the neighbors and try to somehow reason with them, explaining, cajoling, then finally losing his patience, threatening: "You know, Red will come back, he'll break every bone in your body . . ." Nothing helped.

"How's your girlfriend?" asked Guta.

"Who?"

"You know, the one you brought that time . . . The blonde."

"You thought that was my girlfriend? That was my stenographer. She got married and quit."

"You should get married, Dick," said Guta. "Want me to find you a wife?"

Noonan almost replied, as usual, *I'm waiting for the Monkey* but stopped himself in time. It wouldn't have sounded right. "I need a stenographer, not a wife," he grumbled. "You should leave your redheaded devil and come work for me as a stenographer. I remember you were an excellent stenographer. Old Harris still remembers you."

"I'm sure he does," she said. "I had a hell of a time fending him off."

"Is that how it was?" Noonan pretended to be surprised. "That Harris!"

"My God!" said Guta. "He wouldn't leave me alone! I was just afraid that Red would find out."

The Monkey silently appeared—she materialized in the doorway, looked at the pots, looked at Richard, then approached her mother and leaned against her, turning away her face.

"Well, Monkey," Richard Noonan said heartily. "Want a chocolate?"

He dug into his vest pocket, took out a little chocolate car in a clear packet, and offered it to the girl. She didn't move. Guta took the chocolate and put it on the table. Her lips suddenly turned white.

"Yes, Guta," Noonan said, still cheery, "I'm planning to move, you know. I'm sick of the hotel. First of all, it really is too far from the Institute—"

"She almost doesn't understand anything anymore," said Guta softly, and he cut himself off, picked up a glass with both hands, and started pointlessly spinning it in his fingers. "I see that you don't ask how we are," she continued, "and you're right not to. Except you're an old friend, Dick, we have no secrets from you. Not that we could keep it a secret!"

"Have you seen a doctor?" asked Noonan, without raising his eyes.

"Yes. They can't do a thing. And one of them said . . ."

She fell silent. He was silent, too. There was nothing to say here, and he didn't want to think about it, but he was unexpectedly struck by an awful thought: It's an invasion. Not a picnic, not a plea for contact—an invasion. They can't change us, but they infiltrate the bodies of our children and change them in their image. He shivered, but then he immediately remembered that he had already read something like that, some paperback with a bright glossy cover, and the memory made him feel better. People imagined all sorts of things. In reality, nothing was ever the way people imagined.

"And one of them said she's no longer human," continued Guta.

"Nonsense," Noonan said hollowly. "You should see a real specialist. See James Catterfield. Want me to talk to him? I'll arrange an appointment . . ."

"You mean the Butcher?" She gave a nervous laugh. "Thanks, Dick, but it's all right. He's the one who said that. Must be fate."

When Noonan dared to look up again, the Monkey was already gone, and Guta was sitting motionless, her mouth half open and her eyes empty, the cigarette in her fingers growing a long crooked column of gray ash. He pushed his glass toward her and said, "Make me another, dear. And make one for yourself. And we'll drink."

She flicked off the ashes, looked around for a place to throw out the butt, and threw it in the sink. "What's it all for?" she asked. "That's what I don't understand! We aren't the worst people in town . . ."

Noonan thought that she was going to cry, but she didn't—she opened the fridge, took out the vodka and the juice, and took a second glass off the shelf.

"All the same, you shouldn't despair," said Noonan. "There's nothing in the world that can't be fixed. And believe me, Guta, I have connections. Everything I can do, I will . . ."

Right now, he himself believed in what he was saying, and he was already going through names, clinics, and cities in his mind, and it even seemed to him that he had heard something somewhere about a case like this, and everything turned out OK, he just needed to figure out where it happened and who the doctor was. But then he remembered why he came here and remembered General Lemchen, and he recalled why he had befriended Guta, and he no longer wanted to think about anything at all—so he made himself comfortable, relaxed, and waited for his drink.

At this point, he heard shuffling footsteps and tapping in the hall and the Vulture Burbridge's repulsive—especially under the circumstances—nasal voice. "Hey, Red! Your old lady, I see, has a visitor—there's his hat. If I were you, I wouldn't let that slide."

And Redrick's voice: "Take your prostheses, Vulture. And bite your tongue. Here's the door, don't forget to leave, it's time for my supper."

And Burbridge: "Jesus, I can't even make a joke!"

And Redrick: "You and I are done joking. Period. Go on, go on, don't hold things up!"

The lock clicked open, and the voices became fainter—apparently, they had both gone out onto the landing. Burbridge said something in an undertone, and Redrick answered, "That's it, that's it, we're done!" Then Burbridge grumbled something again, and Redrick replied in a harsh tone, "I said that's it!" The door banged, he heard quick footsteps in the hallway, and Redrick Schuhart appeared in the kitchen doorway. Noonan rose to greet him, and they firmly shook hands.

"I figured it must be you," said Redrick, looking Noonan over with quick green eyes. "Ooh, you've gotten fat, fatso! Growing your ass in bars . . . Aha! I see you guys have been enjoying yourselves! Guta, old lady, make me one, too, I gotta catch up."

"We haven't even started yet," said Noonan. "We were just going to. As if we could hope to get ahead of you!"

Redrick gave a sharp laugh and punched Noonan in the shoulder. "We'll see who's catching up and who's getting ahead. Man, I've been dry for two years, in order to catch up I'd have to guzzle a vat . . . Let's go, let's go, why are we sitting in the kitchen! Guta, bring us supper."

He dived into the fridge and stood up again, holding two bottles in each hand, with various labels.

"We'll have a party!" he announced. "In honor of our best friend, Richard Noonan, who doesn't abandon those in need! Though there's nothing in it for him. Ah, Gutalin isn't here, too bad."

"Give him a call," suggested Noonan.

Redrick shook his flaming red head. "They haven't laid phone lines to where he is yet. All right, let's go, let's go . . ."

He entered the living room first and banged the bottles down on the table.

"We're having a party, Dad!" he told the motionless old man. "This is Richard Noonan, our friend! Dick, this is my dad, Schuhart the elder."

Richard Noonan, having mentally gathered himself into an impenetrable lump, stretched his mouth to his ears, shook his hand in the air, and said to the corpse, "Nice to meet you, Mr. Schuhart! How are you? You know, Red, we've already met," he told Schuhart the younger, who was digging through the bar. "We saw each other once, only in passing, however . . ."

"Have a seat," said Redrick, nodding at a chair across from the old man. "And if you talk to him, speak louder—he can't hear a damn thing." He put down the glasses, quickly opened the bottles, and told Noonan, "Go ahead and pour. Give Dad a little, just a nip."

Noonan poured in a leisurely fashion. The old man was sitting in the same position, staring at the wall. And he showed no reaction at all when Noonan pushed the glass toward him. Noonan had already adjusted to the new situation. This was a game, a terrible and pitiful game. The game was Redrick's, and he was playing along, the same way that his whole life he had played along with the games of others—games that were terrible and pitiful and shameful and wild, and far more dangerous than this one. Redrick raised his glass and said, "Well, shall we begin?" and Noonan glanced at the old man in a completely natural manner, and Redrick impatiently clinked his glass against Noonan's and said, "Let's go, let's go, don't worry about him, he won't let it get away," so Noonan gave a completely natural nod, and they had a drink.

Redrick grunted and, eyes shining, went on in that same excited, slightly artificial tone: "That's it, man! No more jail for me. If you only knew, my friend, how good it is to be home! I've got money, I have my eye on a nice little cottage, with a garden, no worse than the Vulture's. You know, I was planning to emigrate, I'd already decided that in jail. Why in the world am I staying in this lousy town? Let them all go to hell, I think.

I get back—hello, they've banned emigration! What, did we all become contagious in the last two years?"

He talked and talked while Noonan nodded, sipped his whiskey, interjected sympathetic curses and rhetorical questions, then started grilling him about the cottage—what is it like, how much does it cost—and he and Redrick argued. Noonan was proving that the cottage was expensive and inconveniently located, he took out his notebook and flipped through it, naming addresses of abandoned cottages that could be bought for a song, and the repairs wouldn't cost much at all, especially if they applied to emigrate, got denied by the authorities, and demanded compensation.

"I see you've even gotten into real estate," said Redrick.

"I do a little bit of everything," answered Noonan and winked.

"I know, I know, I've heard about your brothel business!"

Noonan opened his eyes wide, put a finger to his lips, and nodded in the direction of the kitchen.

"Don't worry, everybody knows about that," said Redrick. "Money doesn't stink. I've finally really understood that . . . But picking Hamfist to be your manager—I almost peed myself laughing when I heard! Setting a wolf to guard the sheep, you know . . . He's a nut, I've known him since childhood!"

Here the old man, moving slowly and woodenly, like a giant doll, lifted his hand from his knee and dropped it on the table by his glass with a wooden bang. The hand was dark, with a bluish tint, and the clenched fingers made it look like a chicken foot. Redrick fell silent and looked at him. Something trembled in his face, and Noonan was amazed to see the most genuine, the most sincere love and affection expressed on that savage freckled mug.

"Drink up, Daddy, drink up," said Redrick tenderly. "A little is all right, please have a bit . . . Don't worry," he told Noonan in an undertone, winking conspiratorially. "He'll get to that glass, you can be sure of that."

Looking at him, Noonan remembered what had happened when Boyd's lab assistants showed up here to pick up this corpse. There were two lab assistants, both strong young guys, athletes and all that, and there was a doctor from the city hospital, accompanied by two orderlies—coarse brawny men used to lugging stretchers and pacifying the violent. One of the lab assistants described how "that redhead," who at first didn't seem to understand what was going on, let them into the apartment and allowed them to examine his father—and they might have just taken him away like that, since it looked like Redrick had gotten the idea that Dad was being taken to the hospital for preventive measures. But when the knucklehead orderlies—who in the process of the preliminary negotiations had hung around the kitchen and gawked at Guta washing windows—were summoned, they carried the old man like a log: dragging him, dropping him on the floor. Redrick became enraged, at which point the knucklehead doctor stepped forward and volunteered a detailed explanation of what was going on. Redrick listened to him for a minute or two, then suddenly, without any warning at all, exploded like a hydrogen bomb. The lab assistant telling the story didn't even remember how he ended up outside. The redheaded devil kicked all five of them down the stairs, not letting a single one of them leave unaided, on his own two legs. Every one of them, according to the lab assistant, flew out the front door as if shot from a cannon. Two of them stayed unconscious on the pavement, and Redrick chased the remaining three for four blocks down the street, after which he came back to the Institute's corpse-mobile and broke all of its windows—the driver was no longer in the vehicle; he had fled in the other direction.

"I recently tried this new cocktail in a bar," Redrick was saying, pouring the whiskey. "It's called Hell Slime, I'll make you one later, after we eat. That, my friend, is the kind of stuff that's hazardous for your health on an empty stomach; your arms and legs go numb after one drink . . . I don't care what you say, Dick, tonight I'll get you wasted. I'll get you wasted, and I'll get wasted myself. We'll remember the good old days, we'll remember the Borscht . . . Poor Ernie's still in jail, you know?" He finished his drink, wiped his mouth with the back of his hand, and asked in an offhand manner, "So what's new at the Institute, have you gotten started on the slime? You see, I'm a bit behind on my science . . ."

Noonan immediately understood why Redrick was steering the conversation in this direction. He threw up his hands and said, "You kidding, pal? You know what happened with the slime? Have you heard of the Carrigan Labs? It's this little private setup . . . Anyway, they managed to get their hands on some slime . . ."

He described the catastrophe, the scandal, how they never figured out where the slime came from—never did clear that up—while Redrick listened in a seemingly absentminded way, clucking his tongue and nodding his head, then decisively splashed more whiskey into their glasses and said, "Serves them right, the parasites, may they all go to hell . . ."

They had another drink. Redrick looked at his dad—once more, something trembled in his face. He stretched out his hand and pushed the glass closer to the clenched fingers, and all of a sudden the fingers opened and closed again, grasping the bottom of the glass.

"Now things will go faster," said Redrick. "Guta!" he hollered. "How long are you gonna starve us? It's all for you," he explained to Noonan. "She must be making your favorite salad, with the shrimp, I saw she's been saving them for a while. Well, and how are things at the Institute in general? Find anything new? I hear you guys now have robots working their asses off, but not coming up with much."

Noonan began telling him about Institute business, and as he talked, the Monkey silently appeared by the table next to the old man and stood there for a while, putting her furry little paws on the table. Suddenly, in a completely childlike manner, she leaned against the corpse and put her head on his shoulder. And Noonan, continuing to chatter, looked at these two monstrous offspring of the Zone and thought, My Lord, what else do we need? What else has to be done to us, so it finally gets through? Is this really not enough? He knew that it wasn't enough. He knew that billions and billions didn't know a thing and didn't want to know and, even if they did find out, would act horrified for ten minutes and immediately forget all about it. I'll get wasted, he thought savagely. Screw Burbridge, screw Lemchen . . . Screw this star-crossed family. I'm getting wasted.

"Why are you staring at them?" asked Redrick in a low voice. "Don't worry, it won't hurt her. On the contrary—they say they exude health."

"Yeah, I know," said Noonan, draining his glass in one gulp.

Guta came in, ordered Redrick to set the table, and put down a large silver bowl with Noonan's favorite salad. And then the old man, in a single motion, as if someone had just remembered to pull the puppet strings, jerked the glass toward his open mouth.

"So, guys," said Redrick in a delighted voice, "now we'll have one hell of a party!"

4.

REDRICK SCHUHART, 31 YEARS OLD.

During the night the valley had cooled off, and at dawn it actually became cold. They walked along the embankment, stepping on the rotted ties between the rusty rails, and Redrick watched the droplets of condensed fog sparkle on Arthur Burbridge's leather jacket. The kid was walking lightly, cheerfully, as if they hadn't just passed a torturous night, full of a nervous tension that still shook every fiber; as if they hadn't spent two agonizing hours on the wet summit of the bare hill in restless sleep, huddling together for warmth, waiting out the torrent of greenide that was flowing around the hill and disappearing into the ravine.

There was a thick fog lying on both sides of the embankment. From time to time, it rolled over the rails in heavy gray streams, and they would walk knee-deep in a slowly swirling haze. It smelled of damp rust, and the swamp to the right of the embankment reeked of decay. They couldn't see anything except the fog, but Redrick knew that on both sides stretched a hilly plain with piles of rocks, and that beyond that were mountains hidden in the haze. And he also knew that when the sun rose and the fog condensed into dew, he was supposed to see the frame of a broken-down helicopter to their left and a train in front of them, and that's when the real work would begin.

As he walked, Redrick shoved his hand between his body and the backpack and jerked the backpack up so that the edge of the helium container didn't bite into his spine. The damn thing's heavy, he thought, how am I going to crawl with it? A mile on all fours. All right, stop bitching, stalker, you knew what you were in for. Five hundred big ones are waiting for you at the end of the road, you can sweat a bit. Five hundred thousand, a tasty treat, huh? No way will I give it to them for any less than that. And no way will I give the Vulture more than thirty. And the kid . . . the kid gets nothing. If the old bastard told me even half the story, then the kid gets nothing.

He took another look at Arthur, and for some time watched, squinting, as he lightly stepped over the ties two at a time—wide shouldered, narrow hipped, the long raven hair, like his sister's, bouncing in rhythm to his steps. He'd begged it out of me, Redrick thought sullenly. He did it himself. And why did he have to beg so desperately? Trembling, with tears in his eyes. "Please take me, Mr. Schuhart! I've had other offers, but I only want to go with you, you know the others are no good! There's Father . . . But he can't anymore!" Redrick forced himself to cut this memory short. Thinking about it was repellent, and maybe that was why he started thinking about Arthur's sister, about how he'd slept with this Dina—slept with her sober and slept with her drunk, and how every single time it'd been a disappointment. It was beyond belief; such a luscious broad, you'd think she was made for loving, but in actual fact she was nothing but an empty shell, a fraud, an inanimate doll instead of a woman. It reminded him of the buttons on his mother's jacket—amber, translucent, golden. He always longed to stuff them into his mouth and suck on them, expecting some extraordinary treat, and he'd take them into his mouth and suck and every single time would be terribly disappointed, and every single time he'd forget about the disappointment—not that he'd actually forget, he'd just refuse to believe his memory as soon as he saw them again.

Or maybe his daddy sicced him on me, he thought, considering Arthur. Look at the heat he's packing in his back pocket . . . No, I doubt it. The Vulture knows me. The Vulture knows that I don't kid around. And he knows what I'm like in the Zone. No, I'm being ridiculous. He wasn't the first to ask, he wasn't the first to shed tears, some have even gotten on their knees. And they all bring a gun the first time. The first and last time. Will it really be his last time? Oh, kid, it looks like it! You see, Vulture, how things have turned out—it's his last time. Yes, Daddy, if you'd learned about this idea of his, you'd have given him a good thrashing with your crutches, this Zone-granted son of yours . . .

He suddenly sensed that there was something in front of them—not too far away, about thirty or forty yards ahead. "Stop," he told Arthur.

The boy obediently stopped in his tracks. His reaction time was good—he froze with his foot in the air and then slowly and cautiously lowered it to the ground. Redrick came up to him. Here, the train tracks noticeably sloped down and completely disappeared into the fog. And there was something there, in the fog. Something large and motionless. Harmless. Redrick cautiously sniffed the air. Yes. Harmless.

"Keep going," he said softly, waited until Arthur took a step, and followed him.

Out of the corner of his eye he saw Arthur's face, his chiseled profile, the clear skin of his cheek, and the decisively pursed lips under the thinnest of mustaches.

They continued going down, the fog enveloping them to their waists, then to their necks, and in another few seconds the lopsided mass of the railcar loomed ahead.

"All right," said Redrick, and he started pulling off the backpack. "Sit down where you're standing. Smoke break."

Arthur helped him with the backpack, and they sat side by side on the rusty rail. Redrick opened one of the pockets and took out the bag of food and the thermos of coffee. While Arthur was unwrapping the food and arranging the sandwiches on top of the backpack, Redrick pulled the flask from his jacket, unscrewed the cap, and, closing his eyes, took a few slow sips.

"Want a sip?" he offered, wiping the mouth of the flask with his hand. "For courage."

Arthur shook his head, hurt. "I don't need it for courage, Mr. Schuhart," he said. "I'd rather have some coffee, if you don't mind. It's very damp here, isn't it?"

"It's damp," agreed Redrick. He put the flask away, chose a sandwich, and started chewing. "When the fog burns off, you'll see that we're in the middle of a swamp. This place used to be swarming with mosquitoes—it was something else."

He stopped talking and poured himself some coffee. The coffee was hot, thick, and sweet—right now, it tasted even better than alcohol. It smelled of home. Of Guta. And not just of Guta but of Guta in her bathrobe, just awakened, with a pillow mark still on her cheek. I shouldn't have gotten mixed up in this, he thought. Five hundred thousand . . . What the hell do I need five hundred thousand for? What, am I going to buy a bar? A man needs money in order to never think about it. That's true. Dick got that right. But lately I haven't been thinking about it. So why the hell do I need the money? I have a house, a garden, in Harmont you can always find work. It was the Vulture that lured me, the rotten bastard, lured me like a kid . . .

"Mr. Schuhart," Arthur blurted out, looking off to the side, "do you really believe that this thing grants wishes?"

"Nonsense!" Redrick said absentmindedly. He froze with his cup halfway to his mouth. "And how do you know what kind of thing we're here for?"

Arthur laughed in embarrassment, ran his fingers through his raven hair, tugged on it, and said, "I just guessed! I don't even remember what gave me the idea . . . Well, first of all, Father always used to drone on about this Golden Sphere, but a while ago he stopped doing that and has started visiting you instead—and I know you two aren't friends, no matter what he says. And he's become kind of strange lately . . ." Arthur laughed again and shook his head, remembering something. "And it all finally clicked when the two of you were testing this dirigible in the vacant lot." He patted the backpack at the place containing the tightly packed envelope of the hot-air balloon. "To be honest, I'd been shadowing you, and when I saw you lift the sack of stones and guide it through the air, everything became completely clear. As far as I know, the Golden Sphere is the only heavy thing left in the Zone." He took a bite of the sandwich, chewed, and said thoughtfully with his mouth full, "The only thing I don't understand is how you're going to latch on to it—it's probably smooth . . ."

Redrick kept looking at him over the cup and thinking: How very unlike they are, father and son. They've got nothing in common—neither faces nor voices nor souls. The Vulture's voice was hoarse, ingratiating, sleazy in some way, but when he spoke about this, he spoke well. You couldn't help listening to him. "Red," he'd said then, leaning over the table, "there are just two of us left, and there are only two legs between us, and they are both yours. Who'll do it but you? It might be the most precious thing in the Zone! And who's going to get it, huh? Will it really be those sissies with their robots? Because I found it! How many of our men have fallen along the way? But I found it! I've been saving it for myself. And even now I wouldn't give it away, but you see my arms have gotten short . . . No one can do it but you. I've trained so many brats, even opened a whole school for them—none of them can do it, they don't have what it takes. OK, you don't believe me. That's fine—you don't have to. The money's all yours. Give me what you like, I know you won't cheat me. And I might get my legs back. My legs, you understand? The Zone took my legs away, so maybe the Zone will give them back again?"

"What?" asked Redrick, coming to.

"I asked: May I have a smoke, Mr. Schuhart?"

"Yeah," said Redrick, "go ahead. I'll have one, too."

He gulped down the remaining coffee, took out a cigarette, and stared into the thinning fog. He's nuts, he thought. A crazy man. It's his legs he wants. That asshole . . . that rotten bastard . . .

All these conversations had left a certain sediment in his soul, and he didn't know what it was. It wasn't dissolving with time, but instead kept accumulating and accumulating. And though he couldn't identify it, it got in the way, as if he'd caught something from the Vulture, not a disease, but instead . . . strength, maybe? No, not strength. So what was it? All right, he told himself. Let's try this: Pretend I didn't make it here. I got ready, packed my backpack, and then something happened. Say I got nabbed. Would that be bad? Yes, definitely. How so? The money down the drain? No, the money's not the issue. That those bastards, Raspy and Bony, would get their hands on the goods? Yes, that's something. That would be too bad. But what are they to me? Either way they eventually get everything . . .

"Brr . . ." Arthur shivered, his shoulders convulsing. "I'm freezing. Mr. Schuhart, maybe I could have a sip now?"

Redrick silently took out the flask and offered it to him. You know, I didn't agree right away, he thought suddenly. Twenty times I told the Vulture to go to hell, but the twenty-first time I did agree. I just couldn't stand it anymore. And our last conversation was brief and very businesslike. "Hey, Red. I brought the map. Maybe you'd like to take a look after all?" And I looked into his eyes, and his eyes were like abscesses—yellow with black dots in the middle—and I said, "Give it to me." And that was all. I remember I was drunk at the time, I'd been binging all week. I was really depressed . . . Aw, damn it, what does it matter! So I decided to go. Why do I keep digging through this, as if poking through a pile of shit? What am I—afraid?

He started. A long, mournful creak suddenly reached them from the fog. Redrick leaped up as if stung, and at the same time, just as abruptly, Arthur leaped up, too. But it was already quiet again, only the sound of gravel clattering down the embankment as it streamed from under their feet.

"That's probably the ore settling," Arthur whispered uncertainly, forcing the words out with difficulty. "There's ore in the cars . . . they've been standing here awhile . . ."

Redrick stared in front of him without seeing a thing. He'd remembered. It was the middle of the night. He'd been awakened, horror-struck, by the same sound, mournful and drawn out, as if from a dream. Except that it wasn't a dream. It was the Monkey screaming, sitting on her bed by the window, and his father was responding from the other side of the house—very similarly, with creaky drawn-out cries, but with some kind of added gurgle. And they kept calling back and forth in the dark—it seemed to last a century, a hundred years, and another hundred years. Guta also woke up and held Redrick's hand, he felt her instantly clammy shoulder against his body, and they lay there for these hundreds and hundreds of years and listened; and when the Monkey quieted down and went to bed he waited a little longer, got up, went down to the kitchen, and greedily drank half a bottle of cognac. That was the night he started binging.

" . . . the ore," Arthur was saying. "You know, it settles with time. From the humidity, from erosion, for various other reasons . . ."

Redrick took a look at his pale face and sat down again. His cigarette had somehow disappeared from his fingers, so he lit a new one.

Arthur stood a little longer, warily looking around, then sat down and said softly, "I know they say there are people living in the Zone. Not aliens—actual people. That they were trapped here during the Visit and mutated . . . adjusted to new conditions. Have you heard of this, Mr. Schuhart?"

"Yes," said Redrick. "Except that's not here. That's in the mountains. To the northwest. Some shepherds."

So that's what he infected me with, he thought. His insanity. That's why I've come here. That's what I need.

Some strange and very new sensation was slowly filling him. He realized that this sensation wasn't actually new, that it had long been hiding somewhere inside him, but he only now became aware of it, and everything fell into place. And an idea, which had previously seemed like nonsense, like the insane ravings of a senile old man, turned out to be his sole hope and his sole meaning of life. It was only now that he'd understood—the one thing that he still had left, the one thing that had kept him afloat in recent months, was the hope for a miracle. He, the idiot, the dummy, had been spurning this hope, trampling on it, mocking it, drinking it away—because that's what he was used to and because his whole life, ever since his childhood, he had never relied on anyone but himself. And ever since his childhood, this self-reliance had always been measured by the amount of money he managed to wrench, wrestle, and wring out of the surrounding indifferent chaos. That's how it had always been, and that's how it would have continued, if he hadn't found himself in a hole from which no amount of money could rescue him, in which self-reliance was utterly pointless. And now this hope—no longer the hope but the certainty of a miracle—was filling him to the brim, and he was already amazed that he'd managed to live in such a bleak, cheerless gloom . . .

"Hey, stalker," he said. "Soil your underpants? Get used to it, buddy, don't be embarrassed, they'll wash them out at home."

Arthur looked at him in surprise, smiling uncertainly. Meanwhile, Redrick crumpled the oily sandwich paper, flung it under the railcar, and reclined on his backpack, leaning on his elbows.

"All right," he said. "Let's say we assume that this Golden Sphere really can . . . What would you wish for?"

"So you do believe in it?" Arthur asked quickly.

"It doesn't matter if I believe in it or not. Answer the question."

He suddenly became truly interested in what a kid like this could ask the Golden Sphere—still a pipsqueak, yesterday's schoolboy—and he watched with a lively curiosity as Arthur frowned, fiddled with his mustache, glanced up at him, and lowered his eyes again. "Well, of course, legs for Father," Arthur said finally. "For things to be good at home . . ."

"Liar, liar," said Redrick good-naturedly. "Keep in mind, buddy: the Golden Sphere will only grant your innermost wishes, the kind that, if they don't come true, you'd be ready to jump off a bridge!"

Arthur Burbridge blushed, sneaked another peak at Redrick, and instantly lowered his eyes, then turned beet red—tears even came into his eyes.

Redrick smirked, looking at him. "I see," he said almost tenderly. "All right, it's none of my business. You can keep it to yourself." And then he remembered the gun and thought that while there was time, he should deal with everything he could. "What's that in your back pocket?" he asked casually.

"A gun," grumbled Arthur, and bit his lip.

"What's it for?"

"Shooting!" Arthur replied defiantly.

"That's enough of that," Redrick said strictly and sat up. "Give it to me. There's no one to shoot in the Zone. Hand it over."

Arthur wanted to say something, but he kept his mouth shut, reached behind his back, took out a Colt revolver, and handed it to Redrick, holding it by the barrel.

Redrick took the gun by the warm ribbed handle, tossed it up in the air, caught it, and asked, "Do you have a handkerchief or something? Give it to me, I'll wrap it."

He took Arthur's handkerchief, spotless and smelling of cologne, wrapped the gun in it, and placed the bundle on the railroad tie.

"We'll leave it here for now," he explained. "God willing, we'll come back here and pick it up. Maybe we really will have to fight the patrols. Although fighting the patrols, buddy . . ."

Arthur adamantly shook his head. "That's not what it's for," he said with vexation. "It only has one bullet. In case it happens like with my father."

"Ohh, I see . . ." Redrick said slowly, steadily examining him. "Well, you don't need to worry about that. If it happens like with your father, I'll manage to drag you here. I promise. Look, dawn is breaking!"

The fog was evaporating before their eyes. It had already vanished from the embankment, while everywhere else around them the milky haze was eroding and melting, and the bristly domes of the hilltops were sprouting through the vapor. Here and there between the hills he could already make out the speckled surface of the soured swamp, covered with sparse malnourished willow bushes, while on the horizon, beyond the hills, the mountain summits blazed bright yellow, and the sky over the mountains was clear and blue. Arthur looked over his shoulder and cried out in admiration. Redrick also turned around. The mountains to the east looked pitch black, while the sky above them shimmered and blazed in a familiar emerald glow—the green dawn of the Zone. Redrick got up and, unbuckling his belt, said, "Aren't you going to relieve yourself? Keep in mind, we might not have another chance."

He walked behind the railcar, squatted on the embankment, and, grunting, watched as the green glow quickly faded, the sky flooded with pink, the orange rim of the sun crawled out from behind the mountain range, and the hills immediately began casting lilac shadows. Then everything became sharp, vivid, and clear, and directly in front of him, about two hundred yards away, Redrick saw the helicopter. It looked as if it had fallen right into the center of a bug trap and its entire hull had been squashed into a metal pancake—the only things left intact were the tail, slightly bent, its black hook jutting out over the gap between the hills, and the stabilizing rotor, which noticeably squeaked as it rocked in the breeze. The bug trap must have been powerful: there hadn't even been a real fire, and the squashed metal clearly displayed the red-and-blue emblem of the Royal Air Force—a symbol Redrick hadn't seen in so long he thought he might have forgotten what it looked like.

Having done his business, Redrick came back to the backpack, took out his map, and spread it on top of the pile of fused ore in the railcar. The actual quarry wasn't visible from here—it was hidden by a hill with a blackened, charred tree on top. They were supposed to go around this hill on the right, through the valley lying between it and another hill—also visible, completely barren and with reddish-brown rock scree covering its entire slope.

All the landmarks agreed with the map, but Redrick didn't feel satisfied. The instinct of a seasoned stalker protested against the very idea—absurd and unnatural—of laying a path between two nearby hills. All right, thought Redrick. We'll see about that. I'll figure it out on the spot. The trail to the valley went through the swamp, through a flat open space that looked safe from here, but taking a closer look, Redrick noticed a dark gray patch between the hummocks. Redrick glanced at the map. It had an *X* and the scrawled label SMARTASS. The dotted red line of the trail passed to the right of the *X*. The nickname sounded familiar, but Redrick couldn't remember who this Smartass was, or what he looked like, or when he'd been around. For some reason, the only thing that came to mind was this: a smoky room at the Borscht, unfamiliar ferocious mugs, huge red paws squeezing their glasses, thunderous laughter, gaping yellow-toothed mouths—a fantastic herd of titans and giants gathered at the watering hole, one of his most vivid memories of youth, his first time at the Borscht. What did I bring? An empty, I think. Came straight from the Zone, wet, hungry, and wild, a bag slung over my shoulder, barged inside, and dumped the bag on the bar in front of Ernest, angrily glowering and looking around; endured the deafening burst of taunts, waited until Ernest, still young, never without a bow tie, counted out some green ones—no, they weren't green yet, they were square, with a picture of some half-naked lady in a cloak and wreath—finished waiting, put the money in his pocket, and, surprising himself, grabbed a heavy beer stein from the bar and smashed it with all his might into the nearest roaring mug. Redrick smirked and thought, Maybe that was Smartass himself?

"Is it really OK to go between the hills, Mr. Schuhart?" Arthur softly asked near his ear. He was standing close by and was also examining the map.

"We'll see," said Redrick. He was still looking at the map. The map had two other *Xs*—one on the slope of the hill with the tree and the other on top of the rock scree. Poodle and Four-Eyes. The trail went between them. "We'll see," he repeated, folded the map, and stuffed it into his pocket.

He looked Arthur over and asked, "Are you shitting yourself yet?" and, not waiting for an answer, ordered, "Help me put the backpack on . . . We'll keep going like before." He jerked the backpack up and adjusted the straps. "You'll walk in front, so I can always see you. Don't look around, but keep your ears open. My orders are law. Keep in mind, we'll have to crawl a lot, don't you dare be afraid of dirt; if I order you to, you drop facedown in the dirt, no questions asked. And zip your jacket. Ready?"

"Ready," Arthur said hollowly. He was obviously nervous. The color in his cheeks had vanished without a trace.

"We will first head this direction." Redrick gestured curtly toward the nearest hill, which was a hundred steps away from the embankment. "Got it? Go ahead."

Arthur took a ragged breath, stepped over the rail, and began to descend sideways down the embankment. The gravel cascaded noisily behind him.

"Take it easy," said Redrick. "No rush."

He carefully descended behind him, balancing the inertia of the heavy backpack with his leg muscles by force of habit. The entire time he watched Arthur out of the corner of his eye. The kid is scared, he thought. And he's right to be scared. Probably has a premonition. If he has an instinct, like his dad, then he must have a premonition. *If you only knew, Vulture, how things would turn out. If you only knew, Vulture, that this time I'd listen to you.* "And here, Red, you won't manage alone. Like it or not, you'll have to take someone else. You can have one of my pipsqueaks, I don't need them all . . ." He convinced me. For the first time in my life I had agreed to such a thing. Well, never mind, he thought. Maybe we'll figure something out, after all, I'm not the Vulture, maybe we'll find a way.

"Stop!" he ordered Arthur.

The boy stopped ankle-deep in rusty water. By the time Redrick came up to him, the quagmire had sucked him in up to his knees.

"See that rock?" asked Redrick. "There, under the hill. Head toward it."

Arthur moved forward; Redrick let him go for ten steps and followed. The bog under their feet slurped and stank. It was a dead bog—no bugs, no frogs, even the willow bush here had dried up and rotted. As usual, Redrick kept his eyes peeled, but for now everything seemed all right. The hill slowly got closer, crept over the low-lying sun, then blocked the entire eastern half of the sky.

When they got to the rock, Redrick turned back to look at the embankment. The sun shone on it brightly, a ten-car train was standing on top of it, a few cars had fallen off the rails and lay on their sides, and the ground beneath them was dotted with reddish-brown patches of spilled ore. And farther away, in the direction of the quarry, to the north of the train, the air above the rails was hazily vibrating and shimmering, and from time to time tiny rainbows would instantly blaze up and go out. Redrick took a look at this shimmering, spat drily, and looked away.

"Go on," he said, and Arthur turned a tense face toward him. "See those rags? You aren't looking the right way! Over there, to the right . . ."

"Yeah," said Arthur.

"That used to be a certain Smartass. A long time ago. He didn't listen to his elders and now lies there for the express purpose of showing smart people the way. Let's aim two yards to his right. Got it? Marked the place? See, it's roughly there, where the willow bush is a bit thicker . . . Head in that direction. Go ahead!"

Now they walked parallel to the embankment. With each step, there was less and less water beneath their feet, and soon they walked over dry springy hummocks. And the map only shows swamp, thought Redrick. The map is out of date. The Vulture hasn't been here for a while, so it's out of date. That's not good. Of course, it's easier to walk over dry ground, but I wish that swamp were here . . . Just look at him march, he thought about Arthur. Like he's on Central Avenue.

Arthur had apparently cheered up and was now walking at full pace. He stuck one hand in his pocket and was swinging the other arm merrily, as if on a stroll. Redrick felt in his pocket, picked out a nut that weighed about an ounce, and, taking aim, flung it at Arthur. It hit him right in the back of the head. The boy gasped, wrapped his arms around his head, and, writhing, collapsed onto the dry grass. Redrick stopped beside him.

"That's how it is around here, Archie," he said didactically. "This is no boulevard, and we aren't here on a stroll."

Arthur slowly got up. His face was completely white.

"You got it?" asked Redrick.

Arthur swallowed and nodded.

"That's good. Next time I'll knock a couple of teeth out. If you're still alive. Go on!"

The boy might make a real stalker, thought Redrick. They'd probably call him Pretty Boy. Pretty Boy Archie. We've already had one Pretty Boy, his name was Dixon, and now they call him the Gopher. He's the only stalker that's ever been through the grinder and survived. Got lucky. He, strange man, still believes that it was Burbridge who pulled him out of the grinder. As if! There's no pulling someone out of a grinder. Burbridge did drag him out of the Zone, that's true. He really did perform that feat of heroism! But if he hadn't . . . Those tricks of his had already pissed everyone off, and the boys had told Burbridge flat out: *Don't bother coming back alone this time.* That was right when he had gotten nicknamed the Vulture; previously he'd gone by Strongman . . .

Redrick suddenly became aware of a barely noticeable air current on his left cheek and immediately, without even thinking, yelled, "Stop!"

He stretched his arm to the left. The air current was more noticeable there. Somewhere between them and the embankment was a bug trap, or maybe it even followed the embankment—those railcars hadn't fallen over for nothing. Arthur stood as if rooted to the ground; he hadn't even turned around.

"Head farther to the right," ordered Redrick. "Go ahead."

Yeah, he'd make a fine stalker . . . What the hell, am I feeling sorry for him? That's just what I need. Did anyone ever feel sorry for me? Actually, yes, they did. Kirill felt sorry for me. Dick Noonan feels sorry for me. To be honest, maybe he doesn't feel sorry for me as much as he's making eyes at Guta, but maybe he feels sorry for me, too, one doesn't get in the way of the other in decent company. Except that I don't have the chance to feel sorry for anyone. I have a choice: him or her. And for the first time he became consciously aware of this choice: either this kid or my Monkey. There's nothing to decide here, it's a no-brainer. *But only if a miracle is possible,* said some skeptical voice in his head, and, feeling horrified, he suppressed it with frantic zeal.

They passed the pile of gray rags. There was nothing left of Smartass, only a long, rusted-through stick lying in the dry grass some distance away—a mine detector. At one point, mine detectors were in heavy use; people would buy them from army quartermasters on the sly and trusted in them as if they were God himself. Then two stalkers in a row died using them in the course of a few days, killed by underground electrical discharges. And that was it for the detectors . . .

Really, who was this Smartass? Did the Vulture bring him here, or did he come by himself? And why were they all drawn to this quarry? Why had I never heard of it? Damn, is it hot! And it's only morning—what's it going to be like later?

Arthur, who walked about five steps ahead, lifted his hand and wiped the sweat from his brow. Redrick looked suspiciously at the sun. The sun was still low. And at that moment it struck him that the dry grass beneath their feet was no longer rustling but seemed to *squeak*, like potato starch, and it was no longer stiff and prickly but felt soft and squishy—it fell apart under their boots, like flakes of soot. Then he saw the clear impressions of Arthur's footprints and threw himself to the ground, calling out, "Get down!"

He fell face-first into the grass, and it burst into dust underneath his cheek, and he gritted his teeth, furious about their luck. He lay there, trying not to move, still hoping that it might pass, although he knew that they were in trouble. The heat intensified, pressed down, enveloped his whole body like a sheet soaked in scalding water, his eyes flooded with sweat, and Redrick belatedly yelled to Arthur, "Don't move! Wait it out!"—and started waiting it out himself.

And he would have waited it out, and everything would have been just fine, they'd have only sweated a bit, but Arthur lost his head. Either he didn't hear what was being shouted to him, or he got scared out of his wits, or maybe he got even more scalded than Redrick—one way or another, he stopped controlling himself and, letting out some sort of guttural howl, blindly darted, hunching over, back to where they came from, the very place they had to avoid at all costs. Redrick barely had time to sit up and grab Arthur's leg with both hands, and Arthur crashed heavily to the ground, squealed in an unnaturally high voice, kicked Redrick in the face with his free leg, and wriggled and flopped around. But Redrick, also no longer thinking straight from the pain, crawled on top of him, pressing his face into Arthur's leather jacket, and tried to crush him, to grind him into the ground; he held the twitching head by the long hair with both hands, and furiously used his knees and the toes of his shoes to pound Arthur's legs and ass and the ground. He dimly heard the moans and groans coming from underneath him and his own hoarse roar, "Stay down, asshole, stay down, or I'll kill you," while heaps of burning hot coal kept pouring on top of him, and his clothes already blazed, and the skin on his legs and sides, crackling, blistered and burst. And Redrick, burying his forehead in the gray ash, convulsively kneading the head of this damned kid with his chest, couldn't take it anymore and screamed as hard as he could . . .

He didn't remember when the whole thing ended. He just noticed that he could breathe again, that the air was once again air instead of a burning steam scorching his throat, and he realized that they had to hurry, that they had to immediately get away from this hellish oven before it descended on them again. He climbed off Arthur, who lay completely motionless, squeezed both of the boy's legs under his arm, and using his free hand to help pull himself along, crawled forward. He never took his eyes off the boundary where the grass began again—dead, dry, prickly, but real. Right now, it seemed to be the most magnificent place on Earth. The ashes crunched between his teeth, waves of residual heat kept hitting his face, sweat poured right into his eyes—probably because he no longer had eyebrows or eyelashes. Arthur dragged behind him, his stupid jacket caught on things, as if on purpose; Redrick's scalded ass burned, and each movement caused his backpack to slam into the back of his scalded head. The pain and oppressive heat made Redrick think with horror that he'd gotten thoroughly cooked and wouldn't be able to make it. This fear made him work harder with his free elbow and his knees, forcing the vilest epithets he could think of through his parched throat; then he suddenly remembered, with some kind of insane joy, that he still had an almost-full flask inside his jacket. My dear, my darling, it won't let me down, I just need to keep crawling, a little more, come on, Redrick, come on, Red, a little more, damn the Zone, damn this waterless swamp, damn the Lord and the whole host of angels, damn the aliens, and damn that fucking Vulture . . .

He lay there awhile, his face and hands submerged in cold rusty water, blissfully breathing in the rotten stench of the cold air. He'd have lain there for ages, but he forced himself to get up on his knees, took off his backpack, and crawled toward Arthur on all fours. The boy lay motionless about thirty feet away from the swamp, and Redrick flipped him onto his back. Yeah, he'd been one good-looking kid. Now that cute little face appeared to be a black-and-gray mask made of ashes and coagulated blood, and for a few seconds Redrick examined the lengthwise furrows on this mask with a dull curiosity—the tracks of hummocks and rocks. He stood up, lifted Arthur by the armpits, and dragged him to the water. Arthur was wheezing and from time to time moaning. Redrick threw him facedown into the largest puddle and collapsed next to him, reliving the delight of the cold, wet caress. Arthur started gurgling and thrashing around, put his arms underneath him, and raised his head. His eyes were popping out of his head; he didn't understand a thing and was greedily gulping air, spitting out water and coughing. Finally, his gaze became intelligent again and fixed on Redrick.

"Ugh," he said and shook his head, splattering dirty water. "What was that, Mr. Schuhart?"

"That was death," Redrick mumbled, and lapsed into a coughing fit. He felt his face. It hurt. His nose was swollen, but strangely enough, his eyebrows and eyebrows were intact. And the skin on his hand also turned out to be OK, just a bit red. I guess my ass didn't get burned to the bone either, he thought. He felt it—no, definitely not, even the pants were whole. Just like he'd been scalded with boiling water.

Arthur was also gingerly exploring his face with his fingers. Now that the horrible mask had been washed away by water, his face looked—also contrary to expectations—almost all right. A few scratches, a small gash in his forehead, a split lower lip, but overall not too bad.

"I've never heard of such a thing," said Arthur and looked around.

Redrick also looked around. There were lots of tracks left on the ashy, gray grass, and Redrick was amazed by how short the terrifying, endless path he had crawled to escape destruction had apparently been. There were only twenty or thirty yards, no more, from one end of the scorched bald patch to the other, but fear and inability to see caused him to crawl in some sort of wild zigzag, like a cockroach in a hot frying pan. And thank God that at least I crawled in the right direction, more or less, or else I might have stumbled onto the bug trap to the right, or I could have turned around entirely . . . No, I couldn't have, he thought fiercely. Some pipsqueak might have done that, but I'm no pipsqueak, and if not for this idiot, nothing would have happened at all, I'd just have a scalded ass—that'd be the extent of it.

He took a look at Arthur. Arthur was sputtering as he washed up, grunting when he brushed the sore spots. Redrick got up and, wincing from the contact between his heat-stiffened clothing and his skin, went out onto the dry patch, and bent over the backpack. The backpack had really taken a beating. The upper pockets were completely scorched, the vials in the first-aid kit had all burst from the heat, and the yellowish stain reeked of disgusting medicine. Redrick had opened one of the pockets and was raking out the shards of plastic and glass when Arthur said from behind his back, "Thanks, Mr. Schuhart! You dragged me out."

Redrick didn't say anything. *Screw you and your thanks! Just what I need you for—saving your ass.*

"It's my own fault," continued Arthur. "I did hear you order me to get down, but I got scared to death, and when it started to burn—I totally lost my head. I'm very afraid of pain, Mr. Schuhart."

"Get up," said Redrick without turning around. "That was a piece of cake. Get up, stop lolling around!"

Hissing from the pain in his scalded shoulders, he heaved the backpack onto his back and put his arms through the straps. It felt like the skin in the scalded areas had shriveled and was now covered in painful wrinkles.

He's afraid of pain . . . *Screw you and your pain!* He looked around. All right, they hadn't strayed from the trail. Now for those hills with the corpses. Those lousy hills—standing there, the jerks, sticking out like a damn pair of buttocks, and that valley between them. He involuntarily sniffed the air. Ah, that rotten valley, it really is a piece of shit. Damn thing.

"See that valley between the hills?" he asked Arthur.

"Yeah."

"Aim straight at it. Forward!"

Arthur wiped his nose with the back of his hand and moved forward, splashing through the puddles. He was limping and no longer looked as straight and athletic as before—he'd gotten bent and was now walking carefully and very cautiously. Here's another one I've dragged out, thought Redrick. How many does that make? Five? Six? And the question is: What for? What is he, my flesh and blood? Did I take responsibility for him? Listen, Red, why did you drag him out? Almost kicked the bucket myself because of him. Right now, with a clear head, I know: I was right to drag him out, I can't manage without him, he's like a hostage for my Monkey. I didn't drag out a man, I dragged out my mine detector. My trawler. A key. But back there, in the hot seat, I wasn't even thinking about that. I dragged him like he was family, I didn't even consider abandoning him, even though I'd forgotten about everything—about the key and about the Monkey. So what do we conclude? We conclude that I'm actually a good man. That's what Guta keeps telling me, and what the late Kirill insisted on, and Richard always drones on about it . . . Yeah, sure, a good man! Stop that, he told himself. Virtue is no good in this place! First you think, and only then do you move your arms and legs. Let that be the first and last time, got it? A do-gooder . . . I need to save him for the grinder, he thought coldly and clearly. You can get through everything here but the grinder.

"Stop!" he told Arthur.

The valley was in front of them, and Arthur had already stopped, looking at Redrick in bewilderment. The floor of the valley was covered in a puke-green liquid, glistening greasily in the sun. A light steam was wafting off its surface, becoming thicker between the hills, and they already couldn't see a thing thirty feet in front of them. And it reeked. God only knew what was rotting in that medley, but to Redrick it seemed that a hundred thousand smashed rotten eggs, poured over a hundred thousand spoiled fish heads and dead cats, couldn't have reeked they way it reeked here. *There will be a bit of a smell, Red, so don't, you know . . . wimp out.*

Arthur let out a guttural sound and backed up. Redrick shook off his torpor, hurriedly pulled a package of cotton balls soaked in cologne out of his pocket, plugged his nostrils, and offered them to Arthur.

"Thank you, Mr. Schuhart," said Arthur in a weak voice. "Can't we go over the top somehow?"

Redrick silently grabbed him by the hair and turned his head toward the pile of rags on the rocks.

"That used to be Four-Eyes," he said. "And over there on the left hill—you can't see him from here—lies the Poodle. In the same condition. Got it? Go ahead."

The liquid was warm and sticky, like pus. At first they walked upright, wading up to their waists; the ground beneath their feet, fortunately, was rocky and relatively even, but Redrick soon heard the familiar buzzing on both sides. There was nothing visible on the sunlight-drenched left hill, but the shady slope to the right became full of dancing lilac lights.

"Bend down!" he ordered through his teeth and bent down himself. "More, dumbass!" he yelled.

Arthur bent down, scared, and that very instant thunder split the air. Right over their heads, a forked lightning bolt shimmied in a frenzied dance, barely visible against the backdrop of the sky. Arthur squatted and went in up to his neck. Redrick, sensing that the thunder had blocked his ears, turned his head and saw a quickly fading bright crimson spot in the shade near the rock scree, which was immediately struck by a second lightning bolt.

"Keep going! Keep going!" he bellowed, not hearing himself.

Now they walked squatting, one behind the other, only their heads sticking out of the muck, and with each lighting bolt, Redrick saw Arthur's long hair stand on end and felt a thousand needles pierce the skin of his face. "Keep going!" he repeated in a monotone. "Keep going!" He no longer heard a thing. Once, Arthur turned his profile toward him, and he saw the wide-open, terrified eye looking sideways at him, and the quivering white lips, and the sweaty cheek smeared with green gunk. Then the lightning got so low they had to dunk their heads in the muck. The green slime plastered their mouths, and it became hard to breathe. Gasping for air, Redrick pulled the cotton out of his nose and discovered that the stench had disappeared, that the air was filled with the fresh, sharp smell of ozone, while the steam around them kept getting thicker and thicker—or maybe things were going dark before his eyes—and he could no longer see the hills either to the left or to the right. He couldn't see a thing except for Arthur's head, covered in green muck, and the yellow steam swirling around them.

I'll make it through, I'll make it through, thought Redrick. Not my first time, it's my life story: I'm deep in shit, and there's lightning above my head, that's how it's always been. And where did all this shit come from? So much shit . . . it's mind-boggling how much shit is here in one place, there's shit here from all over the world . . . It's the Vulture's doing, he thought savagely. The Vulture came through here, he left this behind him. Four-Eyes kicked the bucket on the right, the Poodle kicked the bucket on the left, and all so that the Vulture could go between them and leave all this shit behind him. Serves you right, he told himself. Anyone who walks in the Vulture's footsteps always ends up eating shit. Haven't you learned that already? There are too many of them, vultures, that's why there are no clean places left, the whole world is filthy . . . Noonan's an idiot: Redrick, he says, you're a destroyer of balance, you're a disturber of peace, for you, Redrick, he says, any order is bad, a bad order is bad, a good order is bad—because of people like you, there will never be heaven on Earth. *How the hell would you know, fat ass? When have I ever seen a good order? When have you ever seen me under a good order?* My whole life all I've seen is guys like Kirill and Four-Eyes go to their grave, so that the vultures can crawl wormlike between their corpses, over their corpses, and shit, shit, shit . . .

He slipped on a rock that came loose under his foot, got completely submerged, came to the surface, saw Arthur's twisted features and bulging eyes right beside him, and for a moment went cold; he thought that he had lost his bearings. But he hadn't lost his bearings. He immediately figured out that they had to head to where the tip of the black rock was sticking out of the muck—he realized it even though the rock was the only thing he could see in the yellow fog.

"Stop!" he hollered. "Head farther right! Go right of the rock!"

He couldn't hear his own voice again, so he caught up with Arthur, grabbed him by the shoulder, and demonstrated with his hand: *Head to the right of the rock. Keep your head down.* You'll pay me for this, he thought. When he was next to the rock, Arthur dived under, and the lightning immediately struck the black tip with a crack, scattering red-hot bits. You'll pay me for this, he repeated, ducking his head under the surface and working as hard as he could with his arms and legs. Another peal of thunder rang hollowly in his ears. You'll be sorry you were born! He had a fleeting thought: Who am I talking to? I don't know. But somebody must pay, somebody has got to pay me for this! Just you wait, let me only make it to the Sphere, let me get to the Sphere, I'll shove this shit down your throat, I'm not the Vulture, I'll make you answer in my own way . . .

When they managed to get to dry ground, to the rock scree already heated white-hot by the sun, they were deafened, turned inside out, and clutching each other so as not to fall over. Redrick saw the truck with the peeling paint sunk on its axles and dimly recalled that here, next to this truck, they could catch their breath in the shade. They climbed into its shadow. Arthur lay down on his back and unzipped his jacket with lifeless fingers while Redrick leaned against the side of the truck, wiped his hand as best he could on the broken rock, and reached inside his jacket.

"I want some, too," said Arthur. "I want some, too, Mr. Schuhart."

Redrick, amazed at how loud this kid's voice was, took a sip and closed his eyes, listening to the hot, all-cleansing stream as it poured down his throat and spread through his chest; then he took another sip and passed the flask to Arthur. That's all, he thought listlessly. We made it. We've made it through this, too. And now for what's owed me. You thought that I'd forget? No, I remember everything. You thought I'd be grateful that you left me alive, that you didn't drown me in this shit? Screw you—you'll get no thanks from me. Now you're finished, you get it? I'm going to get rid of all this. Now I get to decide. I, Redrick Schuhart, of sober judgment and sound mind, will be making decisions about everything for everyone. And all the rest of you, vultures, toads, aliens, bonys, quarterblads, parasites, raspys—in ties, in uniforms, neat and spiffy, with your briefcases, with your speeches, with your charity, with your employment opportunities, with your perpetual batteries, with your bug traps, with your bright promises—I'm done being led by the nose, my whole life I've been dragged by the nose, I kept bragging like an idiot that I do as I like, and you bastards would just nod, then you'd wink at each other and lead me by the nose, dragging me, hauling me, through shit, through jails, through bars . . . Enough! He unfastened the backpack straps and took the flask from Arthur's hands.

"I never thought," Arthur was saying with a meek bewilderment in his voice. "I could have never imagined. Of course, I knew—death, fire . . . But this! How in the world are we going to go back?"

Redrick wasn't listening to him. What this manling said no longer mattered. It didn't matter before either, but at least before he'd still been a man. And now he was . . . nothing, a talking key. Let it talk.

"It'd be good to wash up," Arthur was anxiously looking around. "If only to rinse my face . . ."

Redrick glanced at him absentmindedly, saw the matted, tangled hair, the fingerprint-covered face smeared with dried slime, and all of him coated with a crust of cracking dirt and felt neither pity nor annoyance, nothing. A talking key. He looked away. A bleak expanse, like an abandoned construction site, yawned in front of them, strewn with sharp gravel, powdered with white dust, flooded with blinding sunlight, unbearably white, hot, angry, and dead. The far side of the quarry was already visible from here—it was also dazzlingly white and at this distance appeared to be completely smooth and sheer. The near side was marked by a scattering of large boulders, and the descent into the quarry was right where the red patch of the excavator cabin stood out between the boulders. That was the only landmark. They had to head straight toward it, relying on good old-fashioned luck.

Arthur suddenly sat up, stuck his hand underneath the truck, and pulled out a rusty tin can.

"Look, Mr. Schuhart," he said, becoming more animated. "Father must have left this. There's more in there, too."

Redrick didn't answer. *You shouldn't have said that,* he thought indifferently. *You'd be better off not mentioning your father, you'd be better off just keeping your mouth shut.* Although it actually doesn't matter . . . He got up and hissed from the pain, because all his clothing had stuck to his body, to his scalded skin, and now something in there was agonizingly peeling, tearing off, like a dried bandage from a wound. Arthur also got up and also hissed and groaned and gave Redrick an anguished look—it was obvious that he really wanted to complain but didn't dare. He simply said in a stifled voice, "Could I maybe have just one more sip, Mr. Schuhart?"

Redrick put away the flask that he'd been holding in his hand and said, "See the red stuff between the rocks?"

"Yeah," said Arthur, taking a shuddering breath.

"Head straight toward it. Go."

Arthur stretched, groaning, squared his shoulders, grimaced, and, looking around, said, "If I could just wash up a little . . . Everything is stuck."

Redrick waited in silence. Arthur looked at him hopelessly, nodded, and started walking, but immediately stopped.

"The backpack," he said. "You forgot the backpack, Mr. Schuhart."

"Forward!" ordered Redrick.

He wanted neither to explain nor to lie, and in any case he didn't have to. The kid would go as is. He had no choice. He'd go. And Arthur went. He plodded, hunching, dragging his feet, trying to tear off the junk that was stuck firmly to his face, having turned small, pitiful, and skinny, like a wet stray kitten. Redrick followed behind, and as soon as he went out of the shade, the sun burned and blinded him, and he shielded his face with his hand, regretting that he didn't bring sunglasses.

Each step raised a small cloud of white dust, the dust settled on their boots, and it stank—or, rather, it was Arthur that reeked, walking behind him was unbearable—and it was a while before Redrick realized that the stench mostly came from himself. The odor was nasty but somehow familiar—this was how it stank in town on the days the north wind would carry the factory smoke through the streets. And his father stank the same way when he came home from work—huge, gloomy, with wild red eyes—and Redrick would scurry into some distant corner and from there would watch timidly as his father would tear off his work coat and hurl it into his mother's arms, pull his giant worn boots from his giant feet and shove them under the coatrack, and lumber to the bathroom in his socks, his feet sticking to the floor; then he'd spend a long time in the shower, hooting and noisily slapping his wet body, clanging basins, muttering things under his breath, and finally roaring all over the house: "Maria! You asleep?" You had to wait while he washed up and sat down at the table, which already contained half a pint of vodka, a deep dish with a thick soup, and a jar of ketchup, wait until he drained the vodka, finished the soup, burped, and got started on the meat with beans, and then you could come out of hiding, climb onto his knees, and ask which foreman and which engineer he'd drowned in sulfuric acid today . . .

Everything around them was unbearably hot, and he felt nauseated from the dry cruel heat, from the stench, from exhaustion; and his scalded skin, which blistered at the joints, smarted violently, and it seemed to him that through the hot haze that was shrouding his consciousness, his skin was trying to scream at him, begging for peace, for water, for cold. Memories, so worn out they didn't seem to be his, crowded in his bloated brain, knocking one another over, jostling one another, mingling with one another, intertwining with the sultry white world, dancing in front of his half-open eyes—and they were all bitter, and they all reeked, and they all excited a grating pity or hatred. He attempted to break into this chaos, tried to summon from his past some kind of sweet mirage, feelings of happiness or affection. Out of the depths of his memory he squeezed the fresh laughing face of Guta, then still a girl, longed for and untouched—it would appear for a moment but would then immediately get flooded with rust, distort, and turn into the sullen, furry face of the Monkey, overgrown with coarse brown hair. He tried to remember Kirill, a holy man, his fast, certain movements, his laugh, his voice, promising fantastic and wonderful places and times, and Kirill would appear in front of him—but then the silver cobweb would sparkle brilliantly in the sun, and there'd be no Kirill, and instead Raspy Hugh would be staring Redrick in the face with angelic unblinking eyes, and his large white hand would be weighing the porcelain container. Some dark forces burrowing in his consciousness immediately broke through the barrier of will and extinguished the little good that was still preserved in his memory, and already it seemed that there had never been anything good at all—only smirking mugs, mugs, mugs . . .

And this whole time he'd remained a stalker. Without thinking, without realizing it, without even remembering, he would feel it in his bones: On their left, at a safe distance, a happy ghost hovered above a pile of old wooden boards—peaceful, used up, so the hell with it. From the right, meanwhile, a light breeze was beginning to blow, and in a few steps he sensed a bug trap, flat as a mirror and many-pointed like a starfish—a long way away, no need to fear—and at the center of the trap was a bird flattened into a shadow, a rare thing, birds almost never flew over the Zone. And over there, next to the trail, were two abandoned empties—looked like the Vulture had thrown them away on the way back, fear being stronger than greed. He saw it all, took it all into account, and as soon as the disfigured Arthur strayed even a foot from the trail, Redrick's mouth would open by itself, and a hoarse warning shout would fly out of its own accord. A machine, he thought. You've made a machine out of me . . . Meanwhile, the broken boulders on the edge of the quarry kept getting closer, and he could already make out the intricate rust patterns on the red roof of the excavator cabin.

You're a fool, Burbridge, thought Redrick. *Cunning, but a fool. How did you ever believe me, huh? You've known me since I was little, you should know me better than I know myself. You've gotten old, that's what. Gotten dumber. And it has to be said—you've spent your whole life dealing with fools.* And then he imagined the look on Burbridge's face when he found out that his Arthur, Archie, the pretty boy, his flesh and blood, that the kid who followed Red into the Zone, in his, the Vulture's, footsteps, wasn't some useless twerp but his own son, his life, his pride . . . And imagining this mug, Redrick roared with laughter, and when Arthur glanced back at him, frightened, he continued to roar and gestured at him: *Onward, onward!* And once again, a procession of smirking mugs, mugs, mugs crawled across his consciousness, as if across a screen. It all had to change. Not one life and not two lives, not one fate and not two fates—every little bit of this stinking world had to change . . .

Arthur stopped in front of the steep descent into the quarry, stopped and froze in place, staring down into the distance, craning his long neck. Redrick came up to him and stopped nearby. But he didn't look where Arthur was looking.

Right under their feet was a road stretching into the depths of the quarry, formed many years ago by Caterpillar tracks and the wheels of heavy trucks. The right slope was white and cracked by the heat, while the left slope had been partially excavated, and there, between the boulders and heaps of rubble, stood the excavator, tilted to one side, its lowered bucket jammed impotently into the side of the road. And, as was to be expected, there was nothing else to see on the road, except the twisted black stalactites, resembling thick spiral candles, dangling from the rough ledges right by the bucket, and the large number of black splotches visible in the dust—as if someone had spilled asphalt. That was all that was left of them, you couldn't even tell how many there'd been. Maybe each splotch had been one person, one of the Vulture's wishes. This one—that's the Vulture coming back safe and sound from the basement of the

Seventh Complex. That bigger one, over there—that's the Vulture bringing the moving magnet out of the Zone unscathed. And that one—that's the luscious Dina Burbridge, the universally desired slut, who didn't look like either her mom or dad. And that spot—that's Arthur Burbridge, the pretty boy, who also didn't look like either his mom or dad, the apple of the Vulture's eye . . .

"We made it!" Arthur croaked ecstatically. "Mr. Schuhart, we made it after all, huh?"

He laughed a happy laugh, crouched down, and beat the ground with his fists as hard as he could. The tangle of hair on the crown of his head trembled and swayed in an odd and funny way, clumps of dried dirt flew in every direction. And only then did Redrick raise his eyes and look at the Sphere. Carefully. Apprehensively. With a suppressed fear that it would be all wrong—that it'd disappoint, raise doubts, throw him out of the heaven he'd managed to ascend to, choking on shit along the way . . .

It wasn't golden, it was closer to copper, reddish, completely smooth, and it gleamed dully in the sun. It lay under the far wall of the quarry, cozily nestled between the piles of accumulated ore, and even from this distance you could see how massive it was and how heavily it pressed on the ground beneath it.

There was nothing about it to disappoint or raise doubts, but there was also nothing in it to inspire hope. Somehow, it immediately gave the impression that it was hollow and must be very hot to the touch—the sun had heated it up. It clearly wasn't radiating light, and it clearly wasn't capable of floating in the air and dancing around, the way it often happened in the legends about it. It lay where it had fallen. It might have tumbled out of some huge pocket or gotten lost, rolling away, during a game between some giants—it hadn't been placed here, it was lying around, just like all the empties, bracelets, batteries, and other junk left over from the Visit.

But at the same time, there was something about it, and the longer Redrick looked at it, the clearer it became that looking at it was enjoyable, that he'd like to approach it, that he'd like to touch it or even to stroke it. And for some reason, it suddenly occurred to him that it'd probably be nice to sit next to it and, even better, to lean against it, to throw his head back, close his eyes, and think things over, reminisce, or maybe simply doze, resting . . .

Arthur jumped up, quickly undid all the zippers on his jacket, tore it off, and threw it at his feet with all his might, raising a cloud of white dust. He was yelling something, making faces, and waving his arms, then he put his hands behind his back and skipped down the slope, dancing and performing intricate steps with his feet. He no longer looked at Redrick, he forgot about Redrick, he forgot about everything—he went to make his wishes come true, the little secret wishes of a college boy, who had never in his life seen any money, except for his so-called allowance, a kid who had been mercilessly beaten whenever he'd come home smelling even slightly of alcohol, who was being brought up to be a famous lawyer and, in the future, a senator and, in the most distant future, naturally, the president. Redrick, screwing up his inflamed eyes against the blinding light, kept watching him in silence. He was cold and calm, he knew what was about to happen, and he knew he wasn't going to look. But for now, it was still all right to watch, and so he looked on, feeling nothing in particular, save that perhaps somewhere deep inside him a little worm had started to wriggle uneasily, spinning its prickly little head.

And the boy kept going down the steep slope, skipping along, tap-dancing to some extraordinary beat, and white dust flew from under his heels, and he yelled something at the top of his voice, very clearly and very joyously and very solemnly—like a song or an incantation—and Redrick thought that this was the first time in the history of this quarry that someone was going down this road in such a way, as if going to a party. And at first he didn't hear what this talking key was shouting, but then something seemed to switch on inside him, and he heard:

"Happiness for everyone! Free! As much happiness as you want! Everyone gather round! Plenty for everyone! No one will be forgotten! Free! Happiness! Free!"

With that he abruptly went quiet, as if a huge hand had forcefully shoved a gag into his mouth. And Redrick saw the transparent emptiness lurking in the shadow of the excavator bucket grab him, jerk him up into the air, and slowly, with an effort, twist him, the way a housewife wrings out the laundry. Redrick had the time to notice one of the dusty shoes fly off a twitching foot and soar high above the quarry. He turned around and sat down. There wasn't a single thought in his head, and he somehow stopped being able to sense himself. Silence hung in the air, and it was especially silent behind his back, on the road. Then he remembered the flask—without his usual joy, merely like a medicine it was time to take. He unscrewed the cap and drank in small stingy sips, and for the first time in his life he wished that the flask didn't contain alcohol but simply cold water.

A certain amount of time passed, and relatively coherent thoughts started forming in his head. Well, that's done, he thought unwillingly. The road is open. He could even go right now, but it'd be better, of course, to wait a little longer. Grinders can be tricky. In any case, I need to think. I'm not used to thinking—that's the thing. What does it mean—"to think"? "To think" means to outwit, dupe, pull a con, but none of these are any use here . . .

All right. The Monkey, Father . . . Let them pay for everything, may those bastards suffer, let them eat shit like I did . . . No, that's all wrong, Red. That is, it's right, of course, but what does it actually mean? What do I need? These are curses, not thoughts. He was chilled by some terrible premonition and, instantly skipping the many different arguments still lying ahead, ordered himself ferociously: Look here, you redheaded asshole, you aren't going to leave this place until you figure it out, you'll keel over next to this ball, you'll burn, you'll rot, bastard, but you aren't going anywhere.

My Lord, where are my words, where are my thoughts? He hit himself hard in the face with a half-open fist. My whole life I haven't had a single thought! Wait, Kirill used to say something like . . . Kirill! He feverishly dug through his memories, and some words did float to the surface, more or less familiar, but none of them were right, because words were not what Kirill had left behind him—he'd left some vague pictures, very kind, but utterly improbable . . .

Treachery, treachery. Here, too, they've cheated me, left me voiceless, the bastards . . . Riffraff. I was born as riffraff, and I've grown old as riffraff. That's what shouldn't be allowed! You hear me? Let that be forbidden in the future, once and for all! Man is born in order to think (there he is, Kirill, finally!). Except that I don't believe that. I've never believed it, and I still don't believe it, and what man is born for—I have no idea. He's born, that's all. Scrapes by as best he can. Let us all be healthy, and let them all go to hell. Who's us? Who's them? I don't understand a thing. If I'm happy, Burbridge is unhappy; if Burbridge is happy, Four-Eyes is unhappy; if Raspy is happy, everyone else is unhappy, and Raspy himself is unhappy, except he, the idiot, imagines that he'll be able to wriggle out of it somehow. My Lord, it's a mess, a mess! My entire life I've been at war with Captain Quarterblad, and his whole life he's been at war with Raspy, and all he's ever wanted from me, the blockhead, was one thing—that I stop being a stalker. But how do I stop being a stalker when I have a family to feed? Get a job? And I don't want to work for you, your work makes me want to puke, you understand? If a man has a job, then he's always working for someone else, he's a slave, nothing more—and I've always wanted to be my own boss, my own man, so that I don't have to give a damn about anyone else, about their gloom and their boredom . . .

He finished the rest of the cognac and hurled the empty flask at the ground with all his strength. The flask jumped up, gleamed in the sun, and rolled away somewhere—he immediately forgot about it. He was now sitting down, covering his eyes with his hands, no longer trying to think or understand but to at least envision something, how things ought to be, but again he only saw mugs, mugs, mugs . . . money, bottles, piles of rags that used to be people, columns of numbers . . . He knew that it all had to be destroyed, and he longed to destroy it, but he could guess that if it were all gone, then there'd be nothing left—only flat, bare earth. The helplessness and despair again made him want to lean against the Sphere and throw his head back—so he got up, mechanically dusted off his pants, and began descending into the quarry.

The sun was baking, red spots were swimming in front of his eyes, the hot air rippled at the bottom of the quarry, and because of this, the Sphere seemed to dance in place, like a buoy in the waves. He walked past the excavator bucket, superstitiously raising his feet high and taking care not to step on the black splotches, and then, sinking into the crumbly rubble, he dragged himself across the quarry to the dancing and winking Sphere. He was covered in sweat and suffocating from the heat, but at the same time he was chilled to the bone, trembling hard all over, as if hungover, and the flavorless chalk dust was crunching between his teeth. And he was no longer trying to think. He just kept repeating to himself in despair, like a prayer, "I'm an animal, you can see that I'm an animal. I have no words, they haven't taught me the words; I don't know how to think, those bastards didn't let me learn how to think. But if you really are—all powerful, all knowing, all understanding—figure it out! Look into my soul, I know—everything you need is in there. It has to be. Because I've never sold my soul to anyone! It's mine, it's human! Figure out yourself what I want—because I know it can't be bad! The hell with it all, I just can't think of a thing other than those words of his—HAPPINESS, FREE, FOR EVERYONE, AND LET NO ONE BE FORGOTTEN!"

AFTERWORD

BY BORIS STRUGATSKY

The story of writing this novel (in contrast to the story of publishing it) doesn't include anything amusing or even instructive. The novel was conceived in February 1970, when my brother and I got together in Komarovo, a Russian town on the Gulf of Finland, to write *The Doomed City.* At odd moments during evening strolls through the deserted, snow-covered streets of that tourist town, we thought of a number of new plots, including those of the future *Space Mowgli* and the future *Roadside Picnic.*

We kept a journal of our discussions, and the very first entry looks like this:

> . . . A monkey and a tin can. Thirty years after the alien visit, the remains of the junk they left behind are at the center of quests and adventures, investigations and misfortunes. The growth of superstition, a department attempting to assume power through owning the junk, an organization seeking to

> destroy it (knowledge fallen from the sky is useless and pernicious; any discovery could only lead to evil applications). Prospectors revered as wizards. A decline in the stature of science. Abandoned ecosystems (an almost dead battery), reanimated corpses from a wide variety of time periods. . . .

In these same notes, the confirmed and final title—*Roadside Picnic*—makes an appearance, but the concept of a "stalker" is nowhere to be seen; there are only "prospectors." Almost a year later, in January 1971, again in Komarovo, we developed a very thorough and painstakingly detailed plan of the novel, but even in this plan, literally on the eve of the day we finally stopped coming up with the plot and started writing it, our drafts didn't include the word "stalker." Future stalkers were still called "trappers": "trapper Redrick Schuhart," "the trapper's girlfriend Guta," "the trapper's little brother Sedwick." Apparently, the term "stalker" came to us in the process of working on the first pages of the book. As for the "prospectors" and "trappers," we didn't like those terms to begin with; I remember this well.

We were the ones who introduced the English word "stalker" into the Russian language. *Stalker*—pronounced "stullker" in Russian—is one of the few words we "coined" that came into common use. *Stalker* spread far and wide, although I'd guess that this was mainly because of the 1979 film of that name, directed by Andrei Tarkovsky and based on our book. But even Tarkovsky latched on to it for a reason—our word must really have turned out precise, resonant, and full of meaning. It would have been more correct to say "stawker" instead of "stullker," but the thing is, we didn't take it from a dictionary at all—we took it from one of Rudyard Kipling's novels, the old prerevolutionary translation of which was called *The Reckless Bunch* (or something like that)—about rambunctious

English schoolkids from the end of the nineteenth to the beginning of the twentieth century and their ringleader, a crafty and mischievous kid nicknamed Stalky. In his tender years Arkady, while still a student at the Military Institute for Foreign Languages, received from me a copy of Kipling's *Stalky & Co.* that I happened to pick up at a flea market; he read it, was delighted, and right then made a rough translation called *Stullky and Company*, which became one of the favorite books of my school and college years. So when we were thinking of the word "stalker," we undoubtedly had in mind the streetwise Stullky, a tough and even ruthless youth, who, however, was by no means without a certain boyish chivalry and generosity. And at the time it didn't even cross our minds that his name wasn't Stullky at all, but was actually pronounced "stawky."

Roadside Picnic was written without any delays or crises in just three stages. On January 19, 1971, we started the rough draft, and on November 3 of the same year we finished a good copy. In the interim we kept busy with a wide variety of (typically idiotic) pursuits—wrote complaints to the "Ruling Senate" (i.e., the secretariat of the Moscow Writers' Organization), answered letters (which, sitting side by side, we did fairly rarely), composed a government application for a full-length popular-science film called *The Meeting of Worlds* (about contact with another intelligence), wrote three shorts for the popular Soviet television series *Fitil* (or something like it), thought of a plot for the TV movie *They Chose Rybkin*, worked out a first draft of the plot of the new novel *Strange Doings at the Octopus Reef*, and so on and so forth—there were no follow-ups or ultimate outcomes for any of these scribbles, and they have absolutely no relation to subsequent events.

Remarkably, the *Picnic* had a relatively easy passage through the Leningrad *Avrora* (a Soviet literary journal), not encountering substantial difficulties and sustaining damage only during the editing, and minor damage at that. Of course, the manuscript had to be purged of various "shits" and "bastards," but these were all familiar trivialities, beloved by writers the world over; the authors didn't retreat from a single principal position, and the magazine version appeared at the end of the summer of 1972, practically unscathed.

The saga of the *Picnic* at the publisher Young Guard (YG) was only beginning then. Actually, strictly speaking, it began in early 1971, when the *Picnic* didn't yet exist on paper and the novel was only being offered in the broadest of terms in an application for an anthology. This putative anthology was called *Unintended Meetings*, was dedicated to the problem of humanity's contact with another intelligence, and consisted of three novels, two finished—*The Dead Mountaineer's Inn* and *Space Mowgli*—and one that was still being written.

Difficulties began immediately.

> 03/16/71—AS: . . . the higher-ups read the anthology, but are hemming and hawing and saying nothing definite. By their request, the anthology was given to a certain doctor of historical sciences (?) to review—on the grounds that he really likes science fiction. . . . Then the manuscript, along with this review, will come back to Avramenko [the assistant head editor] (probably to give her a chance to reevaluate the existing, but secret, assessment?), and after that will make its way to Osipov [the head editor], and only then will we be apprised of our fate. Bastards. Critics.

> 04/16/71—AS: I saw Bella at the YG. She said there's nothing doing. Avramenko asked her to try to be diplomatic about it: to tell us that there's no paper, and they are all booked up, and so on, so forth, but she told me straight out that somewhere in the upper echelons they suggested having nothing

to do with the Strugatskys for the time being. . . . That's the hegemony bearing down!

And the *Picnic* wasn't written yet, and we're talking, essentially, about novels that have never caused a Big Ideological Disturbance, about little stories that are completely harmless and even apolitical. It's just that the higher-ups wanted nothing to do with those Strugatskys at all, and this overall reluctance was being superimposed on a difficult situation within the publishing house: this was right at the time that the change of leadership was taking place, when they were beginning to root out all the best things created by the then-editorial SF staff under Sergei Georgievich Zhemaitis and Bella Grigorievna Kliueva, due to whose cares and labors flourished the second generation of Soviet science fiction.

At the start of the 1980s, Arkady and I were giving serious thought to the project of gathering, organizing, and disseminating, at least by samizdat, "A History of One Publication" (or "How It's Done")—a compendium of genuine documents (letters, reviews, complaints, applications, authorial wails and howls in written form) related to the history of publishing the anthology *Unintended Meetings*, whose key novel turned out to be the *Picnic*. At one time, I had even begun systematically sorting and selecting the existing materials, but soon gave it up; it was dead-end work, a laborious task with no future, and there was a certain palpable immodesty in the whole project—who were we, after all, to use our own example to illustrate the functioning of the ideological machine of the 1970s, especially against the background of the fates of Aleksandr Solzhenitsyn, Georgi Vladimov, Vladimir Voinovich, and many, many other worthies?

The project was abandoned, but we returned to it once more after the beginning of perestroika in the mid-1980s, during the dawn of the new and even newest times, when there appeared a real possibility of not merely passing around a certain collection of materials but of publishing it according to all the rules, with didactic commentary and venomous descriptions of the main characters, many of whom had retained their positions at the time and were capable of influencing literary processes. We were joined by indefatigable *ludens* [a Strugatsky term indicating a subspecies of humans with superior mental powers —*tr.*]: Vadim Kazakov, a science fiction expert and literary critic from Saratov, and his friends. I relayed all the materials to them—the compendium was for the most part ready—but pretty soon it became clear that there was no real possibility of publishing it; no one had the money for this kind of publication, which was unlikely to be profitable. Besides, things were happening at breakneck speed: the putsch, Arkady's passing, the fall of the USSR, the democratic revolution—a velvet revolution, but a revolution nonetheless. For a period of literally months, our project lost the most minimal relevance.

And now I'm sitting behind a desk, staring at three reasonably thick folders lying in front of me, and am aware of a disappointment mixed with uncertainty and a noticeable touch of bewilderment. Inside these folders are the letters to the Young Guard publishing house (to the editors, the managing editor, the head editor, the director), complaints to the Central Committee of the All-Union Leninist Young Communist League (CC AULYCL), plaintive petitions to the Department of Culture of the Central Committee of the Communist Party of the Soviet Union (CC CPSU), and, of course, replies from all these organizations and our letters to each other—a veritable mountain of paper, by the most conservative calculation more than two hundred documents—and I have no idea now what to do with it all.

At first, I was looking forward to using this afterword to tell the story of publishing the *Picnic*: naming once-hated names; jeering to my heart's content at the cowards, idiots, informers, and scoundrels; astounding the reader with the absurdity, idiocy, and meanness of the world we're all from; being ironic and instructive, deliberately objective and ruthless, benevolent and caustic all at once. And now I'm sitting here, looking at these folders, and realizing that I'm hopelessly late and that no one needs me—not my irony, not my generosity, and not my burnt-out hatred. They have ceased to exist, those once-powerful organizations with almost unlimited right to allow and to hinder; they have ceased to exist and are forgotten to such an extent that it would be tedious and dull to explain to the present-day reader who is who, why it didn't make sense to complain to the Department of Culture of the CC, why the only thing to do was to complain to the Department of Print and Propaganda, and who were Albert Andreevich Beliaev, Pyotr Nilovich Demichev, and Mikhail Vasilyevich Zimyanin—and these were the tigers and elephants of the Soviet ideological fauna, rulers of destinies, deciders of fates! Who remembers them today, and who cares about those of them who are still among the living? So then why bother with the small fry—the shrill crowd of petty bureaucrats of ideology, the countless ideological demons, who caused untold and immeasurable harm and whose vileness and meanness require (as they liked to write in the nineteenth century) a mightier, sharper, and more experienced pen than my own? I don't even want to mention them here—let them be swallowed up by the past, like evil spirits, and disappear . . .

If I did, after all, decide to publish here even a simple list of pertinent documents with a brief description of each one, this list would look approximately like this:

04/30/75	A→B (the editors have "serious doubts" about *RP*)
05/06/75	A letter from A&BS to Medvedev with a request for an editorial response
06/25/75	A letter from Ziberov explaining the delay
07/08/75	The editorial response from Medvedev and Ziberov
07/21/75	A reply from A&BS to the editorial response
08/23/75	B→A (the anthology was touched up and sent to the editors back in July)
09/01/75	A notification from Ziberov acknowledging receipt of the manuscript
11/05/75	A letter from Medvedev rejecting the *Picnic*
11/17/75	A letter from A&BS to Medvedev arguing against the rejection
11/17/75	A letter from Medvedev to B expressing perplexity
01/08/76	A letter from A&BS to Poleschuk with a complaint about Medvedev
01/24/76	A notification from Parshin acknowledging the receipt of the letter to the CC AULYCL
02/20/76	A letter from Parshin about measures taken
03/10/76	B→A (proposing letters to Parshin and Sinelnikov)
03/24/76	A letter from A&BS to Parshin with a reminder
03/24/76	A letter from A&BS to Sinelnikov with a reminder
03/30/76	A letter from Parshin about measures taken
04/05/76	A→B (suggesting a letter to higher authorities)
04/12/76	A letter from Medvedev rejecting the *Picnic*

And so on, so forth. Who needs this today, and who today would read it?

But if not this, then what is there left to write about? Without this tedious/boring list and the gloomy/spiteful commentary on it, how do you tell the story of publishing the *Picnic*—

a story that is in a certain sense almost mysterious? Because this novel probably wasn't without its flaws, but at the same time it was also not without evident merits: it was clearly gripping, capable of making a reasonably strong impression on a reader (it did, after all, inspire a remarkable reader like Andrei Tarkovsky to make an outstanding film); at the same time it certainly didn't contain *any* criticism of the existing order and, on the contrary, seemed to be in line with the reigning anti-bourgeois ideology. So then why, for what mysterious—mystical? infernal?—reasons was it doomed to spend more than *eight* years passing through the publishing house?

At first, the publisher didn't want to enter into a contract about the anthology at all; then it did but for some reason revolted against the novel *The Dead Mountaineer's Inn*; then it seemed to agree to replace *The Dead Mountaineer's Inn* with the previously approved novel *Hard to Be a God*, but then it categorically revolted against the *Picnic*. . . It's impossible here to even give a brief account of this battle; it turns out to be too long—it was eight years, after all. There were unexpected repudiations of the publisher's own demands (suddenly, for no reason at all, down with *Hard to Be a God*!) and five or six renewals of the contract, and even sudden attempts to break off the relationship entirely (all the way up to court!). But mainly, and the whole time, and obstinately and invariably, from one year to the next, from one conversation to the next, from one letter to the next: take the reanimated corpses out of the *Picnic*; change Redrick Schuhart's language; insert the word "Soviet" when talking about Kirill Panov; get rid of the bleakness, hopelessness, coarseness, savageness . . .

I've preserved a remarkable document: the page-by-page comments on the novel *Roadside Picnic* by the language editors. The comments span eighteen (!) pages and are divided into sections: "Comments Concerning the Immoral Behavior of the Heroes," "Comments Concerning Physical Violence," and "Comments About Vulgarisms and Slang Expressions." I can't allow myself not to produce a couple of excerpts. And keep in mind: I am in no way selecting quotes, not looking for idiocies on purpose; I'm presenting the comments in order, beginning with a paragraph from the explanatory letter that accompanied the pages:

> Of course, we [the editors] only copied out those expressions and words that, in our opinion, require either removal or substitution. These comments are first and foremost dictated by the fact that your book is intended for teenagers and young people, for members of the Young Communist League who see Soviet literature as a textbook on morals, a guidebook to life.

> COMMENTS CONCERNING THE IMMORAL BEHAVIOR OF THE HEROES
> [there are 93 comments in all; the first 10 are presented]
>
> must stick your fat ass—p. 21
>
> I'll walk on my teeth, never mind my hands—p. 21
>
> crawling on all fours—p. 32
>
> take out the flask, unscrew it, and attach myself to it like a leech—p. 35
>
> suck the flask dry—p. 35
>
> I need just one more sip—p. 35
>
> I'll get plastered tonight. I gotta beat Richard, that's the thing! The bastard sure knows how to play—p. 38
>
> And I need a drink—I just can't wait—p. 42
>
> I would have been happy to drink with you to that—p. 42

. . . without saying a word pours me a shot of vodka. I clamber up onto the stool, take a sip, grimace, shake my head, and take another sip—p. 43 . . .

COMMENTS CONCERNING PHYSICAL VIOLENCE
[there are 36 comments in all; the last 9 are presented]

grabbed a heavy beer stein from the bar and smashed it with all his might into the nearest roaring mug—p. 179

Redrick felt in his pocket, picked out a nut that weighed about an ounce, and, taking aim, flung it at Arthur. It hit him right in the back of the head. The boy gasped [etc.]—p. 182

Next time I'll knock a couple of teeth out—p. 182

kicked Redrick in the face with his free leg, and wriggled and flopped around [etc.]—p. 185

convulsively kneading the head of this damned kid with his chest, couldn't take it anymore and screamed as hard as he could—p. 185

Now that cute little face appeared to be a black-and-gray mask made of ashes and coagulated blood [etc.]—p. 185

Redrick threw him facedown into the largest puddle—p. 186

may those bastards suffer, let them eat shit like I did—p. 202

He hit himself hard in the face with a half-open fist—p. 202

COMMENTS ABOUT VULGARISMS AND SLANG EXPRESSIONS
[there are 251 comments in all, an arbitrary 10 from the middle are presented]

he suddenly began to curse, impotently and spitefully, using vile, dirty words, showering Redrick with spittle . . .—p. 72

Put in your teeth and let's go—p. 72

the Butcher cursed—p. 74

You're scum. . . . A vulture —p. 74

asshole—p. 76

I'm dying of hunger!—p. 77

The Monkey was dozing peacefully—p. 77

he was dirty as hell—p. 78

To hell with this!—p. 82

beeped at some African—p. 85 . . .

I remember that upon receipt of this amazing document, I rushed straight to my bookshelves and joyously brought forth our beloved and unsurpassed Jaroslav Hašek. With what unutterable delight did I read:

> Life is no finishing school for young ladies. Everyone speaks the way he is made. The protocol chief, Dr. Guth, speaks differently from Palivec, the landlord of The Chalice, and this novel is neither a handbook of drawing-room refinement nor a teaching manual of expressions to be used in polite society. . . .
>
> It was once said, and very rightly, that a man who is well brought-up may read anything. The only people who boggle at what is perfectly natural are those who are the worst swine and the finest experts in filth. In their utterly contemptible pseudo-morality they ignore the contents and madly attack individual words.
>
> Years ago I read a criticism of a novelette, in which the critic was furious because the author had written: "He blew his nose and wiped it." He said that it went against every-

> thing beautiful and exalted which literature should give the nation.
>
> This is only a small illustration of what bloody fools are born under the sun.

Oh, how sweet it would be to quote all this to the gentlemen from Young Guard! And to add something from myself in the same vein. But, alas, this would be completely pointless and maybe even tactically wrong. Besides, as it became clear to us many, many years later, we had completely misunderstood the motivations and psychology of these people.

You see, we had then sincerely assumed that our editors were simply afraid of the higher-ups and didn't want to make themselves vulnerable by publishing yet another dubious work by extremely dubious authors. And the entire time, in all our letters and applications, we took great pains to emphasize that which to us seemed completely obvious: the novel contained nothing criminal; it was quite ideologically appropriate and certainly not dangerous in that sense. And the fact that the world depicted in it was coarse, cruel, and hopeless, well, that was how it had to be—it was the world of "decaying capitalism and triumphant bourgeois ideology."

It didn't even cross our minds that the issue had nothing to do with ideology. They, those quintessential "bloody fools," *actually did think this way*: that language must be as colorless, smooth, and glossy as possible and certainly shouldn't be at all coarse; that science fiction necessarily has to be fantastic and on no account should have anything to do with crude, observable, and brutal reality; that the reader must in general be protected from reality—let him live by daydreams, reveries, and beautiful incorporeal ideas. The heroes of a novel shouldn't "walk," they should "advance"; not talk but "utter"; on no account "yell" but only "exclaim." This was a certain peculiar aesthetic, a reasonably self-contained notion of literature in general and of science fiction in particular—a peculiar worldview, if you like. One that's rather widespread, by the way, and relatively harmless, but only under the condition that the holder of this worldview isn't given the chance to influence the literary process.

However, judging from a letter I wrote to Arkady on August 4, 1977:

> . . . Medvedev has been dealt with in the following way: a) Fifty-three stylistic changes from the "Vulgarisms" list have been made—it's explained in the letter that this is done in respect for the requests from the CC AULYCL. b) Interpretations of corpses as cyborgs for investigating earthlings, and of the Sphere—as some kind of bionic device which detects biological currents—have been inserted; it's explained in the letter that this was done to be left in peace. c) The letter further states that the remaining demands of the editors (concerning violence and so on) are actually an ideological mistake, as they result in glossing over capitalist reality. Everything has been sent with a request for a notification, and judging from the notification, has been received at the YG on the 26th of July of this year. To hell, to hell . . .

That was the very height of battle. Much, much more still lay ahead: further paroxysms of editorial vigilance, attempts to break the contract with the authors entirely, our complaints and plaintive petitions to the All-Union Agency on Copyrights (AUAC), CC AULYCL, CC CPSU . . .

The *Unintended Meetings* anthology saw the light of day in the autumn of 1980, disfigured, massacred, and pathetic. The only thing remaining from the original plan was *Space Mowgli*; *The Dead Mountaineer's Inn* had been lost on the fields of battle more than five years before, while the *Picnic* had undergone such editing that the authors wanted neither to read it nor even simply to flip through its pages.

But the authors prevailed. This was one of the rarest occurrences in the history of Soviet publishing: the publisher didn't want to release a book but the authors forced it to. Experts thought that such a thing was completely impossible. It turns out that it *was* possible. Eight years. Fourteen letters to the "big" and "little" Central Committees. Two hundred degrading corrections of the text. An incalculable amount of nervous energy wasted on trivialities . . . Yes, the authors prevailed; there's no arguing with that.

But it was a Pyrrhic victory.

Nonetheless, the *Picnic* was and still is the most popular of the Strugatsky novels—at least abroad. It's possible that this is due to Tarkovsky's brilliant film *Stalker* acting as a catalyst. But the fact remains: some fifty editions in twenty countries, including the United States (three editions), the United Kingdom (four), France (two), Germany (seven), Spain (two, one in Catalan), Poland (six), the Czech Republic (five), Italy (three), Finland (two), Bulgaria (four), and so on. In Russia, *Roadside Picnic* is also fairly highly acclaimed, although it lags behind, say, *Monday Starts on Saturday. Roadside Picnic* lives on and maybe will even make it to the third decade of the twenty-first century.

Of course, the text of the *Picnic* presented here is completely restored and returned to the authors' version. But to this day, I find the *Unintended Meetings* anthology unpleasant to even hold in my hands, never mind read.